First published in 2017 by Barrallier Books Pty Ltd,
trading as Echo Books

Registered Office: 35-37 Gordon Avenue, West Geelong, Victoria 3220, Australia.

www.echobooks.com.au

National Library of Australia Cataloguing-in-Publication entry.

Creator: Moses, Phillip A., author.

Title: Clancy's hat : the story of Tim's lone journey from Canberra to

Kosciuszko and a special hat / Phillip A. Moses.

ISBN: 9780995414761 (paperback)

Subjects: Voyages and travels--Fiction. Walking--Fiction. Hats--Fiction.
Dreamtime (Aboriginal Australian mythology)--Fiction Canberra (A.C.T.)--Fiction.
Kosciuszko National Park (N.S.W.)--Fiction.

Book layout and design by Peter Gamble, Canberra.
Set in Garamond Premier Pro Display, 12/17 and Minerva Sclptura.

www.echobooks.com.au

CLANCY'S HAT

The Story of Tim's lone journey
from Canberra to Kosciuszko
and a special Hat

PHILLIP A MOSES

ECHO BOOKS

CONTENTS

Clancy's Hat, Original artwork by Jeffrey Frith

ACKNOWLEDGEMENTS

I would like to pay my respects to all peoples who have a connection with Canberra and the Upper Snowy Regions.

A special thank you to: Tyronne Bell for his generosity of spirit in sharing Ngunawal knowledge .

All of the record keepers, historians, authors and poets who have provided context for this story.

Jeffrey Frith for the art work.

The Map Shop for the *How it Was Map.*

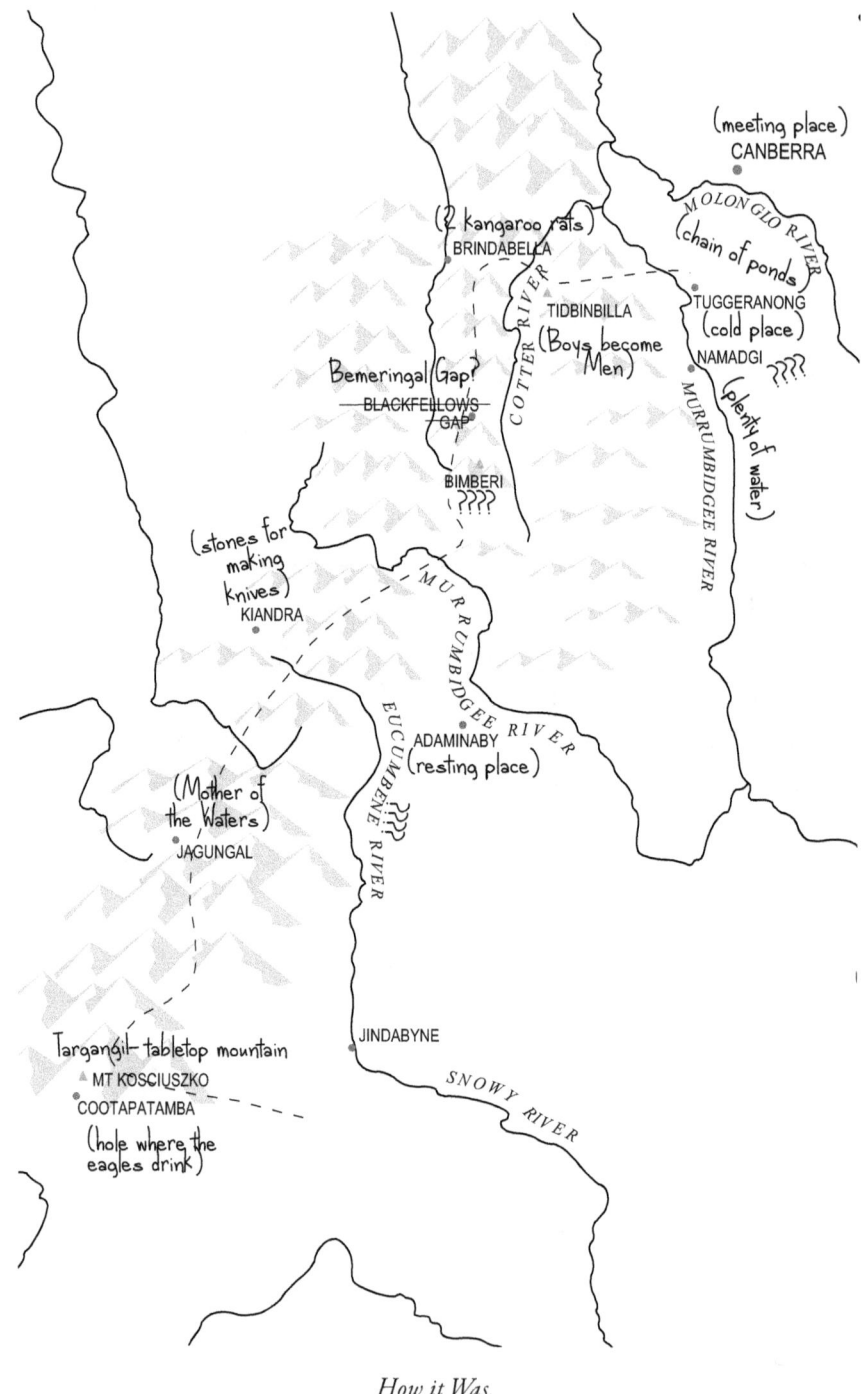

How it Was.

THE GREAT DIVIDE

I COULD SEE THE DISTANT BORDER where the securities of the city ended and a wilderness began. Rooftops ended abruptly and the formidable green-black bush climbed into the mountaintops. Through the office window, elevated on the third floor of the Australia Museum, a thought developed that I alone noticed the Australian bush in this urban setting.

The scrub of the foothills was a barrier and part of a landscape where I was a foreigner. I'd walked, picnicked and even camped on tracks on the far side of that frontier, though I recognised that these tourist paths were not the backcountry. They were not the outback and not the Snowys. They were an introduction to interlopers.

The expanse and the emptiness of the rough country on the other side of the glass intimidated me. The wilds might be a killer and this was just a fraction of the land that extended south from Canberra. Strangely, despite the menace, the bush beckoned to be discovered. This urge took hold even though it had been explored first by the Aboriginal peoples and then by the European settlers.

I could rattle off facts and events that had occurred in this country. This was to be expected from a historian. I knew the bush's past without knowing it. Born and raised in the city, it was a stranger. Perhaps the attraction was that from here the bush looked pristine. It was pure and undefiled.

I shifted my thoughts back to the page of verse I held. It was an exact replica of a document known as *Clancy's Reply*. My eyes began to flicker in tired pain.

A smell tickled my nose. In the hygienic office the slight dank aroma was distinctive. A decrepit hat sat on the corner of the desk. I bent forward to get my face near it. Drawing air through my nostrils, it was clear this was the source. Dirt, human and animal smells combined in an odorous melange.

Focus returned to the poem.

Reading a line, I stopped to let my mind sift each word for new clues. No fresh thoughts came. I'd been reviewing incessantly for hours. It was clear that I'd lost the perspective of distance. I was too close.

I was fruitlessly seeking a hidden meaning that might be conveyed to me by a writer who'd penned these words in 1897. The words were the response of a journeyman to the poem *Clancy of the Overflow*, authored by the famous Australian bard, Banjo Patterson, eight years earlier.

Some historians doubted that the writer of *Clancy's Reply*, Thomas Gerald Clancy, was the character Clancy from Banjo Patterson's verse. Some contended that Patterson's character Clancy was purely fictional.

As a historian I was supposed to be excited about such an argument, though this debate wasn't why I was reading *Clancy's Reply*. All I cared about was that Thomas Gerald Clancy existed. He was a shearer, a drover and a miner before the federation of the states that'd created the Commonwealth of Australia. Most importantly, he'd written to Patterson. These facts were not disputed.

What could I ever truly know of this tough pioneer and his rudimentary life sitting in this comfortable climate-controlled building separated by time and values? In my heart I knew the answer. Nothing.

If nothing, how could I know what he intended by these words to Patterson?

I felt deflated. Adding to my mood the office area was desolate under the harsh glow of fluorescent lighting. The cubicles where people worked had emptied in the last half hour. I'd been abandoned by my colleagues except for John, my boss.

Light still shone in his tiny office.

My thoughts returned to the hat. The well-worn crease at the front of the crown had turned into a hole a century or more before. Stains of dried sweat had been pushed through the leather band that lined the inner rim to the outer felt. These marks caused by the sweat of the owner had mixed with a dusting of mould that'd taken hold during the century of storage. The hatband was a plaid of horsetail hair that the owner had fashioned. The braids were still tight as if completed by someone who'd done the activity often. Perhaps whimsically, while sitting by a fire during a lonely evening on the trail.

I held a strong conviction that a stockman had been the owner of this item of clothing, though I had no proof. The hat was the broad-brimmed type that most Australians associated with the brand Akubra. The maker of this particular hat, like the owner, was a mystery. I was confident that this hat wasn't from the maker Akubra, as laboratory tests had predated the origins of the felt to the years before this famous company was founded. Tantalisingly, the scientists had established the hat to have been made somewhere between 1880 and the turn of the century.

Picking up the hat, I appraised it by twirling it in my hands. The leather band, already crumbling, disintegrated just a little bit more and flecks of broken leather fell on an open book. The fur-felt had lost its prized softness. The stiff abrasiveness spoke silently of its age. I thrilled at the touch. This invigorating sensation had energised me the first time I'd handled the hat last week.

It had been in hand often since then.

The hat had become a fixation.

It was an obsession to be savoured, and revisited, and there was no need to let it go.

What made the hat so special? Was it the care of the maker? The skill and passion of an artisan shaping the hat so it fit just right? Perhaps through the ages I was feeling the attachment of the owner to the item that shaded him all day from the harsh southern sun. The item that'd moulded itself to his head until it was part of him. The piece of clothing that, when it wasn't worn, made nakedness and vulnerability immediately evident.

'Who do you belong to?' I breathed.

The latest retrospective I'd been given to curate at the museum was entitled *The Snowy Region in Australian Culture and Myth.* The exhibition about the Snowy was all about the past, and yet, there were the mountains outside the window. Here was a pioneer's hat on my desk. A pioneer's precious sweat.

Expelling air, I settled into my seat.

John, my boss, approached. He interpreted.

'I can tell from that sigh you're still preoccupied with the hat. Forget it. It's of no historical significance. It's go-home-o'clock. We are the last here again. I'm leaving. You should go too, Tim.'

John's suggestion wasn't tempting.

'I'll be here a little longer,' I offered. 'There's a load of work to do before opening in the morning.'

'It's done,' John smiled. I sensed he was trying to bolster my mood. 'Finished. You've made yourself a walking encyclopaedia on the High Country. It shows in the exhibition. I've learnt so much from your work that I would've altered the title if it wasn't too late. *The Mountains that Changed Us* seems more apt.' John nodded as if agreeing with his own words. 'Every Australian identifies in some way with the Snowy, yet I'll guarantee that there'll be visitors to this exhibition who are going to learn so much more. You've done great.'

I started to speak. John's hand came up in a stop sign.

'We'll open tomorrow. As far as I'm concerned, your work is complete until it's time to pack up. She'll be right. It's the Aussie way. Go home or I'll dob you into Arianne!'

John turned and walked to the exit.

'What about the hat?' I called to his back.

'Leave it out. It's not Banjo Patterson's. This we've established even if it was archived with his belongings. We don't know who wore it. It could be anyone's. It has no historic value. If you hadn't dredged it up from archives the moths would have finished eating it and we'd have thrown it out.' John eyeballed me. 'It'll be thrown out. Here let me show you.'

John strode back and took the hat from my fingers.

The absence of its rough touch instantly registered.

John considered it for a second as if it had surprised him in some way. I detected doubt. Then there was a squint of determination.

With a swift flick of the wrist, John set the hat spinning like a disc through the air.

Holding my breath, I watched it fly a wobbly trajectory towards a distant bin. The hat struck the top, teetered for a moment, and fell to the floor.

I breathed again.

'Go home.' John's voice was soothing and insistent.

I organised an argument.

'John, this is a copy of *Clancy's Reply*. See that stain on the page?' I indicated with a finger a curved yellowing stain that fell across the bottom of the handwritten page. 'I have verified that this duplicate is exactly as the original. That stain matches the curve of the brim of the hat. I think Thomas Gerald Clancy didn't just send a poem. He sent Banjo Patterson his hat, that hat.'

John shook his head. 'Why would he do that?'

'I'm speculating, though I think Clancy is giving up driving cattle. He's challenging Patterson to take up droving. Daring him to stop romanticising the bush like Patterson does in the poem *Clancy of the Overflow*. He's saying to him, 'Have a go yourself and experience the hardships.' I drew breath. 'It's very Australian if you think about it. Stop being a city dweller pretending the grass is greener in the country.'

John's head dipped. 'And the evidence for your theory is?'

My finger jabbed again at the curved stain on the page.

John's head twitched. Scepticism was plainly displayed in his facial expression though he was attempting to hide it.

Scrambling to my feet, I left the desk and went over to the hat. I'd surprised myself with the forceful advocacy and tone of voice. They were covering nagging doubts.

I stooped to reach the hat and it touched my hands. The doubts disappeared. A surge of confidence coursed through me as I strode back to John.

I held the hat against the page.

'See it's almost a perfect match.'

John looked unconvinced. 'Almost. It's not even close.'

Not deterred, I persevered. 'If you bend the brim like this, like you were folding it into a parcel, putting it into the mail, you can see that it's possibly a match. I've a strong feeling about this.'

John gripped both my hands and shook them gently. 'Tim, I love your passion. We are curators at the National Museum. We need evidence. I think we might have learnt that at university in our first history lesson. *Almost* and *possibly* don't make it into a National exhibit.' He took the hat gently from my grasp. 'They make it to the rubbish.'

Once again, I watched the hat fly across the room towards the bin. The hat landed against it and not inside.

I fought the impulse to cheer.

'Tim. I love this exhibition. We don't need that hat. The scientists tell us it's a miracle it has survived this long. It'll fall apart very soon from mould, age and neglect. Nothing they can do will stop it. Why would they stop it? It isn't significant.'

John turned to leave.

I wanted to yell at his disappearing back that there must be a reason for the hat being stored with Banjo Patterson's belongings.

I checked myself because I knew the answer. There were none that could be found.

I plonked down into a chair in frustration.

John's departing back was a rebuke.

John was a good mentor. He was more than that, he was a good friend. I knew instinctively that he was being reasonable. He was a very judicious person and I admired him for it. Recognising John's qualities was a way for me to acknowledge that despite all of my academic training I wasn't completely sensible.

There was a reason John was supervisor. It wasn't just the five years in seniority he held over me. He had a pragmatic wisdom.

I hoped to be as measured one day.

Discouraged, I gazed back through the windowpane. This time it was the uneven battlements of the distant mountains that drew my attention. They were silhouetted as the sun's backlighting of the sky faded. Distant dark clouds were dropping rain on a small section of the ridges. I speculated that at the altitude of the mountains, in the cold air, it was possibly falling as snow. The rest of the sky was clear.

The mountains had no jagged peaks. They were rounded and sometimes table-topped. In this ancient land, erosion had been at work for epochs wearing away at the sharp edges of the most northern extremity of the tallest ranges in Australia.

In the furthest distance, on the horizon, the faint reflection of gold-pink sunrays on snow entranced me for a twinkling. Then the shaft of light from the sun in the west, filtered through the red-brown of the dust in the atmosphere, to the snow clinging to the rounded tip of Bimberi Peak in the south, to my eyes peering out a window in the north, was gone.

I blinked. The spell was broken.

Instinctively I checked the time as if to remember the exact moment.

The sun's position on the right was obscured by buildings. I knew though, that the sun had retreated below the western skyline, fringed by the Brindabella Mountain Range, and that the instant was finished. The connection between me, the mountains, and the sun, was over for another day.

Only from this office, in all of Canberra, could this flash of sun on snow be visible. It was a challenge for me to reconcile the image that we Australians held of ourselves as independent, resourceful, tough Bushmen with the reality of an office, a computer and a deadline. The tamed and the untamed. The safe and the unsafe. The challenge would not be met. I'd only academic knowledge about the other side of the boundary.

I turned to the work on my desk. The tasks to be done were marginal. What I was doing wasn't going to make that much difference to anyone except me. John had stated as much himself and he was right.

Some of the facts I'd found for the exhibition were obscure. Many had been almost forgotten in time. None were totally original and this disappointed me. What I'd wanted was a new discovery that would be ground-breaking.

I swore under my breath. Surely it was hubris that coveted this ambition. Vanity. It was likely just a search for external validation and academic plaudits.

'Put it aside. Let it go,' I whispered. 'You're a historian who sits anonymously in an office. A curator, not a rock star seeking cheers from a crowd.'

My thinking shifted to Arianne. She'd endured absences over many late nights in the last weeks. John was right to remind me of my responsibilities to her. I was being unfair.

The nervous energy of anxiety rose inside of me and I had to fight to suppress it.

One more late night. This assurance came from knowing Arianne would support me as she always had.

I looked across at the discarded hat by the bin. Clancy's Hat. I'd made a fool of myself to John who was such a professional.

I was losing it.

A Hat and a Thief

ISOLATION GAVE A PERSON TIME TO CONTEMPLATE, and self-develop was the idea that struck me as I finished the exhibition's paperwork. The word *self-develop* caused me to pause my thoughts. A modern term, it would hardly have come to the mind of a pioneer.

I considered how many pioneers' lives had been changed by the remoteness of the bush experience. It had defined their existence. Unrestricted by the influence of established society, they'd been required by the rudimentary circumstances to construct a new culture.

In the bush, the deeds of a person in the present had become more important than their past, and because of this the settlers had created an egalitarian culture. The pioneers had taken destiny into their own hands. Remoteness had been used by many as an opportunity to change direction, not as a handicap.

Garrett Cotter, who was a convict and settler south and west of present day Canberra, was one such pioneer. All Canberrans today drink from the river that carries his name as it rushes through the Brindabellas. The inspiring outcomes he achieved with his life were indicative of the characteristics exhibited as the colonies moved peacefully towards federation at the turn of the nineteenth century.

I'd begun to accentuate the positives.

This was the legacy in me of the myth makers who'd worked to establish an Australian ideal. It was a remnant of school education that lecturers at university had asked me to question. Every thought was loaded with bias, perceived and unperceived. I understood that even in thinking that Australia had progressed *peacefully* to federation, that this excluded the original inhabitants.

Despite years of studying history it still tripped me up.

Banjo Patterson, poet and author, was prominent amongst the Australian myth makers. He and others had done such a good job in lauding the positives of bush life that the negatives had been largely overlooked for a century or more.

Life for many settlers in a dry continent with unreliable climate and poor soils was often just hard. Labour often bore no fruit. Clancy in his words to Patterson pulled no punches about this side to life. The relevant words were known to me by rote. The verse streamed through my head as if a play button had been pushed.

> And my path I've often wended
> Over drought-scourged plains extended,
> Where phantom lakes and forests
> Forever come and go;
> And the stock in hundreds dying,
> Along the road are lying,
> To count among the 'pleasures'
> That townsfolk never know.

Sometimes without social contact pioneers became disconnected. There were suicides like the blacksmith at Lanyon on the edge of present day Canberra. He filled his pockets with stones and drowned himself in the Murrumbidgee River in the early days of European settlement. There was alcoholism and murder. There was a spate of bushranging and cattle duffing.

There wasn't a clinical diagnosis of depression, though a modern doctor travelling back in time to visit the pioneers of the region would surely have identified cases. It was clear from research that in a society that had been praised for the good characteristics, a darker side was never far from the surface.

Ironically when researching this exhibition I'd come to relate to the isolation and disconnection shaping the people. I empathised.

I shook my head ruefully.

This observation was of course counter intuitive. The notion that the vibrant modern Australian cities were delivering alienation and aloneness to those who lived within them would've been laughable to an early settler.

The empty office I occupied caused me to shiver involuntarily. It was cold to me even though the climate control kept the temperature perfect for humans. It was twenty-four degrees whether it was winter, spring, summer or autumn.

Despite coming here every day I didn't connect with my fellow office workers. In this area of the museum there were more than twenty employees. I guessed they considered me odd for the long hours I kept. I didn't know if they were suspicious of me for wanting to do things right or whether they supposed I was trying to push ahead of them. It was apparent that some felt a rivalry with me except I didn't intend to participate in any contest. I just wanted to do the job to the best of my ability. Not to be promoted, just for my own satisfaction.

I'd tried to explain this once to a colleague and they hadn't been able to understand.

I'd withdrawn a little more.

I forced my focus back on the paperwork.

Hours disappeared.

In the end, I pushed away from the desk and wiped a sleeve across my brow. The mound of documents in front of me was gratifying, though the lone piece of unresolved work beside it prevented closure. A map I'd tried to make of Canberra and the Snowy. A map of the country as it had been for at least twenty one thousand years. I called it the *How It Was* map. Evidence of Aboriginal occupation dated back that far. More finds were still being found and it was reasonable to believe that older archaeological sites could still be uncovered. The Aboriginal names and places of significance were shown. The meaning of the name was recorded in a red pen amendment in brackets. Finally the modern name used for that place was displayed if it was different to the Aboriginal.

Information was missing on the drawing.

There was the Cotter River. The original name was not recorded. Then there was Bimberi Peak. Its meaning to the Aboriginal was unclear to me.

Recent research into the name Brindabella had raised more questions. The language of the Ngunawal people, pronounced noon-a-wool, was said to use the words *brindy-brindy* to mean water running over rocks. In this version of the origin, *bella* was then added by the Europeans in reference to the mountain range's beauty. Another version was that Brindabella meant *two kangaroo rats*. No one really knew for sure. I recognised that most wouldn't care, though the lack of certainty over the name gnawed at me.

As the map took shape my defeat had been slowly revealed. The impossibility of the task I'd undertaken became evident.

I was using a European format as record.

The original peoples of the region did have a sense of boundaries and land and association with it. It was more fluid than I understood as the clans ranged across territories. The ceremonial circuits and cultural blocs were complex. There were so many layers and it was so multi-dimensional that my attempt at a map could not do it justice.

What to do? I was a historian and I didn't know.

Confounded, I folded the map and placed it into a pocket of the pack I would wear on my cycle home.

There was no closure to be had. I had to stop.

Standing, I picked up the heap of paper for the Snowys retrospective and walked it to John's office.

It honoured the people of the Snowy. There were the Aboriginal peoples, clans and families. Then there were the settlers, a bushranger or two, the cattlemen, the miners, the poets and artists, the leisure seekers, skiers, athletes, conservationists, the hydro builders, the scientists, the immigrants, the wives and children.

I was proud of the work, though with a reservation.

The bulk of the exhibition covered the two hundred years since European settlement. The long Aboriginal association with the Region was under-represented.

I had no solution to this.

I found a paper and pen and wrote 'John, complete, Tim.'

It was already past eleven. I'd struggle to cycle home before midnight.

I rushed to change into cycling attire. I put a layer of Lycra near the skin and then a warmer layer of synthetic fleece to trap air. Finally, a windproof outer layer to stop penetration of the cold was pulled on over everything else. I shouldered my little backpack.

My gaze fell on the hat resting by the rubbish bin.

No value. It could be anyone's. Not Banjo Patterson's.

I was drawn to walk over to the hat. I picked it up and twirled it. Bending to put it in the rubbish, I curbed the impulse. I could feel the buzz from its touch. There was that undeniable tickly sensation in my fingers again.

I looked furtively around.

The next moment I inexplicably took off the sack and stuffed the hat inside.

I was stealing. I was a thief. I'd no right to take the property of the museum home.

John had thrown the hat away. What harm would it do for me to take it and do some more research?

What inquiry? I then questioned. There weren't any other avenues for exploration. I was at a dead end.

Then I invented another rationalisation, this time a defence against future prosecutors.

It wasn't like I was a financial beneficiary from taking the hat.

In the moment this justification made me content enough, so I walked towards the lift.

Perhaps I can turn something up, I promised as solace.

The lift opened and I was confronted with a wall of mirrors. The reflected image of me hidden in layers of the cycling outfit could not hide an athletic medium sized frame. My olive skin, dark hair and ebony eyes were obvious characteristics that confronted me even as I spun to face away from the glass and back toward the entry-exit doors.

My mother proudly pronounced her ancestry to be Second Fleet Irish convicts. When she was inevitably questioned about the skin colour, the olive complexion was explained as a Black Irish heritage.

As a birthday gift for Mum, I'd attempted to complete the family tree. Research by me had closed some gaps in our heredity though not all. With no more ancestors to find and at a dead-end, I'd conducted a DNA test. This had confirmed a lineage that was predominantly Celtic. Genetic links to the Basque people were revealed, though I was informed that these links could date back as far as ten thousand years and were common in people of Irish descent. The test had discovered unique markers. DNA that belonged to people that had occupied Australia for more than sixty thousand years.

Mum had not accepted the science in this exciting find. My belief that knowledge of this unexpected heritage opened up the possibility of a culturally richer life was not shared by her. At twenty six years of age I was uninclined to argue. The rejection had left me flat. Still, a restive curiosity had been awakened in me even though I was unable to find any more ancestors. My accepted identity had been thrown into question, yet finding my exact Australian heritage was out of reach. Mirrors would forever be a reminder of this cloaked past.

I stepped from the lift, out of the building and into the cold winter chill. The temperature was already freezing or close to zero. Despite the high-tech cycle clothing, the cold seeped through the material and onto skin.

It was icy and that was a deterrent to many cyclists.

I didn't care. The cold and the exercise kept me in touch with the real world. It was a world where humans didn't control the climate. The few cyclists I passed on the paths in winter were comrades. They were the fellow journeymen who'd accepted nature's challenge and I was linked to them fleetingly. I knew this briefest of associations was the main reason I enjoyed cycling and walking.

When I drove I was in a bubble and the other motorists were in theirs. This was to me the paradox of urban living. I'd close physical proximity to others and still was emotionally isolated. When I cycled I became linked to strangers and that was more positive than the alternate remoteness.

I unlocked the bike and commenced the homeward journey to the city's southern suburbs.

First I had to leave the peninsular by the lake that the Australia Museum stood on. I pointed the bike north.

Experience had taught me that the pedalling would soon make me warm. I took my gloved left hand off the handle bar and held it to my face. Pressed against the mouth I blew warm air, forcing it through the synthetic and marginally porous material of the glove onto my hand. I put the left hand back on the handlebar. I repeated the process for the right hand. This warmed me for a few seconds and so I conducted the process again for the left hand. It was a well-worn routine. It would carry on until the blood, pumping to the extremities, was sufficient to maintain body temperature without this small assistance.

I looked to the left and tried to picture the area with fires from the first Canberrans. Ngunawal people, the Traditional Custodians of the Canberra region would have been present.

Winter was a time of survival. The Ngunawal had six seasons. Early summer, late summer, early winter, late winter, early spring and late spring. The idea of *Fall* in a land with no deciduous trees didn't exist.

The Ngunawal would have recognised the current season as late winter. This was the cold period of the year with the wind coming from the south and west.

The man-made lake where the Molonglo River once flowed was a very evident mark of the two hundred years of European habitation. The lights of monuments and buildings reflecting in the lake's surface emphasised this observation. The river's name had meant *chain of ponds* to the Ngunawal people. The out-of-sight dam wall had blocked the flow and merged the ponds. The name was now inapt.

It was impossible for me to capture the past, I affirmed in one moment, and then like an addict, I persisted with the mental revision.

More than three thousand known Aboriginal heritage sites had been documented in the Canberra area and they were still being discovered. This suggested extensive occupation by Aboriginal people over time. Most identified sites gave clues to everyday activities. Some were sacred.

At this time of year the men and women would've been covered in kangaroo, wallaby or possum cloaks. The wraps were designed so that when clothed in them, the fur was to the inside, against the skin. Warm air generated by the body from within was trapped by the hairs of the fur providing good insulation. The hide was to the outer offering some protection from rain. Ornamentation of significance to the wearer often marked the outside. The outfit was completed with a head covering from possum fur or matted fibres. Down from local ducks was also used as insulation.

During the research for the exhibition, my understanding of the Aboriginal inhabitants of the region had grown. It'd take toughness and skill to get through a winter in the area of the Australian High Country. The technology to conduct large scale agriculture, to make excess food in the warmer months to be stored through winter, didn't exist. There were no domesticated animals to eat. Canberra region had been populated by a group of people with a resourcefulness that a modern Australian would describe as legendary.

The bike path curled around Lake Burley Griffin and then under the deck of the well-lit Commonwealth Bridge. As I cycled past the pylons that held the bridge I searched the shadows for a homeless man. He was not visible. I saw him often, huddled against the cold with cardboard for protection. I hoped he was in a shelter tonight.

My attention was now drawn to the bridge's reflection in the ink dark water. It was a perfect mirror that pointed south and towards home.

I was soon standing on the pedals to provide momentum to the bike. This speed was needed to negotiate the steep gradient of the entrance ramp of the bridge. Panting a little with the exertion, the cold air was drawn into my lungs. I always enjoyed this little climb. When the ascent ended by arriving on the bridge proper, my body would be warm.

The ramp behind me, I was now on the gentle curve of the bridge deck. In front of me was the attractively lit Parliament House. On the left was the National Library, High Courts, National Gallery and offices that made up the centrepiece of Canberra known as the Parliamentary Triangle.

I never tired of the view. It was an orderly centrepiece to the nation that projected prosperity. The conception of the city by the American architect Walter Griffin, who the lake was named after, was a marriage of New World and European influences. He'd then fused the built environment with nature by nesting it sympathetically into the Australian landscape.

The city and suburbs clung to valley floors. The buildings were partially hidden in parkland. The rocky hills covered in eucalyptus trees overlooked the city. The view wasn't dominated by man-made structures.

One wag had remarked that the architecture was so bland it was best camouflaged behind trees. I didn't agree with this critic.

Lake Burley Griffin honoured a man and his works, yet his name was Walter Griffin. Burley was his middle name and one to all accounts he didn't use. How the lake came to be Lake Burley Griffin when christened in 1964 wasn't simply explained.

Place names had been a passion of mine since I first began studying history. The origin and meaning of a name were often undiscoverable. In some cases, like the lake, there were quirks. If the derivation of a title couldn't be found, it was a fair indicator of the problems to be encountered when trying to find the rest of the history connected with that place.

As one hundred or so years of the capital unfolded, the city was taking on a more Australian flavour. Reconciliation Place was now at the very core. An area was set aside to remind all Australians of the goal of unity between the first Australians and all those who'd arrived in the country later.

The unique Parliament House design of two touching boomerangs fitted sympathetically into the hill on which it'd been built. It stood in contrast to a grand European building that the original plans had depicted. The Parliament had been conceived by a then-Italian architect. He now lived in Canberra and had joined multinational Australia.

The horn of a car blew beside me.

I was pulled out of contemplation and back to reality. It caused me to startle and wobble.

I was on a bike path and separated from the road so there was no immediate threat. In any case, the urgency of sound had brought me to alert. A car whirled past with a passenger hanging out the window yelling abuse.

'Get off the road,' was the nonsensical message swept to my ears on the wind.

I detected the passenger's arm moving. An object detached from the hand. In the darkness I was unable to see what it was. A thud and then a tinkling sound. The object landed on the path, smashing into pieces.

A beer bottle.

The pedalling cadence was broken as I swerved to avoid the mess.

I swore under my breath before quickly re-establishing rhythm.

Most people were going home from partying when I was leaving work.

I was alone in the endeavours at the museum and on this bike.

What was wrong with me?

I had no answer to this question. My mind moved on and then puzzled over another riddle.

I assumed the people in the car didn't mean to injure by throwing the bottle. Why would they hurt me when I had done no harm? They didn't even know me. Maybe they thought that throwing the bottle was funny.

I didn't see the humour.

I kept cycling, all the time wondering why I was different.

LOVE AND DISCONTENT

THE STIRRING THEME SONG from *The Man from Snowy River* reached my ears as I opened the door to home. I'd acquired a copy of the film to watch as part of the exhibition's research. The idea had been to watch it and find a mood for the exhibition. It hadn't worked, even though it was a good film.

The film was based on the story of the famous Banjo Patterson poem. Even as I registered the music, my brain by association caused the first words to come to my lips.

> There was movement at the station for the word
> had passed around that the colt from old Regret
> had got away

This sentence launched an epic tale of jackaroos pursuing wild horses through the Australian Alps. The climax occurred when the skill and persistence of an unlikely hero won through. The man from Snowy River. It was an account of an underdog, a storyline that strongly resonated with Australians more than one hundred years later. The character at the centre of *Clancy of the Overflow*, Clancy, even had a cameo in *The Man from Snowy River*.

Thomas Gerald Clancy, whose poem I'd read this afternoon, and whose hat my conjecture said was in the bag over my shoulder, had been a drover who'd met Patterson. Yet it was Thomas Clancy's brother, John, who'd worked at the cattle station in central New South Wales that bore the name The Overflow. Complicating matters further, it was almost certain that neither of the brothers participated in a chase for wild brumbies across the Snowy region.

I shook my head.

Researching history rarely led to definite answers. My enquiries often uncovered facts that contradicted the accepted accounts. I'd realized that many of the stories that were important to me as an Australian did not withstand scrutiny. Fact gathering had taught me that repetition of a story did not make it true.

The television displayed an image of a bushman wearing a hat just like the one I'd stuffed into my backpack. Instinctively and ridiculously I leaned forward to check if the hat in the film was the same as the one in my bag.

Arianne lay on the couch opposite the door. Her dark hair, still in a ponytail, was falling across a cushion. With eyes closed, she was stretched out facing the television, where the credits for the film were rolling.

I watched Arianne for a second, admiring her contented and peaceful sleep. She was an angel.

I closed the door silently behind me.

She stirred.

Perhaps it was the draught I'd let in or by some telepathy that she felt my gaze upon her. Her eyes half opened.

'You're late,' she remarked sleepily.

Defensively, I analysed her voice for a hint of reproach. I found none.

'I know. Sorry.' The need to apologise was urgent. 'It's finished now.' I went to her and kissed her tenderly on the forehead. 'Thank you for all of your support. It means so much.'

Arianne winced at the kiss. 'Your nose and cheeks are freezing.'

'My hands are cold as well,' I confessed as I touched her arms.

She jumped and yelped, half in admonishment, half playfully.

I sat on the lounge next to her.

'Finished, you said.' Her brown with a hint of green eyes searched mine as she settled. 'Happy that it's all over?' Without allowing an answer, she said, 'We should have a glass of red to celebrate.'

Eventually I spoke. 'Finished, yes. But I'm not ready to celebrate. Perhaps we should have a nice dinner when the exhibition closes.'

Arianne was still.

The need to explain myself to her further was obvious. 'The exhibition is good.' I hesitated. I knew what I wanted to say. It was about her and not work. Then, in the same moment, I knew I wouldn't say the words that I longed to.

I elected to use the word that captured my feelings for her, and I'd never spoken to her, by hiding it amongst other meaning. 'You'll love it ... the exhibition. I can't wait for you to see it.'

Arianne beamed. I supposed that the joy wasn't at the report on the exhibition. It was at the fact that she read me so well. 'Love it,' she responded, and let it play for a long moment. 'And yet that pause suggests reservations. You aren't entirely sure of yourself. You know a man who is sure of himself is so much more attractive.'

Her smile gave away her playfulness.

I groaned. 'And to think you still chose indecisive me.' I kept talking, not allowing her to re-join the repartee. 'A few things happened today that confuse me. I can't say *that'll do*. John was trying to assist me in letting go and I couldn't. This time I'm fixated about the origins of a hat.'

I could feel Arianne's breathing as she waited. I recognised that what had just been verbalised made little sense.

I persisted. 'These fellows threw a beer bottle at me just now as I was cycling across the bridge and I don't understand it. I obsessed over that all the way home. I'm not like everyone else. Un-Australian somehow.'

Arianne laughed and took my hand reassuringly.

'Don't over think it,' Arianne offered as a platitude.

'Can you over think something? We could solve many more problems if we all thought a little bit more.'

Arianne shook my hand. Her furrowed brow showed concern. 'Thanks for the deconstruction. I'm here with you because you're different. You always act with a reason. You then assume everyone else acts with a reason. What if they don't?'

I looked into Arianne's deep eyes. They showed tolerance and humour. She persisted. 'Being obsessive doesn't have to be a bad thing. I can handle it.'

I nodded.

Arianne continued. 'And I can explain for you the beer bottle being thrown.'

I waited in anticipation.

'They're drunken idiots,' Arianne grinned, though her forehead was still wrinkled with concern for me. 'Come to bed.'

I unpacked the cycling gear and took out the hat carefully.

'It's a hat that was in Banjo Patterson's belongings. It's not his so it's to be thrown out.' I broke off and deliberated over the next words. 'You just told me that I act with reason. Is it rational to steal this hat from the museum because I get a tingling sensation when I touch it? On the strength of that feeling I think that it must have some significance and I can't stand the possibility of it being in the rubbish.'

Arianne touched the hat. She looked serious. She touched and rubbed it some more. 'It's scratchy with age, but I see what you mean. So there's a reason.'

I wondered if she'd had the same sensation or was just being compassionate.

'I was going to try and turn up some more info on this hat.'

'Tonight?' Arianne frowned.

I didn't answer.

Standing, she reached and took the hat. Then she poked a finger from the inside of the hat through the well-worn hole in the crown.

'Look, it's talking to me.' She wriggled a finger like it was a puppet and feigned a deep voice. 'It's saying, go to bed Mr OCD.'

I laughed. I wanted to say, 'I love you,' but held back.

Arianne bent at the knees and let the hat drop softly to the floor.

I had an uncomfortable sensation.

The hat shouldn't be on the floor. Not on the floor and not in a bin. It should be looked after.

I refrained from saying anything. I was clearly the sole individual who felt this way about the old hat.

Picking it up, and then the cycling pack, I opened the door to the garage. I reached in and placed them on a workbench inside the door.

Arianne watched without saying a word.

THE IDEA OF A JOURNEY

LYING IN THE DARK, I WAS DISORIENTED by time and purpose. I registered my surrounds, though I wasn't sure of the hour or what I'd do when I went to work in the morning. I guessed it was between two and three. These were the darkest hours. The time long experience had shown me when the brain became overactive. At this time of the day I more than usual blew things out of proportion and fretted about small issues. I made major problems out of off-tune words or an out of place action.

Gradually stretching, I reached for the watch on the bedside table. Once in hand, I fumbled to select the light function.

It was 2:41.

For a flash, I was pleased with the guess. Then I understood that knowledge of these habits wasn't a cure. Self-awareness just irritated me more.

I turned for the hundredth time. Each time I moved it was as gently as possible so as not to disturb Arianne. This act of restraint provided no release for my energy. Frustration continued building. Arianne's regular breathing was a reproach to my restive discontent and I rolled over again.

The warmth of Arianne's body beside me was comforting, particularly as the icy air of a Canberra winter's night was transmitting through the window and blinds. Once radiated inside it brought a chill to the warmer air of the room.

Cycling to and from work, I'd become sensitive to changes in temperature. On a ride, the lake near work was warmest, Woden Valley cooler and Tuggeranong Valley where home was, colder again. It was said that Tuggeranong meant *cold place* to the Ngunawal. They had that observation right I had confirmed to myself on many occasions. These changes were no more than a degree or two, yet they were distinguishable to the first people in the area even if they'd possessed no thermometers. The changes in temperature were known to me. They were important to notice as they allowed me to estimate just the right amount of cycling gear to wear so I was neither too cold nor too hot. Tonight had the bite of sub-zero temperature. Creeping frosts would be forming in the darkness.

I was stupid, I admonished. Why did work have to consume me when it consumed so few around me?

I turned again.

Why was I so insecure that John's remark, *She'll be right. It's the Aussie way,* unsettled me so?

Was John having a go at me and inferring that in some way I wasn't Australian? Was the olive skin the reason? My black skin.

Why were my eyes drawn constantly out the window to the mountains?

Why did I take the hat? Why was I disturbed when John put it in the bin and Arianne placed it on the floor?

Why was I disconnected from those around me?

Why was I restless? The idea of staying where I was seemed claustrophobic?

I was angry at myself and I couldn't pinpoint why. Staying still, staying put, felt wrong. Going somewhere, anywhere, seemed the right thing to do.

I twisted over.

I looked at the shadow of Arianne in the blackness.

This last observation wasn't meant for her. I wanted to be near her. I was guilty I'd made it, even if merely to myself in the middle of the night. I was being unfair to John as well. He wasn't having a go at me.

I rotated to observe Arianne better. She shifted slightly.

I cursed for disturbing her again. I was irritated at not declaring my love to her earlier this evening. 'You'll love it ... the exhibition.' It was feeble. Maybe I was hoping that if she loved the exhibition that she might love me.

Now I instigated a debate I'd hosted in my head often.

It was circular. No answer ever presented itself.

Arianne had never communicated to me that she loved me over the two years we'd been together. She was an independent Australian woman of the twenty first century. She was more than capable of speaking her mind. And she did. If Arianne wanted to say that she loved me, then she would.

If I told Arianne that I loved her would I look needy? Weak?

Arianne was so strong. She didn't need an uncertain man. She'd intimated as much herself this afternoon.

Progressively I lifted the blanket, gradually moving my feet to the floor.

I crept out of the room.

I didn't want to turn a light on and risk waking her. Feeling the way so as not to bump into a wall or door, I made for the garage in darkness.

Shutting the door to the rest of the house, I found the light switch.

Turning it on, I squinted adjusting to the suddenly bright light.

In the back corner of the space, near a sink, in an old wooden cupboard was where I stored all of the hiking equipment.

Accessing the gear took a little time. I had to move the golf clubs, tennis rackets, gym machines and canoe to one side.

Finishing the task, I rubbed my hands together to remove the dust that had been picked up from all the items. The dust was so tenacious I washed my hands in the sink.

Finally I reached the shelving where the pack and other equipment had been stored. Before long the floor was covered in equipment, maps and dehydrated food. I was rummaging around in it for fun and to release energy. Inspecting a food pack of dehydrated lamb roast I noticed the *best before* date was December of the previous year. The next food pack was the same and the next.

I picked up the snowshoes that I used on day trips near the resorts. Safe trails well-groomed for novices to give a taste of a mountain experience.

I scanned the equipment. My brain acknowledged and was horrified that I'd purchased so much. I'd bought all of the other sporting gear that'd hardly been used. I'd subscribed to the experience of the outdoors by procuring stuff.

Inspecting the first aid kit I noted that the seals on the tablets packaging was still intact. They'd been stored for a while and I hoped they were still OK. A space blanket tightly wrapped in a tiny bundle interested me for a moment. Not for the first time I wondered how big it was when expanded. I suspected I'd never be able to pack it away as neatly so I never checked and I wouldn't now. Various bandages were turned over in my hands. They looked serviceable. A set of hand warmers was scrutinised. A chemical reaction was triggered when the plastic wrapper was breached and the items exposed to air. A date on the package informed me they were expired but I left them. They still might work.

My attention went back to the snowshoes. I tested the bindings. They were serviceable. Next I inspected the aluminium frame, the stretched vinyl deck, and the metal claw on the underside that gripped the snow. All was in order. My life might depend upon it functioning properly, I rationalised. Perhaps I'd picked up that idea from the salesman as well. In reality I'd always visited safe, designated, controlled sightseer zones. In these areas the car and relative safety was only a short hike away.

I recollected John telling me work was done at the museum until it was time to pack up. That was two weeks before the exhibition finished.

What could I do in two weeks?

I knew what I'd be doing at work. Endless rounds of escorting media and dignitaries to the Public Affairs area of the museum. Public Affairs would then present talking points I'd written for them while I stood and watched. A spare wheel. It had happened before.

I found the map of Namadgi National Park. This park encompassed the Brindabella Mountains and the river valleys south of Canberra that I'd beheld through the window this afternoon. Besides being a haven for flora and fauna, the Brindabella Ranges were the source of water that was so important for an inland capital to be created in this, the driest of continents. Shielding this water catchment by excluding farming and grazing meant that the capital's bush became protected early in Canberra's development.

A group of scientists, bushwalkers and skiers came together in the 1960s to set up an association with a view of establishing a National Park in the Australian Capital Territory. The dream of this alliance to conserve the unique environment of the alpine and sub alpine regions was realised in 1984.

I'd walked in the Park on the occasional weekend with Arianne. We weren't alone. Hiking the trails of Namadgi was a recreational activity for some of Canberra's population.

I perused the map. It wasn't creased and worn like a map that'd been folded and refolded many times. It was practically new.

Immediately my attention was drawn to the contours that marked Bimberi Peak. The highest mountain in the Australian Capital Territory and the snow-capped summit I'd seen from work this afternoon. I visualised a few different routes to reach the feature. Then my fingers touched the map as I traced squiggly lines, mentally checking off the kilometres to get to her. It'd be thirty kilometres that way or fifty five kilometres down the Mount Franklin Road. The longest Road in the Australian Capital Territory.

I'd never journeyed to Bimberi Peak. It was a long way out and I couldn't drive there and do tourist walks. I'd have to shoulder a pack.

This was unlike Mount Franklin, another mountain of the Brindabellas that was marked on the map. Arianne and I had visited this mountain in summer. We drove the car to the base of the final hill before walking a few kilometres to look around the old ski fields and at the view. Then we'd enjoyed a picnic and a drive home.

It was a bush experience for city residents. A bush experience for the likes of me.

The planning process absorbed me. It was enjoyable and a relief.

Leaning from the waist I stretched with my arm and selected the adjoining map of Kosciuszko National Park. This map too had few signs of wear. There were large swathes of the territory it covered that I'd studied for the exhibition. I knew the history, though I'd never been there.

The Parks joined each other along the state boundary. Kosciuszko National Park was in New South Wales and Namadgi in the Capital Territory. I noted the huge reservoirs of the Snowy Hydroelectric scheme that were so prominently marked in blue. I read the title *Jagungal Wilderness* and scanned the close contours of the Mountain that gave the wilderness its name. This indicated steep terrain. Touching this spot on the map I then let the fingers shift south to Mount Kosciuszko. This mountain was the highest on mainland Australia.

The High Country. The Main Range. The Snowys. The Man from Snowy River Country. All of these names were common Australian vernacular. These different nomenclatures each provided a nuanced picture of the alpine and sub-alpine area of Australia. Many peaks were well above the fifteen hundred metre mark.

The name Muniong didn't spring to mind, though it was attributed by early Europeans as the name for the area by the original peoples of the region. Several records suggested it meant Big White Mountain. Some believed that it should more correctly have been spelt Munayang and that this was the word used to refer to meeting places.

I walked across to the cycle pack on the bench and pulled out the *How It Was* map I'd drawn at work. I unfolded it. I returned to the floor and placed it beside the other maps.

There were wooded valleys and open plains. Fast flowing rivers and waterfalls. It was country to be enjoyed. I'd hiked the periphery of it during spring, summer and autumn. On a few occasions I'd walked around the resorts in winter using the snowshoes that now rested on the floor. I stared at them again. Was it possible to walk to Kosciuszko in winter? By myself carrying everything?

My mind lost itself in the adventure and the mathematics of it.

Two hundred kilometres.

Two hundred and seventy five thousand steps.

A week's supply of food would weigh about five kilograms.

Camping gear would be fifteen kilograms.

Snowshoes and walking poles another five kilograms.

A total load of twenty five kilograms.

A walk in winter would see temperatures ranging from minus fifteen degrees Celsius to plus fifteen degrees Celsius. A dangerous range that meant there was snow, ice and freezing weather at night followed by melting during the day. The melting meant that there would be a dampness that couldn't be avoided. Sometimes it rained and sometimes it snowed. Add this to airstreams that were sometimes more than one hundred kilometres per hour and there was a wind-chill danger that might cause an unwary hiker hypothermia in half an hour.

The Australian Alps were affected by the fast south-westerly winds known to mariners as the Roaring Forties. These strong winds were at about latitude forty degrees south of the equator though they varied in location between summer and winter. The winds shifted to a more northerly track in winter and a more southerly track in summer.

Used by sailors to make good time in the era of sail they were dangerous and unpredictable. The speed of the winds and storms caused many a ship wreck along the southern Australian coast.

The airstream of the Roaring Forties collided with the north-south spine of the Australian Alps. The sides of the mountains acted as a wall that the gusts lashed, searching for gaps and the heights to rush through and over. Bush walkers had died of exposure in storm events caused by this weather system. It was a constant danger.

An expedition to Kosciuszko in winter would be a challenge. Alone it might be dangerous, even foolhardy.

I shifted position to be central amongst the gear and started running checks.

The maps covered the entirety of the journey.

There was an emergency beacon for safety. A note to Arianne would tell her where I was each day. I knew where the mobile telephone had some coverage from previous visits. Admittedly those areas were near the road and resorts and would be of limited use for much of the journey.

I had the best light-weight equipment. This would enable me to make quicker time than if I was weighed down with heavier kit. The salesman had found a good customer who'd bought the gear and the story.

Impulsively I began packing. I checked each item for serviceability. The absolute need for it was weighed in my head. Only then would it be stuffed into the pack. No need for extra load on an expedition like the one I was imagining.

Heavy items went in first and against the frame so it was as close to the back as possible. This helped lower the centre of gravity and meant that my back wouldn't strain to keep the load in an upright position. I'd be as stable as possible. All of this had been learnt on an introduction to camping and bush survival course I'd purchased once.

Soon the floor was empty and the pack was bulging.

I was fit. The cycling all year round helped build leg strength and aerobic fitness.

I lifted the load and tested it on my shoulders. At the same time I glanced over the floor to ensure that nothing was left behind.

I jumped up and down on the spot to test if there would be any annoying rattles when I walked. There were none. The pack clung to me as I bounced. It was noiseless. This was evidence that it was tightly packed and wouldn't move under the repetitive motion of walking.

The hat came into vision. I dwelt on it for a second.

I unbuckled the pack and placed it back down.

Packing for the imaginary hike to Kosciuszko had been a fun diversion. All up the activity had been a good distraction from the many unwanted thoughts that'd crowded around me when in bed.

Striding over to the hat I picked it up and then placed it on top of the pack. The display of the pack with the hat on it was satisfying. It looked like it all belonged to me. It did, apart from the hat. The ensemble was whole.

The battered hat attracted the eye and drew the attention away from the hardly used pack. The hat gave the impression that the gear was in use by an expert.

A mountain man!

Sinking to the floor, I propped against the wall of the garage to view the pack.

I went across to it pulled out a dehydrated food pack, pot and stove. I filled the pot at the sink, lit the stove and sat waiting for water to boil.

Planning

I ATE THE REHYDRATED FOOD and noted that while past the *best before* date it was still good. Food finished, I remained motionless ... passive. I was content, from a distance, to admire the pack and hat as an image of adventure. It was a contemplation of indeterminate length.

I realised the assembled sculpture was more than an image. It was a collection of commodities that'd been sold to me as a dream. The fantasy of a holiday that'd never come. The idea of being a rugged outdoor man of legend. The chance to be someone I wasn't. The possibility of being someone who was truly Australian.

The merchandise had made adventure available.

The pack and all the equipment were hardly used. They were hardly worn, though in theory they were designed to be rugged and long lasting. *Last a lifetime* the salesmen had pitched over and over. The one piece of equipment that'd been exposed to the elements was the hat.

I'd been to lessons on camping. It was these that'd taught me to pack the gear so carefully. I'd learnt navigation, first aid and survival skills. The lessons were largely forgotten. The acquired knowledge hadn't been practised. It was starkly obvious that I was an imposter.

Eventually the cool of the concrete seeping through my pyjama trousers caused an involuntary tremor. This reflex reaction pulled me out of the reverie and into the present.

The question of what to do with all of that neatly packed equipment and food needed answering.

Obviously I might unload it all and put the equipment back where I'd taken it from. This was sensible, though unsatisfactory, as it was wasteful of the good job I'd done.

There was the possibility of an expedition, though I didn't know anyone who'd accompany me at this time of year.

Since the Dreaming, winter wasn't the time to travel to the High Country. The peoples of the region had noticed when the mists rose from the valleys to the crests. For some Aboriginal people in the region this was the Spirit of the Mountain awakening. It was a warning that the huge body of the Spirit would block the sun and freeze the ground. It froze those people who chose to go there. The Spirit lay as snow until it returned into the mountain again. That was the time to go to the Australian Alps. Not now.

The awakened Spirit of the Mountain wasn't the only reason to avoid the ranges in winter. Walking alone was against all of the conventional wisdom of bush travel.

As I sat on the floor of the garage, the image of the red and white posters that adorned the inside walls of High Country huts came to mind. I'd seen them on visits. The poster was titled *Back Country Travel*. The first line of advice was *Never Travel Alone*. Always travel in a party into the Australian bush. The theory being that the group offered safety. If a member was hurt they could carry the injured person to help.

I smiled.

I'd tried rescuing a person on the survival course. The instructor had nominated Arianne to be a simulated casualty. The rest of the group had set about rescuing her. We'd fashioned a stretcher and then stumbled onward carrying her. Despite Arianne's slight build, and her weight being shared by four bearers, it was difficult. For us office workers she was still heavy. The stretcher had restricted vision, making it hard to see where to place the feet safely. All in all it'd been an awkward lesson in how difficult a rescue would be.

The activity had ended up with more people hurt. This time not simulated. Carrying an injured person on a rough trail was hard, heavy and dangerous work.

The instructor had suggested that someone might stay with the injured person. Others in the group would go for help. This he imparted was the best course to take in such circumstances.

I countered this argument with the knowledge that the emergency beacon I'd put in the pack would alert rescue teams of a life threatening situation more promptly than any companions racing for help. At maximum it should take twenty minutes for the signal to leave the beacon, be picked up by a satellite and re-transmitted to earth for processing at the National Emergency Centre. The possibility of someone taking hours or days on foot to get help was ever present in sparsely populated Australia.

I imagined how reassuring the presence of another might be especially if injured, but determined that I'd do without it.

Companions might be better when doing navigation, I hypothesised. Arianne and I had shared the map reading on our short hikes. On the other hand, during that same survival course, we had managed to convince ourselves we were in the right place even when we were proven to be in the wrong place. Some in the group had pointed out features as they saw them, related them to the map before declaring where they believed we were. I had doubts. Yet I found myself nodding in agreement with the rest. Later we discovered that we were quite wrong.

The group later conducted an inevitable post-mortem. It came to the consensus that we were mostly right and everyone dropped the subject happy. To this day I remained concerned about how we'd all convinced ourselves we were correct when in reality my navigation skills were poor.

Due to my concern I'd later spent time thinking about this experience. The difficulty with being almost right was that when bushwalking I either knew where I was or I didn't. Mostly right wasn't much good. I grunted as the saying that was sometimes quoted sprang to mind. *A problem shared is a problem halved.* Actually a problem shared was still a problem.

A group wasn't necessarily an aid to navigation. A group just gave me people to share the nagging doubts with. Alone, the sole person to consult was me. Just my own skills and deductive reasoning to reach the right answer.

Rather than companions I decided a good map was the most essential navigation aid. Experience with tourist maps had taught me that there were plenty of ordinary maps that didn't show the right level of detail to move around accurately.

Map reading also required diligent attention to the ground as I walked: the features around me, the sun's position in the sky, the length of time spent walking, and knowledge about how fast I walked per hour. They all aided accurate navigation. Add to this a compass to confirm direction.

I'd purchased a GPS device as backup after the confusing map reading experiences. I acknowledged it wasn't a cure for being lost. It was another aid that needed to be used in conjunction with all of my skills.

I can do it, I avowed, knowing that this assertion was made to drown out doubts.

Then in the next moment I conjured the media headlines. *Foolhardy man rescued in mountains.*

I grinned ruefully. The self-deception hadn't worked.

It was certain that if I needed to signal help with the beacon that this would be the angle the media would focus in on. I'd watched the phenomenon with bushwalkers and solo sailors. *Lone Sailor Rescued in Southern Ocean. Costs Taxpayers Millions.*

Ambulances were summoned every day to assist people who'd hurt themselves unnecessarily. Some injuries were accidents and others misadventure. These misfortunes by and large didn't attract much attention or criticism.

Why did society adversely judge a well-equipped visitor to the bush having to be rescued? Why would it judge me negatively?

Perhaps it was because I'd be discovered alone. I knew that was a problem.

The modern world advocated individualism. This implied to me singularity and that our society was pro people being separate. I knew though that the public were suspicious of aloneness.

This inconsistency had once troubled me. I spent so little time alone. On the few occasions when I was spotted by others alone they had commented on it.

'Was it you that I saw at the movies by yourself on Saturday afternoon?'

It was an accusation.

I always felt the need to explain. 'Arianne was with friends and she didn't want to see that movie.'

Perhaps I was just overly defensive.

I liked being alone. I also liked good companionship. I didn't prefer one over the other. Companionship offered the joy of sharing. Solitude offered the elation of the discovery that I could rely on myself.

Conceivably, the imagined headlines were because the bush was unfamiliar to us modern Australians and therefore we'd become fearful. We weren't comfortable there anymore. It was a strange and unaccustomed environment that held many dangers. We could become lost, bitten by snakes, die of exposure and starvation. Death in the bush had become dramatic. The much more common death in the urban environment from car accident, electrocution, trapped in burning building or murder was humdrum in comparison.

Few of us knew how to survive in the outback anymore.

I realized, it was recognition that in the bush we'd lost control. In the city we controlled the climate in our house, car and office. We couldn't govern the climate of the bush. We were at the whim of nature. The city's built environment was about taming nature. Pretending we had control over it and our lives. Maybe we didn't like to expose ourselves to an environment where this illusion might be lost.

I shivered again from the cold concrete. This time it caused me to stand and walk to the pack.

I hesitated. A hat was a very personal item. It was like a pair of socks. If it wasn't yours, you shouldn't wear it.

Reaching down I placed hat on head.

I adjusted it up and down. No matter where it sat, on the forehead, tilted back or frontward, or on an angle to the side, it was very comfortable. Without doubt, it was a very good fit.

Instinctively, I could tell when an item was perfect. This hat was right for me. It was as if I'd visited every store in Canberra to find the precise hat for my head.

I hadn't, and there was a magic in that knowledge.

Bending, I picked up the pack, swinging it onto my back.

The hat caressing my forehead and the weight of the pack on the shoulders made me feel self-reliant. It was an unfamiliar sensation.

I wondered if the weight of my pack was the cause of this confidence. Perhaps the knowledge that all I needed to live was contained within it elicited the emotion. Maybe it was some association I had of hiking with holidays. Holidays I'd never had. Possibly it was a sense of relief at not having to go to work rather than confidence.

My mind was drawn back to the hat.

It sat so snugly. There was no feeling of irritation around the forehead from the old felt or worn leather band. The hat wasn't as soft as it would've been when new. Yet it was, I judged, still top rate. It was a testament to the craftsmanship of the makers.

Impulsively, my hand reached upward for the brim. The now familiar tingle in the fingers as the tips brushed against it started again.

Was it the hat that made me self-reliant?

I dismissed the idea as it formed.

I was ready for a journey. The challenge of climbing a snow-covered mountain. The magical mountain I'd seen with shafts of light illuminating its gold-pink summit. I might embark on a quest to find the wild brumbies and have the adventure of discovering the bush for myself.

The sense of purpose was palpable. Excitement began to rise.

I quelled these expectations by removing the pack from my shoulders and returning it to the concrete flooring.

This sobered me and I started to think.

The expedition appeared doable.

Then it was a dream.

Then next moment I believed it was possible again, though not in the pyjamas that I wore. It was obvious that I'd never know the answer until I tried.

Walking to the rear of the garage area, I pulled from a drawer a set of gardening trousers and shirt. I dressed in them and then I put on the new hiking boots.

I tiptoed from the garage into the main house. In the kitchen I raided the pantry and refrigerator for extra foods.

I wrote a note for Arianne. It was more difficult than I expected and it took a good hour.

Then with letter in hand I trod quietly to the front door.

Stopping, I put an envelope on the ground where Arianne wouldn't miss it. Her name was printed neatly on the front.

I stepped through the door into the dark and cold. Stealthily, I locked it behind me.

THE LETTER

Dear Arianne,

I couldn't sleep.

I was tossing and turning and disturbing you.

Sorry.

Sorry I came home in such a strange mood. It was unworthy of all the support you've shown me. You've been amazing these last few months and I appreciate you sharing in my passion. I hope I haven't been too much of a pain.

I should be pleased about the opening of the exhibition tomorrow. The truth is I can't face being there. It's a good exhibition. At least everyone tells me so. I still have doubts. At the heart of it is the nagging question, how can I produce an exhibition that people like when I don't understand them? I don't even understand myself.

John said I was done until the exhibition is over so I'm going walkabout. I need to be in the mountains to get my head straight. I'm thinking about hiking to Kosciuszko, as you'll tell from the itinerary I've put on the next page. I might get home before then depending on circumstances. I'll have the mobile and will give you a call when I can. As you know mobile coverage is limited away from the city. I'll do my best to call. Please explain to John—I think he'll understand. I hope you do. This restlessness is not about you.

I count on your support and hope you'll indulge this impulse.

I won't leave the trails and I'll stay in the abandoned bushmen's huts when I can.

I'll not walk in a storm to be safe. If a storm hits the mountains, assume that the itinerary will slip while I wait for it to pass.

I'll be careful.

I'll talk on the mobile when I can—thank you for your understanding.

I care about you so much.

Tim

PS. I've attached an itinerary, a list of equipment I'm carrying and the details of the emergency beacon.

PPS. Please tell John I took the hat he threw out. I'm sorry. I shouldn't have. I'll return it when I'm back.

I'll stay on the itinerary below unless there's a storm:

Night 1—Pryor's Hut; Night 2—Oldfield's Hut; Night 3—Witzes Hut; Night 4—Happy Jack's Hut; Night 5—Valentine's Hut; Night 6—Guthega; Night 7—Thredbo Village via Mount Kosciuszko

I'm carrying:

Pack and weather proof pack cover

Walking poles, snowshoes and plastic sandals for river crossings

Socks and underwear (three spare pairs), Long Johns

Gloves and balaclava, polar-tec vest and warm shell

Sunglasses

Tent, foam sleeping mat, sleeping bag, inner sheet

Emergency beacon (EB 2014-SN0016016370), torch, mobile telephone

Maps, compass, GPS

First aid kit, snow shovel

Pot, cup, water bottles, stove and fuel, fork and knife
Seven days food
Trowel, personal toiletries
Camera
Hat

THE ESCAPE

FROM THE WARMTH OF THE MODERN HOUSE and into the age-old cold of a damp mist, I moved. It swallowed me. With a walking pole in each hand, I awkwardly adjusted the pack on my shoulders as I moved towards the scrubby ridge that was just behind the suburb. Soon I was away from the glow of the street lighting. Dropping my head, I concentrated on the ground directly in front. Vision was just a few metres and I needed to stare intently.

Native grasses covered in a thick layer of frost crunched underfoot. A cloud of vapour rose from my mouth and danced in front of my nose before joining with the fog. The Spirit of the Mountain had awakened as it had for millennia, I observed.

My nose had almost lost all feeling except I had a sense it was about to drip.

Stepping slowly, and after a little stumbling on the uneven ground, I found the flat sandstone rock I was looking for. It was level with the soil. The sandstone was grooved.

Halting, I knelt and took off the glove on my right hand. Fingers dwelled above the grooves. I checked myself. *Nangingattai*. The Ngunawal word for look and listen came to mind. I listened. A still hush surrounded me. Out of reverence I did not touch.

These marks were evidence of tool making. The indentations had formed from countless years of rubbing stone on stone. Incalculable generations of peoples had visited this site to fashion axes and spearheads.

The stone was unlike the more usual granite-like rocks of the region. The location of this rare sandstone outcrop in the Canberra regional landscape would've been passed down from father to son through word-of-mouth.

I stroked the dirt near the grooves. This wasn't the exciting thrill I had when I touched the hat. This was altogether different, though no less satisfying. The gritty touch of the dirt conveyed sureness that grounded me. This place always had. Here on the edge of the suburbs, on the edge of the Alps, was evidence that humans had been in this country fighting to survive for eons. Perhaps some of the peoples who'd come here were my ancestors.

No one had sign-posted this most ancient site.

Not for the first time I pondered why.

Maybe no one cared. Possibly it was because some scratch marks in rocks were not considered to be very spectacular and worthy of a sign. Conceivably there was fear that if this site was known to the broader public it'd be vandalised.

I didn't know for certain. In the end I decided that it hadn't been sign-posted for millennia so it didn't need to be sign-posted now.

I recognised that all of this speculation was dominated by modern cultural ideas. In any case, I'd come to understand that when I touched the dirt in this place that the earth touched me in turn. The possibility that the many toolmakers who'd crafted here had left some kind of a presence occurred to me. This was similar to how I'd come to think about the hat.

My hand stopped touching the dirt and reached up to brush the brim of the hat.

There it was again—that feeling. I touched the hat and the hat touched me back. Possibly the maker who'd tenderly softened, worked and shaped the felt had also left a presence that I detected.

I regarded this internal discussion as not rational or fact-based. How else to explain it?

The cold seeped into my bones, interrupting this thinking.

I examined my watch instinctively to mentally record the start time. 5:10. The journey began from here and now.

I stood, placed on gloves and walked towards the lights. Back into the suburb. Little streams of cars drove past in the direction of Civic, the city centre. Parallel beams extended from the fronts of the cars through the fog. They came as blobs of vehicles that'd been gathered together at a red traffic light and then released by the green.

In the grey-black confusion of the early morning I guessed no driver had seen me walking in the opposite course. They'd have tunnel vision as they peered into the gloom on their way to work.

They were warm and I was cold.

Today I'd left the commute and I was heading in a different direction.

The moist vapour on my face was invigorating. My nose was dripping and I used the glove as a wipe. The damp cold penetrated the jacket and trouser legs. Despite the fact that the effort of walking was generating heat, my extremities were cooling. A fast pace was needed just to maintain body temperature. At least that'd be the case until the sun rays were high enough and strong enough to poke through.

My feet were going as fast as they'd move. Probably I was doing about five kilometres an hour, though I knew this would slow as the day wore on and reduce further when I hit the mountains. I might do three and a half kilometres an hour on the undulating dirt trails of the mountains and even less in the snow.

A risk to the success of this expedition was blisters on the feet. I ran a mental check of the boots. The socks inside of them were smooth and fitted.

There were no wrinkles around the skin. The laces were tied firmly holding the feet in place without too much movement. The boots were secure as the leather tongue flexed against the cords. Everything was in order.

I shouldn't get blisters today.

Next I evaluated the walking poles that were in each hand. The alternate arm extended to the horizontal in cadence with each step. The shafts, gripped in fists, were punching forward of me. They were almost bashing a path for the rest of the body to follow.

I gauged that the walking poles were at the correct height. Hikers had expressed to me different ideas about the need for these lightweight, adjustable aluminium shafts. It was suggested that they were OK when walking on a trail yet were of limited value when walking cross-country.

I had doubts. Still I purchased them because the sales person was so convinced of their worth.

Since then, on day hikes with Arianne, I'd come to learn that they took a little weight off the knees. They provided balance on dirt tracks and steep downhill paths. It was true I'd never bush-bashed with them, though I guessed if they were a hindrance, I'd just collapse them and tie them to the pack.

Lastly I did an audit of the pack. The weight was sitting on my hips and not the shoulders. This was the more correct position I'd learnt on the camping course. The straps across the shoulders were even on the left and right. Overall I judged the load in the pack to be well enough distributed.

I'd been advised on the survival course that most people packed better on the second day of a hike. I'd never hiked for two days in a row so I hoped that this would prove to be true.

I panted as I walked. The freezing temperatures were causing the lungs to burn a little.

The road traffic disappeared and the streets were now empty except for me. The last streets of Canberra's outer southern suburbs rose upwards off the valley floor and I puffed a little more. The concrete paving gave way to gravel and I was soon heaving the pack over a gate before climbing it.

I'd crossed the line from well-ordered suburbia to the bush. My vision tunnelled in on the track ahead. Mild anxiety caused my stomach to spin. I suppressed a sense of trepidation.

Adjusting the pack back onto shoulders by shrugging and tugging at the straps I headed up a short steep climb. This slight climb was the rise that ringed most of Canberra's suburbs. Across the top of this hill was a downward slope where water ran into the catchment of the Murrumbidgee River untreated. The limits of Canberra were to some extent constrained by the need to ensure preservation of water cleanliness in the important corridor. Farmers and townsfolk downstream accessed this water to drink. Sheep, cattle, orchards and vineyards were all reliant on the water from the Mountain regions. Yass, Gundagai, Wagga Wagga were all large inland populations in New South Wales whose residents drank from the water. The water of the Murrumbidgee then flowed into the Murray River. This was the border between the states. Next towns from the state of Victoria drew from the combined Murray and Murrumbidgee River flows. Then South Australian towns consumed the water. It was syphoned a myriad of different ways before the remnant water flowed into wetlands and then out to sea.

In recent years residual water didn't exist. The water turned to mud, the wetlands dried out and the river for many years didn't link to the ocean at all. The damaging outcome was a dying river caused by the conjunction of the increasing demands by humans, changes in rain patterns, warm weather leading to more evaporation and politics. Federal Government, State Governments and Local Governments rarely agreed on how to conserve the scarce resource of water in this parched land. The media reported the certainty of each level of government that something needed to be done.

I crossed the ridge. I'd normally have expected vistas before me of open pastures sloping to the river. In the gloom and fog vision was limited.

On I strode faster now on the downhill. Puffing decreased to panting. Soon all of the breathlessness disappeared.

In the dark, quicker than expected, I found myself standing on the banks of the river.

I took a spell, taking the opportunity to rest and observe.

From my vantage point, the water was a murky slate grey below. There'd been rain in the last few days and the run-off of many mountain creeks had swelled the river causing it to flow strongly. It was apparent that the river would be deeper than normal. The Ngunawal meaning of Murrumbidgee, *plenty of water*, would be true this morning. Adding to this worry, I'd happened upon a section of the river that had steep banks. The old Bushman's adage was steep banks meant deep water.

I swivelled my head to left and right.

The sheer edges extended in this section in both directions. In the darkness it was impossible to tell how far I'd need to walk before I came to a better area for crossing. I judged the best course was to have a go at wading through it here.

Carefully I descended to the river.

I stopped and stripped off.

The solitary item of clothing I now wore was the hat. Shivering in the cold I scrunched the clothes into the pack. The boots were tied onto the pack by the laces so they'd remain dry.

Finally I placed on my set of plastic sandals and donned the pack. Pausing, I gathered courage for a second before stepping into the flow.

I winced as the icy cold water touched my toes and ankles. I pushed further into the river, eyes fixed on the far bank.

The water soon came to the knees.

Advancing further, the water reached just short of the waist. I'd been holding my breath, so I paused to concentrate on drawing in air for a moment. I was aware that the next steps would immerse my genitalia in freezing water. Most importantly it'd be lapping at the pack and its contents. I couldn't afford to have it get wet.

The eddying black water spun on the river's surface towards me and around me. The grey fog swirled above it. I registered the tonal difference in the shades, though the slow dance made them as one. My mind tried to categorise and separate each movement and failed. Eyes unsuccessfully searched for a focal point.

I swayed.

I steadied by tightening my stomach muscles and staring straight to the front.

I took the pack off and balanced it on my head. The weight of it squashed the hat further down on my forehead, though not as far as the eyes. I could still see. I kept the left hand on top of the pack to secure it and the right hand contained the two walking sticks that I prodded the stream with for balance.

Going back wasn't an option.

I advanced again.

The cold caused me to grimace and I promised myself that the worst was over.

There wasn't any evidence that this self-assertion had any basis in fact.

To the contrary, as I progressed, the water rose to my chest. My judgement was that I was halfway across the river and the depth was still increasing.

My neck muscles ached from the strain caused by the weight of the pack. I halted and carefully adjusted it. Despite my caution, it almost overbalanced before I steadied it with effort.

Stepping onward again, I fought the current with every tread for firm footing and stability. Unseen rocks beneath the surface shifted beneath my feet.

The water had now risen to my chin and I was numb all over.

I had no choice now. I had to continue.

Misgivings rose with the rising water. The strength of the river's flow dragged at me. Down and to the left it tugged.

With alarm I registered that the water now covered my mouth. It reached to a point just below the nose.

I took a deep breath just in case the next step took me under.

The next step was taken and the next. Then another. The water level was back at my mouth, though my numb lips and brain couldn't be certain.

I dared to think that the depth was less.

Encouraged, I ploughed on in desperation.

The water fell to my chest and kept falling.

The numbness was now in every part of my limbs and I sensed the muscles weakening. My footing was less sure and I stumbled. Just in time I caught myself from falling by jamming the walking poles against a rock.

In my semi-delirious state I had time to think that they were well worth the money.

A few more crawling, splashing steps and I collapsed on the far bank. The pack hit the ground with a thump and a cracking sound. My muscles were weak from the cold. I looked back across the river and saw the glowing grey-orange orb of the sun trying to press through the fog. It was dawn.

'Are you right?'

I looked in every direction for the voice.

On higher ground near some bushes I believed I saw the dark shadow of a man in full length oil-skins. His face was silhouetted black and featureless.

I tilted the hat backwards.

'I'm not sure,' I tentatively offered.

There was a long pause. 'You'll be right then.'

'What does that mean?' I stammered. My voice was weak and uncertain. It was so low it was barely audible even to my own ears. It sounded like I was talking to myself.

The stranger seemed to hear every word. 'You're uncertain because you're frightened. I reckon you need to be scared in the bush. Fear is a form of respect. You must be respectful of this country or it'll punish you. The mountains and the weather have slayed many before. It kills those that disregard the danger. Now get your clothes on and move. Move like a startled Brumby until all the cold has left your limbs. Go,' he ordered.

Responding to the command, I hastily pulled on my clothes. In silence, fingers fumbled at the buttons and zips. It took concentration to achieve the simple task of dressing. I had to think through every step of tying the bootlaces. Left over right, now through, pull to tighten, loop, then left over right again.

I picked up the pack.

The figure of the man in the fog was visible and so I carried the pack forward to him.

Arriving a few paces short of the figure, I stopped. It was a rock.

I looked around, confused.

THE OTHER SIDE OF A RIVER

NO PATH EXISTED from the southern river bank to the top of the next ridge. Though I was just out of town, I was in the wilds. Anxiety rose within me at the situation I'd chosen.

I was cold, I was on the bank of the Murrumbidgee River and I didn't know exactly where. The path ahead would be the one I made. My whereabouts were not known to anyone. I was alone.

Going back was discarded as a possibility. I wasn't going to cross the cold river again. I doubted that I could. I was now certain that if I'd known what I was plunging into when stepping into the river, I wouldn't have. I would've looked for a shallower crossing or gone home. Now forward towards the south was the only course to take.

Searching, I chose a spur to climb out of the river corridor. Progress was upwards, always upwards. Legs strained with the steep ascending grade that was never relieved by a flat or downward section. The weight of the pack added to the difficulty.

Branches I pushed through intermittently whipped backwards, flicking at my cheeks and eyes. Breathing shortened to gasps. Vision concentrated on the next few metres except when on a frequent break. Then I'd tilt my head upward to examine the steep grade. Fallen trees, scrub and boulders filled the view. The slope and obstacles extended in front of me with no end in sight.

When off a trail the general convention in the Australian bush is to move to the high ground. Walk on the crest. Stay on the spurs that connect the ridges. Water ran off the ridges and spurs, leaving them with fewer trees and bushes and therefore making it easier to walk through.

I'd been taught at school this was how Blaxland, Wentworth and Lawson had crossed the Blue Mountains for the first time in 1813. This successful expedition had opened up the colony to the economic development made possible by the access to pastures across the range that'd hemmed the settlement of Sydney against the coast since its establishment in 1788.

The Aboriginals had at least two routes that they used to pass through the mountain barrier. According to the discovery myth, not one colonist had considered asking for assistance in a path. Crossing the Blue Mountains was a European achievement.

The shortcomings of history aside, this convention had a practical modern application. If disoriented, I was to head for the high ground in the Australian bush. Most trails followed ridges and spurs because that was the easiest place to build them, just as it was the easiest place to walk.

So the theory goes, I thought irritably. The knowledge I'd gained from books and a lesson on camping was being tested by the reality of bashing through the scrub in real life. The experience of putting the information into practice was tiring and frustrating work. The bushmen who'd made these conventions were hardened by years of tough living. Their experience was different to my life in every way. Maybe this was easier going for a pioneer though not for me.

Bush fires had been through this area a decade earlier. Big trees had fallen before its force. All around me was dense regrowth. Saplings obscured the loose rocky ground making the footing treacherous.

Halting, I drew breath. I packed the walking poles away. They were of no use in this mess of rocks and bushes. Hands were better used pushing branches aside, or grasping stronger ones to pull myself upwards.

Hardy Australian flora was heat resistant and required less water. This was often achieved by having small waxy pointed leaves that had the same effect as thorns when brushed against. My hands were now bleeding from cuts and scratches. Threads were running in the trouser legs where sticks and prickly leaves had penetrated.

Views of the ridge were obscured and I had no sense of how far I had to travel before I reached the top and an expected fire trail. The upside was that the exertions had left me warm. The cold of the river was a memory.

With frequent stops to draw breath and to select a route, I moved uphill in a zigzag. Sometimes the log of a fallen tree would provide a path higher. Sometimes a patch of rocks, bare of vegetation, was easier to scramble over than bashing through the bush. No good routes and no rules existed. The brain just worked constantly making quick decisions. It weighed up the many negatives to find a best path from the numerous bad options.

My steps became more deliberate as the relentless slope wore on. Make haste slowly. Pause and choose—time spent finding the easiest route is seldom wasted, I thought.

It took a good hour ploughing upwards before I spied the point where the slope met the sky. I was relieved and elated even though it still took another ten minutes to achieve the ridge on the western side of the Murrumbidgee River.

At the top of the ridge I came upon a trail that ran in a southerly direction.

Taking the pack off, I sat on a rock to recuperate. It was a relief to be free of the load. I guzzled water. It spilled from my mouth and across the chin. I nibbled on a biscuit.

When I finished eating there was silence.

The whisper of sound that was everywhere in a city was gone.

A feeling of calm swept through me.

Still the sun had not completely penetrated the mist. The grey glow of filtered light was providing an eerie radiance. I was surrounded by shadowy trees. The illumination wasn't bright enough to show the common olive greens of the Australian landscape.

Views of the Tidbinbilla Valley could be seen below and to the west. Through the mist it too was shades of grey and white. Wisps of impenetrable fog sat in some hollows and the grass of the valley floor was covered in a thick frost. This valley ran south to north. The early settlers had referred to this area of the mountains as Tidbinbilly. It was now a family park. Some said the spelling that most closely reflects the Ngunawal pronunciation for that valley was *Jedbinbilla*. The meaning, where boys became men, was unknown to most visitors of the family park. It was a ceremonial location where aspirants were initiated into society.

To the north poking above the tree tops were the white dishes of the NASA facility at Tidbinbilla. One of these antennas had been moved from Honeysuckle Creek Station that was twenty kilometres east and south of where I stood. It'd been the antenna used to transmit the film and voice of the Apollo eleven lunar landing. I stared at the white parabola of the dish. Here in this ancient landscape the technology existed to talk to another world.

I shivered. Swallowing more water I then shouldered the pack. I followed the fire trail south. It went slightly downhill before it veered west and then steeply descended into the valley and the mist.

In time, I came to the Cotter Road. Crossing, I found another road pointing south. I selected this route. I knew from picnic trips that this road would take me to Corin Dam.

In front, vision narrowed to the bitumen of road disappearing into fog. A lone cyclist appeared from the gloom silently hurtling downhill towards me. Both of us were surprised. We did not acknowledge each other. My brain registered his name, a brand name or a sponsor's name on the vest.

'Beaumont.'

Then he was gone somewhere behind me and I was left thinking about the name that'd been automatically registered. My conditioning was to read every word and yet I hadn't taken the time for the social communication of a nod of recognition.

Momentum continued for stride after stride.

On my right was Birrigai. My eyes searched the rocky steep slopes. In those rocks archaeological digs had uncovered signs of human habitation for more than twenty thousand years. Old fireplaces, bone from hunted animals and stone tools all provided evidence of a long association by humans with the area I was walking though. It was hypothesised that the ancestor population had lived in the area using the rocks as shelter. The enormous rocks had naturally fallen in such a way as to form habitations.

It was easy to say twenty thousand years, I reflected.

There would be people in Canberra who wanted to visit Stonehenge in the United Kingdom. It was certain that some Canberrans and many Australians had travelled around the world to see that site. The oldest known part of Stonehenge was four thousand years old. Here, on the edge of Canberra, was evidence of human habitation five times longer than Stonehenge. Few knew of its existence.

Evidence of occupation of the shelter by Aboriginals dated its use throughout the last ice age. At that time, with the temperatures significantly colder, there would've been deep snow in winter followed by grass in the valleys in summer. Probably occupation of the shelter would've been seasonal with the inhabitants living near the warmer coast during the colder months.

This seasonal use was for some clans and peoples the pattern until the nineteenth century. Then, many Aboriginals were forced off the grasslands around the city of Canberra by Europeans and their cattle.

Some Aboriginals worked for the settlers. Others discovered that the spearing of cattle for food brought the risk of being shot, so it was probable that they retreated to these foothills for shelter.

A culture that had lived for thousands of years, with no exposure to European agriculture or sense of ownership or diseases, was on a collision course that would nearly destroy the population in a seventy year period from first contact.

Up the valley I progressed always heading south. The sealed road was on my left side. I walked facing towards the traffic as a precaution. Apart from the cyclist there'd been no traffic in either direction.

The morning was advancing and the sun still had not bathed me in warmth.

I spied small waterfalls in the distance that occasionally disappeared from view behind trees.

In time I arrived at Gibraltar Creek. A sign pointed to a picnic area that had been established near the waterfalls. Hunger pangs and my senses suggested it was lunch time.

I checked my watch. It was five minutes past eleven in the morning. I'd been walking for almost six hours without breakfast.

I hadn't been walking. I'd been marching at a frantic pace. Almost running, though from what was hard to explain.

The little viewing platform for the falls invited me to stop. I downed the pack and pulled out some bread and cheese for lunch. The cheese was still cold. I recalled the culinary recommendation of taking cheese from the refrigerator to ripen at room temperature for hours before eating. The cheese wouldn't ripen as the current temperature was no more than a few degrees Celsius. In my judgement the temperature was still cooler than most fridges. No sun penetrated into the steep valley and an impromptu shiver racked me from head to toe.

I sipped from the water bottle. The cold liquid hit the stomach. It drained more heat from me, from my core. I shuddered violently.

The warm pocket of sweat on the back, from where the pack had been pressing against it, was already chilled.

Unzipping the pack's main storage compartment, I reached for a vest that was strategically near the top.

My hand touched fragmented pieces of plastic.

I pulled the pieces into view and recognised the distinctive yellow colour. The GPS.

I remembered the cracking sound as I dropped the pack at the side of the river. That must have done it.

Pulling the device from the pack, with hope I pushed the button that would turn the GPS on. Nothing happened.

I swore.

I grabbed the vest and pulled it on. Instantly, I felt warmer.

'Where are you heading?' A deep, strong and reassuring voice questioned.

I looked over my shoulder and saw a squat man in park-ranger uniform not ten paces away. He was balding and crease marks from years of smiling lined his face. His name tag identified him as 'James.'

'Up to the High Country,' I offered with a shake of the head in the direction of the mountains to the south. I was a little sheepish and didn't want to seem foolish. I wasn't sure how many went to the mountains by themselves in winter. I expected a negative reaction. To be frowned upon. None came.

'You're *Bemeringal*?'

'I don't know that term?'

'*Bemeringal*,' reiterated the ranger. 'The coastal people have used it as a name for the Mountain Men since the dreaming. Mountain Men are different. They have their own name.'

'No. City slicker,' I corrected. 'I don't think there was a term for that in the Dreaming.'

James's head jiggled good-humouredly in agreement. 'You're heading for the country of the Corroboree Frog. *Dyirri* my grandparents used to call him. Do you know of the Corroboree Frog?'

'Yes.' I filled the silence with as much knowledge as I knew. 'They're yellow and black and painted as if for a Corroboree. Unusually they don't hop. There are two populations, one population in the mountains near here and one near Kosciuszko. The population near Kosciuszko are green and black. The frog is endangered because it's reliant on wet bogs and never travels far from them. The bogs are drying out with less snow fall and therefore less moisture. Recently a newly introduced disease has sent the numbers into further decline.' I paused, 'would you like some lunch?'

James shook his head.

'Do you mind if I keep eating?'

James shook his head again. He started to talk.

'You know the science. I know the reality before that. The truth as it was to my people for thousands of years. *Dyirri* was created as an ordinary brown spotted frog. One day he was restless. *Gudba* the bad spirit came to him and offered to make him a different frog by sprinkling a magic powder over him. *Dyirri* consented and fell asleep. When he woke he was yellow and black and full of mischief.'

James's deep voice had a melodic quality. Still chewing, I closed eyes as the story developed.

'*Dyirri* knocked the old green frog off his reed and chased the young tadpoles scaring them. Then he tried to sing with the other frogs as the sun went down and he made such a terrible sound all the other frogs refused to sing. They threw rocks at *Dyirri* to make him go away. *Jundar* the spirit of the Billabong offered to help. *Jundar* put a dust on *Dyirri* that made him so thirsty that he drank the water and moved far away in search of more. He kept going until he found the mountain streams. He drank them dry, forming wetlands. There he remains hiding in the grasses. That's how *Dyirri* came to the mountains and created the wetlands.'

Silence fell.

Slowly it registered that the story was complete and so I opened eyes to acknowledge James.

He was nowhere to be seen. I was perplexed. Why had he left? Did James think I didn't like the story? I had liked it very much.

Then realising I was cold, reached for the hat and placed it on. I was warmer and comforted.

Where had James disappeared to?

I couldn't explain where he'd appeared from or where he'd gone. He certainly hadn't arrived or left in a car. I would've heard the sound of the engine.

I couldn't explain James's presence.

What the hell was going on in my brain?

I shook my head in confusion as if trying to jiggle it awake.

Impulsively, I adjusted the hat by pulling it down further on my head.

I drank from the water bottle. It was emptying rapidly. I shook it in a reflex action as if that somehow made the assessment more accurate. There was only a gulp left.

I went over to the waterfall and held the bottle out to fill. The cold water soon made my fingers sting. Persisting despite the discomfort, I held the bottle under the water until it overflowed. It was crystal clear and was some of the purest water in Australia. Even so it might still have giardia and cryptosporidium and wasn't to be trusted. Reaching into a pocket I took out a chlorine tablet and dropped it into the bottle. It'd treat the bugs in the water in the next hour.

I shouldered the pack. As I commenced walking again, gently at first to let the warmth begin again in the muscles, I checked the time.

11:09.

Lunch had taken four minutes.

How could that be?

I shook the watch as an impulse to make certain that it was working. This was a silly reflex. The watch was digital and not mechanical.

The visual check had shown the display to be working perfectly. It had taken four minutes in this shady valley to get cold. Four minutes to eat lunch and to get the story of *Dyirri*.

Logic told me that this wasn't possible.

What was happening to time?

The Boundary of City and Bush

THE ROAD LEVELLED OUT as I reached a pass at the altitude of twelve hundred metres. My footfalls on the road lengthened as the long tiring climb I'd been struggling up turned to a flat stretch. Patches of snow clung to the shade under trees. It was the remnants of a bigger fall.

Past the Corin Forest family play area I strode. Here man-made snow was created in a paddock for recreational purposes. I saw a few cars and mud. Some screams of children having fun could be heard. My eyes automatically searched for them. They remained unseen.

At this point a locked gate across the bitumen road blocked car access. It was evident that the road had been shut for reasons of safety as snow was across the tarmac. Rangers with the key were the only people I could expect past this point. The road now dipped down for seven kilometres to the Cotter River and the Corin Dam. The wall of the dam would be the bridge to the far side and true wilderness.

I pondered the loss of the GPS. It was not needed at the moment, though it would be valuable backup when deep in the backcountry. I pushed the thought aside. I didn't want to dwell on the carelessness that had caused me to break the device.

I was tiring, though I had to keep going to reach the destination before dark. I remembered from an earlier appraisal of the map that the long downhill stretch now in front of me was the last for the day. It was all uphill once I crossed the Cotter River. From that point the track would climb more than five hundred metres in the two kilometres past the dam wall. I had the toughest section of the day to negotiate and the walking pace must continue as fast as possible. I used arms to pump with their walking poles as a means of increasing stride. The faster I pushed the walking poles the faster my legs moved to catch up.

The snow-capped Mount Gingera towered over the road. At irregular intervals I looked up to the long rounded mountain for inspiration. I loved the look of snow. It was a novelty in this hot dry continent famed for its rolling plains and deserts. I associated snow with Christmas, even though the festive season was in the middle of an Australian summer and the temperature was likely to be around thirty degrees Celsius. The southern hemisphere winter and Australian snow fell at this time of year, from June to September.

My destination, Pryor's Hut, was in the lee of Gingera. I'd be in a mountain retreat surrounded by snow tonight and the idea thrilled me.

My attention was drawn to litter on the roadside. Hurled from car windows there was a beer bottle here, an empty pack of cigarettes there. A few metres further on a can of drink, or a piece of plastic. Then, as this rubbish disappeared behind me, a wrapper from a chocolate bar and cardboard coffee cups would appear. All of the waste was emblazoned with eye-catching design and colours. Titles calculated by marketers to appeal and attract notice. Habitually I read each logo and my brain registered the product.

I recollected the beer bottle hurled at me just last night. I hadn't understood that event and my mind struggled to understand the garbage as well.

It was dangerous to throw objects from a moving vehicle.

It was illegal.

More than that, the rubbish could have been kept in the car and placed by the occupants in the bin when the car returned home. In fact most of what I surveyed was recyclable.

Soon the waste I walked past would be washed into Canberra's water supply, polluting it. I considered picking it up and taking it with me. I dismissed the idea. I didn't have time and I didn't know where I'd carry it. The pack was already full and heavy.

Was there a respect for the cleanliness of the car and not for the bush? Did the person littering think that the rubbish wouldn't make a difference because the bush was so big?

Why was I walking past with excuses? After all I wasn't making any effort to cleanup.

How had we forgotten what the Aboriginal people had known for thousands of years? If you look after Country, Country will look after you. *Gurragan malier*. Take nothing and do not disturb the ground.

I forced myself to stop thinking about the issue. This was recognition that I'd find no satisfactory answer.

Don't over think it. I could hear Arianne's voice.

A longing for the company of Arianne poured into my brain, filling it up. She'd have found a way to rationalise or make me laugh.

Perhaps civilisations' rubbish was all that marked the city-country divide.

My gaze shifted from the litter and advertising to the bush.

Beautiful trees, large rocks on the hillsides, and the odd wallaby who bounced away startled by a human's presence, was entertainment enough.

Gingera was getting closer.

Distant rocks engrossed my mind for a time. I admired their shapes and automatically categorised them. Small, large or ginormous. Square, rounded or triangular.

Time went swiftly.

After an hour I crossed the Corin Dam wall. Named after William Corin, a pioneer in Australian Hydroelectricity development, this dam was built to capture Canberra's water supply in 1958.

Halting, I rested my back on a large flat rock. Taking off the pack, I stretched and then made use of the public toilets that had been built by the roundabout at the end of the road. I was on track from here. Another milestone ticked off.

I refilled the water bottles from a tank that fed the amenities.

It was already past two in the afternoon. Anxiety coursed through me. I had eight kilometres to go and it'd be gloomy in two and a half hours. Dark in three. Doubts rose within me about whether I could reach my destination before nightfall.

I chomped nervously on a chocolate bar and steeled myself for the scramble upwards. I twisted my neck to peer up at the mountainside. I traced the route of the track until it disappeared into cloud. I adjusted the walking sticks to make them shorter. By doing this I'd get maximum use out of them. I'd use them for leverage upwards.

A blue and red feather poked from under a bush. I bent and picked it up. It was from a crimson rosella. I took off the hat and pushed it into the braided band. I twirled the hat with satisfaction. I was ready. Re-energised by the rest and the chocolate I shouldered the pack with purpose and strode off.

A sign-in register for visitors to the National Park halted me. I stopped and notated my name and intention to walk to Kosciuszko. A notice to the inside of the register drew my attention.

BIOSECURITY ALERT: Hawkweeds. Report all sightings of the mouse-ear hawkweed and orange hawkweed. Introduced from Europe, they stop the potential regeneration of native grasses. They are a threat to the Australian Alps and have been sighted in nearby Kosciuszko National Park.

I closed the lid to the register and resumed upward.

A little sign advertised *2km of steep trail.*

No more than a hundred metres past this sign my purposeful steps had shortened. I was puffing hard. I realised that attempting to keep a rapid cadence wouldn't succeed. I had to accept that it wasn't possible to go faster on such a grade despite my wishes.

My arms punched with the walking poles and I used them to get every bit of leverage available.

I dared not stop.

I gauged my upward progress by watching the dam waters disappear into the distance beneath me. When I lost sight of the dam I turned my attention to the hills on the opposite side of the Cotter River. I measured my progress by drawing an imaginary line from that hill and noting the increasing elevation.

The arm muscles strained as I pushed off.

The legs muscles, already tired, burned with the exertions, and now the arms did as well. Tension built in the shoulder blades as they tried to do their bit to help with the climb.

Drawing breath became harder and a tremble in the leg muscles began. I was going into oxygen deficit and lactic acid was building. I fought to regain breath. I had to slow the pace.

I stopped.

A kookaburra high in the treetops commenced its distinctive laugh. I scanned the branches but couldn't find the bird. It was easy to imagine that it was laughing at me. This feeling was reinforced when another kookaburra in the distance joined in. It was as if they were sharing a joke, and that joke was me.

The tremble became uncontrolled shaking in the left leg. It was a sign that I'd pushed too hard before resting. In the moment it might just as easily have been from the humiliation of the kookaburras.

I moved forty or so paces upward before stopping again.

On one of the frequent halts I saw a man, this time with a hat, to my front. I stared hard.

After a little thinking I realised it was my own faint shadow caused by the sun low in the horizon over the right shoulder.

I'm tired, I conceded.

Pull it together, I urged in frustration.

Touching the hat, I saw the shadow do the same. This was reassuring and so I touched the hat again to gather extra confidence.

Soon I was resting every twenty paces. There was a strong inclination to bend at the waist to alleviate the strain on my back, but I refused to give into this need. Instead I forced myself to straighten. The bent position would obstruct my airways and prevent the all-important oxygen from reaching my lungs.

Breath regained, I stepped off again.

I looked upward at the trail as I hiked with ever shorter paces. I maintained this posture for a burst and then I was leaning against a tree and puffing again.

The dark slid in, surrounding me. It was getting gloomy and the shadows were causing my field of vision to narrow and shorten. The colours of the trees, the grasses and the sky were merging. I wanted to stop to observe the wonder of day turning to dusk. Instead I pressed on. I was running out of time.

At a point in the climb I registered that the vegetation had changed to snowgums. Growing at altitudes from thirteen hundred to nineteen hundred metres, the twisted gnarled snowgum, beaten by weather and with its mottled red, chocolate, olive bark trunk was an image that was associated with the Australian High Country. After slogging all day, I acknowledged that this was the alpine zone.

Patches of snow were on the path. Avoiding them, I maintained the ascent. As the altitude increased, the patches of white became larger before they eventually joined.

I was now walking on snow. Progress became harder still in the mushy low altitude, ankle-deep snow. The wet snow caused my boots to lose traction and I stumbled as gravity tried to pull me down and back.

I pushed on.

An internal debate about whether I should stop to put on snowshoes began. The steel claws would stop me slipping. Then I determined that the snowshoes would be ungainly amongst the trunks and branches.

I kept going.

A faint waft of air brushed my skin as I clambered higher. Now, as I gained altitude, an airstream was stretching across the crest towards me. The leaves in the trees were moving from the breeze passing through.

The strength of the wind increased, then there were gusts and finally I was surrounded by constantly shaking branches and leaves. The weather was from the south and sucking the warmth out of me. Straight from Antarctica!

A reverberation filled the air from the timeless creak of gums.

My mind drifted as I heard imagined conversations hum.

Concentrate, I cautioned.

Walking faster I reasoned would generate warmth. I kept thrusting into the wind.

It didn't work. It wasn't possible for me to walk faster. I was too tired, up too high and the wind too cold.

I heard the sound of footfalls as someone followed behind me.

I halted. So did the sound.

I walked and the sound I was listening for commenced in the same moment.

I took another break. The noise from the stalker died away.

I listened intently. What or who was pursuing me?

The brain and ears attempted to filter sounds unsuccessfully. The rustle of leaves filled the air.

I chided myself for being delusional. No person was following me. There wasn't a soul for miles. I pressed on. The imagined stalker followed again, though this time I reassured myself that the noise of footfalls was just mine.

As a distraction I compelled my mind to debate the decision of when to put on the snowshoes. Within a minute it was raging inside my head. At every step I assessed whether fitting the snowshoes would be an advantage or a hindrance.

In the end it was the cool of the wind that forced me to stop. I opted to put on an outer waterproof layer of clothing. The barrier of waterproofing was also windproof. It'd help me retain body warmth.

This worked magically.

I felt better.

I reached into the pocket of the rain jacket and took out a set of gloves and a balaclava. I put on the balaclava and then plonked the hat on top. The head was warmer. I sensed that I'd staunched the loss of heat.

In this period of respite, I chose to take the snowshoes off the pack where they'd been strapped. They were placed parallel to each other on the snow. Stepping onto them I pushed the toes of the boots into the bindings. With a little fiddling I tensioned the straps.

The gloves I'd just put on increased the difficulty. My fingers were still cold and fumbling.

First I adjusted the toe ties. Next I tightened the heel mechanism that ratcheted the shoes into place.

There was a delay of a few minutes to get the snowshoes fitted right. The straps needed to be firm so the shoes would stay parallel and not twist when walking. I kicked each shoe into the snow to test they were attached to satisfaction. Eventually I was ready to walk again.

The time spent in fitting snowshoes when walking out of a warm building or getting out of warm car wasn't a problem. There was warmth stored in the body. Here though I had no stored warmth except that from my own exertions. The warmth ebbed away from my core and I realised how vulnerable I was at this moment and for the rest of this trip from hypothermia. This realisation made me impatient to move again.

The feet were now encumbered with an additional one and a half kilograms of steel, plastic and bindings strapped to each boot. Walking was now slightly ungainly. Wider and longer to disperse bodyweight, my feet were unable to rest in their natural position. Additionally, I needed to lift my legs marginally higher to move. This combined with the extra weight increased fatigue at the top of the thigh.

Despite the weight and the adjustment to stride it was clear immediately that the snowshoe offered distinct advantages. I now walked on top of the snow without sinking into it. The metal claws underneath provided grip. The slipping around had ceased and I was stepping more confidently. The problem I'd had of gravity trying to pull me backwards was fixed.

Swirls of clouds swept in. I watched them with foreboding as they choked the last of the light.

It was ever darker. The day was dead.

The path was faint. It flattened out.

I guessed that I now must be at the height of the hut.

The clouds twirled and the trees swayed. I heard a cry for help in the distance. Without checking momentum I listened intently. The sound came again. I recognised it this time as the hollow wailing creaks of dead gum trees swaying in the wind.

Leaves of the nearby swaying eucalyptus trees rattled together to create a whisper that played on the ears. In the gloom the sound was sinister.

Hit by a gust, I was off balance for a moment. I braced the muscles in my legs and back.

Mentally, I regathered.

This wasn't the time for anything except pure attentiveness.

I stepped deliberately.

My eyes peered with desperation for the path. Indications were it curved to the left, though a gap on my right could have been its direction.

I moved tentatively to the left. Could I find the hut in these conditions?

Steps were now short and uncertain.

This is dangerous, my mind yelled. Stop! You're about to lose the path, it screamed.

Lingering to gain composure, I mentally reviewed the map and path. I was cold and desperate for shelter. I was close to the hut and that added temptation.

I drew steadying breaths.

Go on or pitch a tent?

It didn't seem to be super dangerous. Still I had to know when to stop before an accident happened. Stopping after an accident happened wasn't going to be much help.

A sotto voice spoke. 'You're on track. It's a bit confusing in these parts. Twenty more paces and you'll be on a fire-trail. Go left up a slight rise and you'll see the hut to the right.'

Was it the wind I'd just heard?

It couldn't be. It was the same voice from by the river. I raised my head.

The voice had been distinct. It was reassuring and not ominous like the undertones of the wind.

I scrutinised the dark to the front, the left and then right. I saw a shadowy figure by a tree.

My eyes flicked back to the spot and stared. The human shape was gone.

My eyes were playing tricks as well.

Then I guessed that maybe this was who had been following me up the ridge.

'Hello,' I yelled, with all my strength. A blast of air took the sound and threw it back in my face. It was gone over my shoulder.

Standing expectantly, I waited for a response from this companion who I sensed was ever present.

Only the sounds of the gum-forest could be heard.

Sighing in disappointment I steadied and walked hesitantly into the gloom. The shaft in each hand felt the way like a blind man's cane.

It was the sense of touch that was helping me with the obscured ground under foot. I needed to find a firm footing before stepping to minimise the risk of falling.

I wished the GPS wasn't broken.

Then I pushed the thought aside. It might tell me where I was, but it wasn't going to help me see in the dark.

Slow progress was made as first one shuffling step and then another.

More forward movement as feet tentatively slid to feel for obstacles.

The prodding with poles found it first and then the feet. I was standing in a distinct impression in the ground. I felt around. It extended left and right. There was a bump upwards in the ground and another long dent horizontal to the first.

Staring, I could now see it indistinctly. Masked beneath the snow were the wheel ruts of four wheel drive vehicles. The fire-trail!

I didn't step down to the left as instructed. I hesitated.

Was I delusional? Were my senses being tricked in the dark?

I searched around with my eyes and poles. I allowed myself to believe that the two lengthy indentations could be nothing else.

I turned as instructed.

My paces took me up a shallow rise.

Some of the tenseness within me ebbed away.

The trail flattened.

Desperately I delved into the darkness. At first there were only trees and then I made out a black box. It was the silhouette of a structure.

Every step required concentration as I willed my feet towards the hut. All the energy I could muster expressed itself in the legs as a desperate shuffle.

Opening the door I fell inward, coughing and then vomiting in a bitter release of the tension of the last hour.

I had time to wish that there wasn't anyone in the hut to see this undignified display.

REFUGE

THERE WASN'T A WITNESS to critique the unseemly arrival in the hut. No arbiter was present to assess me. The ridiculous paranoia of the last moment was exposed for what it was. I chided myself for such irrational thoughts. I was at seventeen hundred metres on the edge of the Alps with a storm brewing outside.

Spluttering the last of the vomit, I wriggled free of the pack. It was a relief to be rid of it for the day. I still lay on the floor out of energy and thinking. I took time to consider what had just occurred. My mind switched to the voice in the forest just down the hill.

Was he judging me? It seemed not. He was helping me.

Would he join me in the hut? I dismissed the question. If he intended coming to the hut he would have shown me where it was.

This was different to the city and I needed to acknowledge the change in circumstances. In town there were others present. It was easy to imagine that other people were reviewing my words and actions. It might well be a reasonable guess. Out here though there was just me appraising my own efforts.

I must stop constantly referring to what others thought.

Then I affirmed that I'd do this in Canberra as well.

It was indeterminate how long I lay on the floor.

A branch, flung by the wind, landed on the tin roof with a thump. This caused me to stir. I picked myself up.

My right leg was cramping from the exertion of the day, the cold, the lactic acid and the fear. Stiffness had set in.

The relief at being safe for the night was substantial.

I removed the snowshoes.

Hobbling around inside the hut, little by little, I stretched the legs. At the same time I willed the muscles to relax. I picked up the hat that had fallen onto the floor and put it back on in the hope it'd provide some extra warmth.

Fumbling inside the pack, I found a small torch.

The beam shone around with the shadows receding before it.

I took the time to evaluate Pryor's Hut, my home for the night. The steps to the front door, legend had it, were in the Australian Capital Territory. The hut I now stood in, still favouring the leg that hadn't been cramped, was in New South Wales. The door I'd just fallen through marked the border and provided entrance into a tiny room. Another door then led me to the main room with a fireplace. A table fashioned out of crudely cut timber sat below a window. A door at the far end led me into a bedroom. A bunk and a mattress was in this area. I examined the mattress with the torch. It was an unexpected luxury.

The mattress was mouldy and there was excrement from native marsupials sprinkling the surface. I chose the floor in preference to the bed. The thin piece of foam that I carried for insulation from the ground would be sufficient. It was the cleaner option.

Automatically the knowledge I'd researched about the hut came to mind. Lindsay Pryor, who this hut was named after, had built here in 1952. It was a shelter for those who worked in the Alpine Botanical Gardens, a section of the National Botanical Gardens that had been created in Canberra. Pryor at the time of building was the Superintendent of Parks and Gardens for the Australian Capital Territory and the Hut was a base for planting and studying botany in the alpine zone. His knowledge of Australian flora was renowned and he would later be a professor at the Australian National University.

I would always appreciate Professor Pryor for building this hut.

It was reassuring being in the relatively familiar surrounds of a man-made structure after the day in the bush. It was smaller and more basic then a city dwelling, yet I was accustomed to the form and function. It was homely. The hut gave me comfort in a way that a tent wouldn't have. I was at ease.

But I was cool and getting colder.

Fumbling in the pack I found the lightweight stove. The broad based water bottle that doubled as a pot was next to it. I placed the stove on the table and lit a match with trembling fingers. I poured water into the pot.

Next I placed out warm clothes for the evening. The thermal pants and undershirt were prominent in their bright colours. I drew breath, preparing myself to be naked in the cold hut, and then changed hurriedly.

The events of the day had left me with no illusions. The fragility of the human body made it vulnerable. In the High Country, at this time of year, when the Spirit of the Mountain was awakened, the first thoughts and actions were always to address safety. Anything less would be foolish. In particular, the preservation of the body's warmth was paramount. It was certain that for the Aboriginal and the early settler, this too must have consumed their thinking. The modern clothing I wore gave me assistance, though they had the advantage of being tough and familiar with the country.

Now that I was dressed in a dry, warm and clean under-layer with still more jackets on top, I was satisfied that I wasn't in danger of hypothermia.

Dipping a finger into the water, I checked to see that the water wasn't close to boiling. It was still tepid.

I thought of Arianne. I'd left her a note of my intentions, though a conversation would have been better. Was it possible that there was mobile phone coverage? I turned on the device and checked for reception. There was none.

Stepping outside the hut, I held the phone extended in a gloved hand to better view the screen. Expectantly I watched for the icon showing a signal to appear. No electronic bars appeared to indicate signal reception.

The letdown was instant and real.

A wave of remorse hit me.

This was crazy.

Why was I putting myself and Arianne through this?

Then I forced my mind to change tack. These regrets were not going to resolve anything in this moment in these mountains.

Holding the phone above my head, I peered hopefully upwards at the screen. With excitement I saw a single bar. This disappeared the next second, though I still held the phone high. I twisted the phone to face different directions. The bar reappeared and then vanished again. A minute later the bar was back.

I pulled the arm and phone down, typed a message with rapidly freezing fingers.

'At Pryor's Hut. Safe.' My fingers stopped as I deliberated on the next words. Indecision frustrated me in the cold. I typed, 'Luv u.'

I held the phone above my head again and pushed send. Waiting I cursed the stinging cold.

Would the text message go? Could the tower pick it up? Did the phone have enough capacity to push the signal that far? These were all speculative questions as I had no real technical knowledge. I used these modern tools and had no understanding of how the science that made them work was harnessed. The Aboriginal and the pioneer knew their tools intimately. I couldn't say the same about myself.

After a few minutes, with fingers stinging from cold, I returned inside the hut.

The pot had a stream of vapour escaping from around the lid toward the roof. I turned it off to save on precious fuel. Everything was tight for this journey. Fuel, food. I hoped that I'd packed enough ... just enough. Every kilogram of weight extra was going to be a hindrance when I hit the snow on the higher slopes upwards to Mount Kosciuszko. I'd brought the minimum.

I emptied a satchel that combined sugar, instant coffee and creamer into a mug. Finally I poured the steaming water into the vessel.

I enjoyed the reinvigorating smell wafting on moisture from the mug to nose. I sniffed hard. Then I relished the sweet coffee on the tongue. Caressing the mug in both hands near my face I eked every ounce of warmth out of the potion. The heat penetrated the body through the hands. The steam floated onto face and eyes. A sip warmed mouth and tummy.

I was stronger and more alive.

This brew was perhaps the best I'd ever drunk. I couldn't discuss with anyone the merits of the origins of the coffee or the type of beans. How it had been roasted, or whether it was fair-trade or organic. This coffee was pleasurable, and that's what mattered to me right now.

Mug in hand, I reappraised the hut. The dark grey light coming through an east-facing window made little impression on the interior, so I shone the torch around.

A good stone fireplace was available.

Small piles of kindling and wood were stacked neatly.

It was my judgement that the immediate danger of hypothermia had been averted and I was now safe for the night. I took a moment to celebrate this small victory. This firewood might be needed by someone in an emergency and that wasn't me.

I imagined the cosy atmosphere that a fire would bring to the hut. Mulled wine and companions accompanied the image.

I had no wine or companions. In addition it'd be smoky and the hut wouldn't hold much heat unless it was kept going all night. Tired after the day's exertions I'd fall asleep. I knew my limits.

I elected not to light a fire.

The instant I made this decision the remembrance of an Australian backcountry book I'd browsed sprang to mind. It had offered the guideline, *the bigger the fire the bigger the fool.* My brain extrapolated the notion that the smaller the fire the smarter I was. In this case it followed that no fire at all made me a genius. I smiled. No one would walk into the cold hut and come to that conclusion.

There was marsupial excrement on the table I'd set up the stove on and in little patches on the floor. A broom rested by the fire. Using the broom first on the table top and then the floor I swept the offending excrement out the hut door.

I selected a place on the wooden floor for a bed. It took just minutes to make. I unrolled the thin foam mattress. Across this I lay a sleeping bag. The weight of the bag prevented the foam bouncing back into the curled position it'd been holding all day for carriage. I hunted around inside the pack and found an inner sheet that I inserted into the sleeping bag. This would keep me comfortable and warmer. An outer sack was then placed around the externals offering extra protection and trapping warmth. Stuffing some clothes into the sleeping bag cover I made a pillow. The bed was complete.

My rumbling tummy drew my attention.

I took a bag from the pack. In this I had placed the food and beverages. Appraising the food satchels on offer I selected a pack of freeze-dried roast chicken and vegetables.

I filled a cup of water. My cup held two hundred and twenty millilitres. This was the quantity needed to make a satchel of dehydrated foods expand. I needed to boil the exact amount. More mass of water meant more fuel and I must save this for emergencies. The water was put into the pot and the stove restarted.

The simple meal process that'd be repeated each evening was to boil water. I'd then tear open a satchel, pour water, stir, reseal and wait ten minutes for the food to rehydrate.

The wait for the minutes to tick past was a test of patience. Ten minutes was an eternity when sitting staring at a dark room. Without conversation, distractions or entertainment, I willed the meat and vegetables to plump up and become edible.

When finally ready, the food was consumed in much less time than it took for it to be prepared. Attempts to eat slowly failed. I chewed the rehydrated mush and attempted to savour the taste of each spoonful.

Dinner was finished all too soon, but I was warm on the inside.

Another torch beam assessment of the hut was initiated. I saw the building with different eyes now that my stomach was full and the emergency of my arrival had receded.

It looked gloomy and the smell of smoke from past fires hung in the air. The hut was shabby compared with the well-lit modern housing that I enjoyed in Canberra. I shone the beam into each corner. The dark retreated and the foreboding that there was some danger lurking was demonstrated to be pure imagination.

I felt the cold on my hands and nose. I checked my watch. It was just past 6:00. There'd be no more light until seven in the morning. No TV, no games, no company to consume the hours. There was nothing practical to do other than to climb into the sleeping bag to stay warm.

I took off my boots and the toes revelled in new found freedom.

Lying on the foam mattress I wriggled into the inner sheet, then the sleeping bag, and then the outer bag. As I progressed through each layer I closed zips to seal in the heat my body would produce. The zipping required contortions. There was a fair amount of wriggling before I was cocooned.

Straightening, I aligned my body squarely in the middle of the foam mat. The hardness of the floor beneath me was evident. The foam offered insulation but not much cushioning. I puffed the sack of clothes doubling as a pillow by bouncing it a little. It was still uncomfortable when I lay on it.

I stared at the blackness of the room and ceiling.

What next?

Propping myself up, I rummaged around in the pack until I withdrew a little notepad and pencil.

It was reasonable without companionship that I might write my thoughts.

Mentally I ran through the beginning of the day and stepped chronologically through all that had happened.

Today fear had driven me. I'd been afraid from the time I entered the river this morning. Out of my depth, out of control and I didn't like it.

A tree branch fell onto the tin roof, banging loudly. I flinched.

My mind turned to the wind. I'd been made uncomfortable by the wind in the past, though I'd never been scared of the wind in the way I'd been today. It had alarmed me. It was a breeze, then a stronger wind and then powerful gusts, though never quite a storm. In the coming gloom of the clouds and nightfall, I'd feared it could kill me.

Pushing all of these thoughts out of mind, I focussed on the sound of the blasts of air outside the hut. It was stronger now than when I was exposed to it this afternoon. A billion leaves rustled and then the noise subsided before a crescendo of noise rose again. The hut shuddered under its power. The wind had a rage to kill and I was pleased to have beaten it by finding this shelter.

Arianne popped into mind. She would be secure at home in comfortable surroundings. I was pleased and then I craved to be with her. I pushed the idea aside as it was a desire that would not be satisfied.

I wrote a sentence about fear and the wind. A fear that was very real. The wind's chill might have brought on hypothermia this afternoon and it was a multitude of times fiercer now. This observation was very clear when I contrasted the relative warmth in a sleeping bag to the state I'd arrived at the hut.

I finished writing a sentence and then reread it.

It was unsatisfactory.

I used the pencil to cross out the words and started another.

The next sentence was equally inadequate.

The jumble of fear and awe were fragments in the mind. The expression of this flotsam whirling around the head was complicated. It was all related somehow. The words were disjointed and yet to be connected. The phrases had a beat like the interminable rhythm of feet on trail. The words and phrases came in gusts and then they poured relentlessly like the wind over the slopes.

I stared in frustration for a while and then started doing something that I hadn't done since school.

I wrote the first line of a poem.

Wicked wind whispers

Looking Back

GREY BEARDED ELDERS IMPARTED KNOWLEDGE to me at significant points in the landscape. Sometimes I was beside a creek or waterhole and at other times in open grassy valleys. First I was hunting kangaroos. Then I was trying to make fire from rubbing two sticks together. All the while an audience of men scrutinised my sporadic progress. Not in a judgemental way, but in a fatherly way. Sometimes I was offered helpful counsel. At first I thought it was a quest, though it troubled me that I didn't know what I was seeking. Now I was creating a scratching sound as I rubbed stone spear heads against other rocks in an effort to sharpen them.

The question of what these linked activities were about had barely formed when the deep sleep disappeared in an instant.

The scratching noise remained, but the dream had finished. It was apparent that the sound wasn't from the making of spear heads. An irregular scurrying, scratching of tiny feet on the wooden floor brought me to alert.

The lightest of quick touches across the lower half of the sleeping bag, followed by a quick pitter-patter, made me kick with my feet.

I was alarmed and defensive. I attempted to connect the brain to my eyes, ears and nose. Senses readied for fight or flight.

The sudden awakening in the pitch black was disorienting. Awareness returned after a few moments. The dream, though seemingly real, was illusory. The recollection that my bed was on the floor of Pryor's Hut rushed into my consciousness. Only then could I start to put the sound in context.

Rats.

Actually, it was probably a little marsupial of some sort, or possibly a saw-tooth rat. The name sounded fearsome, though pictures I'd seen showed them to be a very cute endangered native animal.

Freeing my arms from the cocoon of the sleeping bag I reached for the torch. My fingers fumbled for its button before it flicked on.

The light caused a flurry of sound. I detected some movements on the edges of the beam without necessarily seeing the little creature.

The noise died down quickly. I shone the torch around the room, letting it linger on the food bag that I had left on the bench near the stove. It was an orange sack that popped from the surrounds when hit by the light. From where I lay all was in order. The temptation to go and check the contents of the sack came to me, but the warmth of the sleeping bag held me. I reassured myself that the food was safe. Now I focussed the beam of light onto the pack to ensure that by some accident food hadn't been left inside. There didn't appear to be anything near it and there was no scurrying noise.

The room appeared empty except for me. I wasn't fooled. The problem was that doing something about it meant going into the cold chasing little creatures around the hut, knowing that they'd return as soon as I lay down again.

Lying back, I adjusted the makeshift pillow and turned the torch off.

The scurrying and scratching started the moment it was dark.

I reached for the torch again.

The light caused another flurry of sound. A tinkle was made as an unseen creature ran into the cooking pot.

Then the noise died away.

I committed to ignoring the noise and rolled over to get comfortable and try to sleep. At the same time I hoped that the marsupials wouldn't scurry over me again on the floor. There were no reports I'd ever read of a camper being harmed by a native marsupial. They were benign. Yet somewhere in my human makeup I didn't like noises in the night. Especially not from little creatures I couldn't see.

In all likelihood, I guessed they were just curious about the invader of their home. I wished they'd be curious about something else.

Slowly I came to terms with the scratching sounds of my companions. At some point the worrying about the noises ceased. At another I dozed before falling into a deep sleep.

The grey light of morning coming through the window of the hut caused me to shift. My face was cold. The temperature was well below freezing and I willed myself awake.

The initial reaction was to pull the sleeping bag over my head in an attempt to surround it with warm air. I enjoyed this sensation for a minute. The time was used to bring my brain into the present.

I had a long day in front, I realised. It was not nearly as long as yesterday though it'd test endurance.

I tried to spring out of bed and put on some water for porridge and coffee. It was more complex than that, as I had to negotiate all of the zippers and layers to be finally free to stand.

Once I had a blue flame licking at the base of the pot, I shot back to the warmth of the sleeping bag. Out of the corner of my eye I watched the flame and waited for the emission of steam that'd be the signal it was ready for use.

I reached for the map case and thought through the coming day's walking.

It'd be easy going on the Mount Franklin Road to the east, a steep climb to the south through Leura Gap, a downhill towards the northern most part of the Snowy Scheme and then a night at Oldfield's Hut. It'd be a good thirty plus kilometres and would require a steady pace all day. This was daunting, though I'd covered more ground and steeper elevations yesterday.

I did an audit of my body and judged that despite a crick in the neck, perhaps caused from the makeshift pillow, I was feeling OK. A shoulder was sore from the weight of the pack. This inconvenience wouldn't hinder progress today and my body would adjust. The legs were stiff, though they were largely rejuvenated after the cramps. I resolved to persist with the journey. I'd get through today as long as I looked after the feet, rested regularly and kept the walking steady. I knew that I couldn't repeat the frantic pace of yesterday and I needed to walk smarter.

Steam bellowed from the pot.

Leaving the sleeping bag, I shovelled down a quick breakfast. The porridge was followed by a satchel of coffee drunk from the same cup. The remnants of the oats floated around the coffee. Breakfast wasn't much, but it was hot and rejuvenating.

After eating I packed as rapidly as possible. Movement was needed to retain the warmth inside of me created by the porridge.

As I crammed items into the pack, I noticed a hole had been chewed through its side by little teeth. I placed my fingers against it. Right through the fabric and into some biscuits I'd forgotten were inside. The fabric was damaged beyond my ability to repair it, though I assessed that the thread wouldn't run and the hole widen any further.

Breathing a curse, I threw my head back in frustration. It was then I noticed hooks hanging off beams on the ceiling. I realised these were to hang food bags to protect them from the little bush rats. I swore at my poor powers of observation.

This ineffective admonishment was all I could do. Of course it was futile.

It was done and there was no one else to blame. This wouldn't be the last mistake I'd make on this trip. I needed to be attentive, stay alert and learn for next time.

Be kind to yourself for these blunders, I affirmed. If I didn't like myself I'd forever have the company of an enemy. We all made mistakes. My head rocked from side to side weighing up these thoughts.

Mollified, I reached for the boots.

They were frozen solid. The moisture of sweat and snow on yesterday's climb had soaked the leather. Combined with the freezing conditions overnight they'd turned into an inflexible mass. Try as I might, I couldn't squeeze my feet into them.

In desperation I reached for the stove, lit it and held a boot high above the flame to warm it. I made certain that I kept the synthetic laces well clear of the heat so they didn't accidentally melt. When the leather was pliable, I slipped it on and reached for the other boot to repeat the process.

After what felt like an eternity of preparation, I was ready for the trail.

I swept the hut. At the same time I glanced over it to ensure I'd left nothing behind. It was pleasing that it looked tidier than when I arrived.

A log book in the corner of the table drew my attention. I took time to write my name, the date and destination. It was a safety measure for searchers.

At the door of the hut, I stopped.

I conducted a cautious check from head to toe. Once I left the safety of the shelter I needed to be totally prepared.

I wore the hat. The pack was fitted and straps tightened. All the zips were closed so no items would fall out. The boots were on and the laces firmly tied. I was as ready as possible for the day ahead. From the door I could see a magically white world with snow in every direction. Eucalyptus trees were surrounding the hut and a few hundred yards away was a perfect square of pines. The work of Professor Pryor. Stepping through the door, I stood into and fitted the snowshoes. I tested the walking poles by thumping them at the snow. They were locked firmly and at a good height.

I evaluated the wisps of high altitude cirrus clouds filling the sky. Cirrus clouds meant fine weather I recollected from a lesson at school. It was almost windless. The weather looked good and I took my first steps with high spirits.

Snow covered the fire trail that was evidenced by two parallel dents cleared of trees and bushes heading to the east and the distance. It was an obvious path in the light of day. It was exactly where I expected the route to be. The snow was frozen hard in the morning's cold temperatures. It was about forty centimetres deep, though in places it'd collected into drifts that were almost a metre deep. I walked into a drift and found myself sinking into the softer snow. The snow was not dense enough to hold my weight with pack. I learnt to avoid them. In other places the wind had blown the trail clear so that it was just exposed mud for a little section.

I viewed the mud with an automatic distaste. Then I detected a frosting on the surface. I went across to a section. Curious, I prodded it with the snowshoe. The mud was frozen solid. This was a good outcome from the cold. Even in adversity there were advantages to be found if I took the time to notice. I focussed on the positives. No droning flies and no buzzing mosquitoes. It was hard to believe this was the Australian bush. I included no snakes, though I was aware at lower altitude they had been known to come out for a sunbake in winter, though not on snow.

The thinking process cheered me and I marvelled for a moment at the simplicity of life here in the mountains.

In the next moment this happiness turned to worry. My feet were numb in the cold boots. I wriggled the toes downwards and back in a curling motion. I couldn't feel anything. Concerned, I determined to move at pace with the intention of getting the blood pumping to the body's extremities. I drew unpleasantly cool air into my lungs to fuel the extra efforts.

After fifteen minutes of walking, I reached a gate that showed the branch where the Mount Gingera trail curved upwards to the summit. Just as Mount Gingera could be seen from Canberra, Gingera was reputed to have some of the best views of the city. There was no need to haul the pack to the peak so I took it off and turned down the branch track.

The extra steepness of the slope soon had me puffing.

Intermittently, I paused to catch my breath. At each stop, by twisting at the waist, a better view of Canberra was revealed. Eventually I reached the crest of the mountain. Topping the apex of the ridge a panorama extended south to the Tantangara Reservoir far below. In the distance behind the black water of the dam was a distinctive lone peak. I assumed this was the famed Mount Jagungal. A white smudge on the horizon, well past Jagungal, might have been Kosciuszko or a cloud. In the next few days, if I followed the plan, I'd walk past all of these landmarks.

The Brindabella's had been my horizon at work. Now that I was here there was a new horizon pulling at me. I sensed the distant peaks calling me in the same way that Bimberi Peak had drawn me into the mountains.

Jagungal was a one hundred kilometre walk and Kosciuszko one hundred and seventy. I instinctively leaned forward as if this would bring me closer to the beauty of this dramatic scene.

Turning one hundred and eighty degrees I faced north. Back the way I'd come yesterday.

To my front and left was Mount Franklin covered in patches of white. This was the location of Canberra's old ski club. Built in the 1930s, the chalet had been burnt in the blaze that tore into Canberra in 2003. From this angle, at a twenty kilometre distance, the scars where the hillside had been cleared to create ski runs were apparent. The slopes were abandoned and so were the tows.

Their time had come and so had the snow's.

Yet in the city in the shadows below, the debate on climate continued in political rows.

Moving to the right a little, I viewed the sprawl of Canberra from above. I was now in the bush looking across to the city. This was the opposite view from the vantage point at work. I recognised the peak of Parliament House and the peninsular by the lake where I worked. The National Museum and suburbs I knew so well. There below me was the landscape I was familiar with. Not the snow and storms and creatures of the mountains I'd experienced yesterday.

I was looking down and looking back.

The introduced deciduous trees that concealed the city in summer had dropped their leaves exposing the hidden. It looked immaculate in the early morning glow. Canberra was a silvery glimmering radiance of cold concrete and glass. From the mountains, the city looked pristine.

It was an optical illusion, however. There was the homeless that I cycled past. There was graffiti. There was corruption, crime and dirty politics. Lastly I included the discarded rubbish into my observations.

I dragged air into my lungs. I gauged it against that of the city. Below the air smelt of fumes emitted from the exhaust pipes of cars. This was so pervasive and considered so necessary that no one acknowledged it much. It contributed to the deaths of thousands in Australia, yet it wasn't spoken about.

I considered the viewing of objects from a distance. This had set me on this journey and I was doing it again now.

From a distance granularity was lost. Pixilation occurred.

When I'd looked at the mountains from the office they'd looked pure, though yesterday's walk had exposed the rubbish that blighted the boundary. I didn't remember the climb of yesterday for its beauty. The wind was a memory of deadly brutality. None of this had been evident from the safety of an office.

To understand anything it had to be experienced, not admired from a distance and even then there were still unanswered questions from the observations.

From here I recognised the familiar landscape of urban Canberra. This knowledge aside, I knew no more about the people and their motivations than I knew of the wanderings of hut marsupials in the night.

I stared at the city for a long moment.

I lived there. I worked in my dream job. I enjoyed Canberra. I admired its design and designer. Arianne was there. It was home, except that in some unexplainable way I was estranged. Even with its faults I didn't want it to change. There was the rub. It'd change. It was a city. It must change, yet how did I ensure that it'd change for the better?

My gaze moved onto the mountains. I admired their beauty at the same time as I was daunted and fearful of them.

They changed slowly. They'd change even though I didn't want them to.

Where did I belong?

Not here ... though I wasn't sure if I belonged in Canberra either.

The day before yesterday I'd raised my eyes from the computer screen to the horizon. Still, now that I'd walked to the horizon, where was I?

Perplexed, I put my head down and retraced the tracks down to the main trail.

The walking poles were both placed ahead of me. I pushed them hard into the snow. When I was sure they had firm purchase on the snow, I stepped to them.

Most accidents happened when descending, not ascending, I remembered from a lesson on the survival course.

Despite the caution I slipped many times before I was able to retrieve the pack at the junction. I hesitated and then stepped off down the main trail.

Away from Canberra, and deeper into the wilderness with each step. Tracks of animals crossed mine.

- = - = - = - =

The small deeper indent into the snow at the rear was the two back legs coming together with the weight of the creature, as it reached ahead to do another movement that created the parallel lines to the front.

The evidence suggested that a hop had created this track. A rabbit, I guessed from the size. A hare would've been larger.

This deduction was pleasing. I was right and I knew it.

Spontaneously, a quick review of history was triggered.

Introduced into Australia, the rabbit was a pest that had destroyed the farmer's fragile pastures, causing erosion. It had beaten many attempts to eradicate it. There'd been hunters, encouraged by the government-provided bounties for pelts. They'd failed. The release of Myxomatosis and then Calicivirus had each worked for a time. Then the population bred resistance and bounced back. It was all to no avail.

Another set of prints a little further along crossed the path.

$$= \quad = \quad = \quad =$$

This was a larger, heavier animal than the rabbit. Upright it left two large parallel marks. A bush wallaby, I guessed. On I walked, delighted at this game.

I spied two parallel lines of arrows on the snow.

$$-> \quad -> \quad -> \quad ->$$
$$-> \quad -> \quad -> \quad ->$$

Confused, it took me a moment to realise they weren't arrows. They needed to be turned around.

$$<- \quad <- \quad <- \quad <-$$
$$<- \quad <- \quad <- \quad <-$$

Lyrebird tracks joining with the trail, following it for a little and then disappearing into the bushes on the left. I'd never seen this creature outside a zoo, though I could envision its feet. Miles Franklin in her novel *Childhood at Brindabella* set in the 1880s had mentioned seeing lyrebirds. She'd written in disapproving tones of trappers who collected lyrebird feathers for markets.

In the cold of the morning I included *conservationist* to Miles Franklin's feminist credentials. Then I dismissed the conjecture. That was guessing. Complete fabrication. Something historians didn't do, I reminded myself.

I reached up and touched my hat, the symbol of my greatest speculative folly. *My hat.* I checked myself. When had it become my hat?

'What are you doing?' I questioned out loud. The sound of my voice startled me into stopping.

I stood very still, thinking.

Yesterday had been harder than I expected. The broken GPS was a handicap that I hadn't anticipated. There was now extra danger to this trip.

Reaching up I took the hat off my head and analysed it again. It was unchanged. Worn and moth-eaten it looked nothing special. My head was instantly cold now that the forehead was exposed to the crisp morning air.

'You're mad,' the force of the reproval came from speaking the words.

'You should go home,' I declared with authority, as if trying to convince a stranger. I was still staring at the hat.

A shiver wracked my whole body, turning into a shrug.

'I should go home,' I whispered, as I turned and looked back down the track in the direction I'd come. The track looked inviting. My lone footprints had been left as a trail to home and I realised all I had to do was follow them. They'd lead to my front door. To the life I shared with the wonderful Arianne.

The cold caused me to shudder again.

Facing the front, I gave the path one last look. I'd already half determined to return home.

A robin redbreast sat perched on a tree ten or so metres away. The bird's head cocked in my direction and one eye was clearly observing me.

I wondered how I'd missed him, or had he flown in while my back was turned staring at the trail home. My mind retrieved the data it had stored.

I knew the bird was more correctly known as a Flame Robin. Measuring just over ten centimetres, this was a male specimen as the females were an inconspicuous grey.

The little bird let out the tweets of a beautiful song and I felt my mouth move impulsively upward in delight.

The song, combined with mentally revising knowledge, made me confident.

The hat was returned to head as an instinctive reaction.

Immediately I was comforted.

I was warmer.

The track didn't look so forbidding. Actually, as I stood staring, the trail of snow with no footprints looked like a challenge. What lay behind me was known. Ahead there were endless possibilities.

I had no company except this bird. No one was following. I was very much alone and that was disconcerting. Still that didn't seem so bad when excited by what lay ahead.

Behind was just a trail of footprints. It led to work and home. They were both fine. I was content with life, a wonderful partner and a stimulating career.

In front of me lay the unknown. Anything! It'd been explored, though it hadn't been revealed or travelled by me. A tiny species of spider, the peacock spider, had been found and documented for the first time in this national park in 2008. There was more to be discovered.

I stepped off.

The Flame Robin left the branch and flew a playful course to another tree a little further down the track. It was maintaining its distance from me. I maintained the advance. The Flame Robin skipped ahead again.

I watched my feet make a new trail in the snow. Is this how the first peoples felt? How Clancy felt?

I touched the hat almost without knowing it.

Face to the unknown. Face to adventure.

COMMITTED

THE TRAIL TWISTED AND TURNED in an easterly direction, all the while gradually losing height. As the altitude dropped, the snow thinned and turned to patches. Taking off the snowshoes, I stowed them on the pack and walked on. At intervals I tried the mobile phone to see if it could pick up a signal. It didn't. I hoped Arianne had received the text message last night.

The last in vain attempt to get reception on the mobile was at Blackfellows Gap where I took the first large break of the morning. I walked around in open areas with the phone in hand. This failed so I tried the same dance with the device held above my head. No matter how hard I stared at the screen I clearly had no signal. Disappointed, I turned the phone off to conserve battery.

Returning to the pack, I sat on it for comfort and had a snack. Swigging mouthfuls of water, I washed down the biscuit that I was chewing. I took the time to look at the surrounds. The high ground was covered in frost. In clumps near the trail were grey coloured shrubs about one metre or more in height. They were strewn with remnants of spidery red flowers. They were grevilleas and native to the region. The grevillea flowers were a stark contrast to the grey greens of the bush and added cheer in the same way the flame robin had lifted spirits earlier.

I took out the map of Namadgi and beside it I placed my unfinished map. The *How It Was* map. I leant back with hands clasped around my knees, comparing the two. My current location, Blackfellows Gap, could be seen easily on the Namadgi Map. On the *How It Was* map there was just a question mark. The research I'd conducted into the area had revealed no new information. It was a high mountain pass. It was probable that this would've been part of a pathway for peoples in the Canberra region to access the High Country from the north and east during summer. Other groups may have used it as access from the south. In all likelihood it was *Guru Bung Dhaura* in Ngunawal language. Stony ground—a path.

I'd been unable to find the Aboriginal name for this particular place. Thinking of yesterday and the term *Bemeringal* I wondered whimsically if it might have been called *Bemeringal Pass*.

Detailed history of this place where I sat had vanished. Under threat, the knowledge might have been hidden to protect it. In any case the inherited verbal story of the first peoples had been disrupted. Remnants were still to be discovered though they had to be found, recorded and put back into the knowledge bank.

I folded the maps, stood, lifted the pack and stepped back down the track.

On the side of the trail I came upon tussocks of alpine grass and ground that'd been churned into long patches of mud. I hadn't seen this before, though I'd read articles where this was described. This must have been snout ripping. It was caused by feral pigs foraging for food, usually the roots of native orchids and lilies.

The Namadgi National Park authorities had been trying to control the feral pigs by using poisons for more than twenty years. Their success was frustrated by hunters who'd release sows and boars into the park so that they could continue with their sport. Before release, the ears of the breeding animals were cut off by the hunters to ensure that dingoes and feral dogs couldn't use these as leverage to pull the animal down. This improved the chances of survival.

I weighed the opposing effort from these two groups. The custodians of the National Park attempted to protect the wilderness. This was the duty they'd been designated by society. At the same time, others in that same society worked furtively to prevent their success.

The frustration of not understanding why society and people couldn't match the stated goals with behaviour rose within me again. Conceivably part of why I'd walked out of Canberra yesterday was my inability to reconcile these types of contradictions within human behaviour. My mind wanted to align what people said with what they did. What I said with what I did. If I couldn't, it was reasonable to suppose that I had no idea of what they were thinking, what I was thinking. I recognised that my brain latched onto differences between words and actions and then spun up in a never ending question and counter question cycle, trying to reconcile the unresolvable.

The length of stride and cadence of pace increased as I brooded over the National Park pig puzzle. I'd become agitated. I forced the pace to slow while I tried to accept that human behaviour couldn't be neatly packaged. I allowed a grin. Just like my action of walking into the wilderness.

As I travelled eastward I rounded bends in the trail, catching sight of the snow-capped Bimberi Peak. The mountain I'd seen from the office and the inspiration in many ways for this walk. It was closer now and even more inviting. At nineteen hundred and eleven metres, it was the highest mountain in the Australian Capital Territory and even more beautiful now that it was closer. It was a common myth that the central axis of the Griffin town plan for Canberra ran from Mount Ainslie to Capital Hill where Parliament House now sat. In fact, the central axis of the Griffin plan went through Capital Hill and finished on Bimberi Peak. A red arrow on the original drawings inscribed with the words *to Bimberi Peak* were able to be viewed in Canberra at the exhibition centre. Walter Griffin, and the architect-drawer

Marion Mahony, who was soon to be Walter's wife, had never been to Canberra. The beautiful drawings depicted a mountain in the background that dominated the landscape somewhat more than in reality.

The sight of Bimberi Peak energised my steps. The pace picked up again, though this time it wasn't from frustration. It was from the excitement of discovery.

A stream crossed the track and I knelt by it to fill up the emptying water bottles. A trail junction was visible to the front. This was as I expected from the map. The direction of travel was to the right where the track would then ascend through a eucalyptus forest in an extended steep climb to Leura Gap.

Purification tablets were plonked into each bottle of water; I screwed on the caps and stood. Rising to full height, I dragged air into my lungs and marshalled strength. I stepped onto the junction.

The march upward warmed me.

The once-numb toes could be felt in damp socks. Blood was carrying oxygen and warmth to all parts of the body. I was functioning as a human should. I tramped with determination and not with the desperate need that'd driven me yesterday. Something was changing inside of me as the feet carried me further into the forest.

I'd fled from the city. That part of the journey, the escape, was now complete. I was far from town, deep in the wilderness and going deeper. It was now up to me to conserve energy, resolve problems and get myself to Mount Kosciuszko safely.

The trail peaked at a gate. The track went downhill from this point. Opening the gate that marked the border of the Australian Capital Territory and New South Wales was another artificial and satisfying milestone of the journey. I was crossing the state boundary.

I chose to stop and sit in the sunshine. The rays had penetrated the clouds. Feeble though the warmth was, it was glorious, and made even more so from the morning exertions that'd left me tired. I squinted for a few moments before pulling sunglasses out of the pack and putting them on.

I made a note to myself that I was possibly passing onto pathways of a different group of nations about now. I unfolded the *How It Was* map. Pen marks illustrated the uncertainty. Around here or near the Goodradigbee River down the hill were likely paths of Wongalu, Monero Ngarigo, and Maneroo-Ngarigo. The signs that marked this change were not known to me.

I hesitated. In the end it was better to be cautious. I stood.

In my mind I offered deference to the ancestors and the traditional custodians of the land and requested safe passage through Country.

I was self-conscious about this act as I stood on the empty hillside.

I assured myself that this was my secret and it was the right thing to do. It did no harm. Courtesy cost me nothing. Safe passage should never be taken for granted in the mountains. I returned to the sitting position.

The very near Bimberi Peak that dominated my view was a reminder that jogged this last point. An accidental death had occurred there in January of 1896. Christy Goody, when crossing the mountain on horse had been injured when he attempted to adjust his saddle. His horse had kicked him. There on the side of the exposed mountain he'd lain until the injured man was discovered by Henry Oldfield. Oldfield nursed him through the night and then carried him down the mountain to his house in the Cotter River area. It was there that he died. Henry Oldfield had then made the burial arrangements.

I considered the story. Christy Goody was Aboriginal. It was recorded and described as *neighbourliness* at the time of the inquest. In the present we might describe Oldfield's actions as mateship.

At the very beginning of the arrival of European settlers in the mountains, a complex relationship with the first peoples developed. Garrett Cotter, the former convict and stockman who was the first European to enter the region had a rapport with an Aboriginal, Honyong. It was Honyong who, in the late 1820s, guided Cotter west of the Murrumbidgee River into the foothills around the Cotter River valley during a drought. Cotter was seeking summer pastures for cattle. In a sense, the relationship between Honyong and Cotter created the opportunity for the tradition of summer cattle grazing in the High Country. When the pastures at lower altitudes had dried out in the heat of the summer sun, the migration of cattle began.

Conceivably, the challenges of the alpine terrain meant that all were just trying to survive. There was no need for unnecessary conflict though as European population numbers increased this occurred. Honyong himself was reported to have carried a bullet in his leg from when a settler shot at him.

I lay in the sun longer and pondered humans in history. What we modern Australians knew of our history and what we'd lost.

Honyong was not from Canberra. Yet it was he who introduced Cotter to this new country by guiding him through the land, other Aboriginals would've done the same for other settlers. It was likely that many of the paths through the mountains, including the route I was following, had been Aboriginal. European settlers had come and leveraged these routes that'd been known for millennia.

Across Australia there were scant records of the more than three hundred Aboriginal languages spoken when colonised. Fewer than twenty of those languages were *living* by being handed down to the next generation.

When curating the exhibition I'd visited the Institute of Aboriginal and Torres Strait Islander Studies. There a mountain of film, sound and video recordings were held. In that mountain were nuggets of gold for people like me, though much of it was not catalogued. This material needed to be digitised or it would be lost. Only a small portion of the funding needed for such a task was available.

Loss of culture hadn't happened. It was still happening.

The recordings of place names, a reminder of this vanishing history, was in large measure due to the Surveyor General of the colony of New South Wales, Thomas Mitchell. In 1830 he gave instructions for surveyors to always record the native name of rivers and places. In some parts of the colony this instruction would've been too late. The first Australians' numbers were already in decline. In this region, with the limestone plains of Canberra first visited by Europeans in 1820 and settlement west and south dating after that year, Mitchell's edict seems to have been followed to some extent. Some of the original names are recorded. The meanings are occasionally known. The entire context of these beautiful and unique names seemed to be gone. I'd only found a jigsaw with missing pieces.

I stood and placed the pack on my back and headed downhill. I was deep in thought. Were the pieces of the jigsaw lost or hidden?

I twisted and turned steadily for many long winding kilometres. The going was particularly easy after the lengthy climb. The track was well defined and the temperature had now risen. At walking pace I was neither too warm nor too cool. There was undeniably a chill in the air, though it was more invigorating than dangerous on this wide fire trail as I loped downhill. The trees were tall and healthy. Around many of the bends in the path I'd see a little creek. Looking up and down the banks I'd marvel at the clarity of the water while listening to the sounds of it splashing against rocks.

I monitored my body constantly; no hot spots on the feet, my back wasn't sore, the legs were strong. I was well placed to continue with the journey. The shoulders were still tense from the unfamiliar weight of the pack. I hoped that'd soon go. There was nothing to do about it in any case. The tightened muscles stayed or worked themselves out. Visiting a physiotherapist, sports medicine expert, chiropractor or masseuse wasn't a possibility so I needed to cope with the situation.

Rounding a bend I came face to face with a group of seven or more wallabies. They looked up, startled. Clearly the family wasn't expecting a human to encroach upon their winter wilderness. Dark in colour, almost black, they simultaneously started hopping in different directions. Then as one, the group achieved consensus by following the leader.

Just like me most of the time, waiting for a lead and then following. Not now though. There were no leads on this journey by myself.

On another bend in the trail I noticed indents in the wet clay. The marks were near a dip with a slither of water. The moisture had clearly made the trail softer at this point and susceptible to leaving observable imprints of heavy animals. They were irregular and semicircular.

ɔɔ ᷄ɔ ɔ ɔɔ
ɔ ɔɔ_ɔ ɔɔɔ ɔ

It wasn't just one animal. There were many. Some prints were scuffed where the animals that'd created them had slipped.

The hooves of horses. There were many horses in the mob travelling in the same direction.

Brumbies were nearby. My pace lengthened with anticipation.

Past some concrete culverts I walked. These constructions were made as part of the Snowy Scheme. Down the end of this valley, still many kilometres away, was the man-made Tantangara Dam, the northern most water storage in the Snowy Hydro Electric Scheme. My mind though wasn't on the Snowy right now; it was instead excited by the nearness of wild horses.

Free ranging feral horses were not native to Australia. They were the offspring of lost or escaped horses belonging to the European settlers. The horses had arrived with the First Fleet in 1788. At least seven were known to have been brought along. They did not fare well as three years later a stallion and a mare survived of the originals with two young colts. This inauspicious start didn't give any hint to the large numbers of wild horses that'd eventually flourish across the continent. Australia now had the largest feral horse population in the world with upwards of four hundred thousand. Here in the Kosciuszko National Park estimates varied from fifteen hundred to five thousand.

Only the strongest animals survived initially and this helped in making healthy breeding stock from horses as diverse as South African 'Capers',

Indonesian 'Timor Ponies', English ponies, draught horses, thoroughbreds and Arabians. Horses had become a famed part of the landscape of Australia and the Alps.

In this area, expeditions to trap Brumbies were mounted through the Brindabella Ranges, as well as New South Wales and Victorian Alpine areas. Stockyards were used for the capture, though the remains of these were now virtually all gone.

The origin of the word Brumby was obscure. Banjo Paterson in the introduction to his 1894 poem, *Brumby's Run*, stated Brumby was the word for free-roaming horses. Others believed Brumby derived from the Pitjara word *baroomby*, meaning wild. According to another story, James Brumby, a settler of New South Wales, left horses that he was unable to muster or dispose of when he sailed for Van Diemen's Land. Folklore had it that these were known as Brumby's horses and later as 'Brumbies'.

The lineage of the horses in the Australian Alps is as obscure as the name Brumby. The horses in the mountains are believed to be descendants of horses owned by the pastoralist and pioneer Ben Boyd. No one could say for certain.

The reverie on this subject was interrupted as I entered a clearing with the Goodradigbee River crossing the centre.

On the far side was the mob of wild horses.

They faced me, ready for danger.

Progressively, so as not to startle them, I reached for a camera.

Don't run, I willed a tall shiny brown horse with white markings that looked like the leader. Shorter, stocky brown horses, with long winter coats stood ready on either flank.

Stay and let me get a photo.

The dirty river water and the churned mud around the Goodradigbee River's banks couldn't be missed. This erosion and ground compression damage the horses' heavy hoof prints caused was foreign to the fragile alpine landscape. Many now viewed the horses as a pest to be exterminated, while others staunchly defended them as part of Australian heritage and sought more humane treatment.

My eyes met those of the charger. A link, a magical bond, was instantly created. I reminisced for the first time in years about my childhood dream of riding a horse free. No saddle, no bridle, just me and a horse and an endless plain. It was a dream that had no basis in reality as I'd never ridden a horse and doubted I could. Still perhaps the impossibility of that dream was what made it so enchanting. I imagined for a fleeting second me riding this charger bareback. At the same time a hand found the pouch that contained the camera.

The horse opposite shook its head as if to break the spell between us. It turned its back on me. The rest of the mob followed as one.

The camera was now in hand and I fumbled for the power button. I whipped the camera to my eye, peering through the aperture and snapped a picture of horse tails.

Then I ran in pursuit.

The rumbling of hooves throbbed at my ears. The air and ground shook as the mob gathered momentum. Reaching a crest that was partly obscuring my view, I halted. Puffing hard from the sprint, I could see the hinds of the horses disappearing into the scrub.

The distance was too far for the photograph that I wanted. I stood and watched for a moment before bending over to catch my breath.

Eventually I straightened. I looked in the direction of the horses. I was disappointed they hadn't stayed for a photo.

Continuing along the track, piles of smelly horse manure were an unpleasant reminder of the Brumbies' recent presence. The manure was mounded in many places past knee height as the animals marked their territory.

I'd discovered in researching the Brumbies that each animal produced more than twenty kilograms of manure a day or about eight tonnes a year. A family of horses could cover a large area with manure in a smelly unsightly manner.

Patterson had omitted this accompaniment, with flies in summer, to the romantic bush he portrayed. I recalled *The Silver Brumby* by Elyne Mitchell as the journey southward proceeded. These much loved Australian books were about horses in the Alps. She hadn't mentioned manure in the stories she'd written.

The beauty and the commanding presence of a horse made them emblematic for the whole country to Elyne Mitchell. Man's attempts to tame the horses, tame the country, frequently failed. The horses of Elyne Mitchell were free, despite the battle with man who wished to ensnare them. Perhaps because horses in her books represented beauty and freedom, manure was an unwanted distraction. Maybe her eyes didn't see the mess the horses left across the landscape. It was the modern nose that absorbed the smell. The urban eyes saw the obvious damage.

The horse in the Snowy region was now the subject of a tug-o-war between romanticists about Australia's heritage and conservationists.

Over time the romanticist position had evolved to the concept of gaining recognition for the Brumby as part of Australia and the Snowy's heritage. They accepted that damage was caused, though wanted a place to be found for the horses by controlling numbers through trapping.

The conservationist position was that the wild horses didn't belong in this ancient and delicate landscape. They should be removed as the damage caused was unacceptable.

All around me was the evidence of the conservationist position and still the heart kept making the case for the horses. The excitement at seeing them, my want to take a photograph to record the moment, revealed to me that I had a boot in each camp.

A pragmatist.

The trail wound on into a valley. The rays of the feeble sun disappeared behind clouds. A little waterfall attracted attention so I broke trail to appreciate its beauty and eat a muesli bar. Without the heat from the sun, the moment I ceased exertions I cooled. It was an uncomfortable chill.

A solitary Water Dragonfly fluttered near the surface. This was not the season for insects. A lonely presence, I remembered that dragonflies near water had been a sign that it was of good quality to the nations of the mountains. It meant the water was safe to drink.

I took out my water bottles to fill them. I stopped. I let my hand immerse itself ever so slowly into the water. I felt the waters clear depths. I replenished my water bottles while debating the idea of not purifying the water as a test. I then thought of the feral animals and urged myself not to be silly. The land was not as it had been.

I was about to move on when a flurry of noise broke behind me and to the left. A large grey kangaroo hopped at full tilt. I admired the lines and grace of its agile and rapid spring followed by the short flight. I'd scarcely had a moment to ponder what had caused it to be startled when a wild dog appeared in pursuit. Then another dog broke through the bushes at pace. The eyes of both animals were focussed on the quarry and their ears were pinned back. The fangs could be seen even at the distance that I was observing from.

My immediate reaction of willing the kangaroo a good escape turned to anxiety.

What would I do if the pair of dogs turned and came back for me? The advice from the survival course was to fold arms, eye the dog, and calmly back away. I was to hit them with a stick if they came too close. This had been adequate guidance at the time, though after seeing the teeth and the size of the animals, I now knew it wasn't.

My gaze fell on the pond at the base of the waterfall. The dragonfly danced back and forth across the pond. If I stood in the middle of the body of water the dogs would have to swim to attack me. I could eyeball them from out there and my arms would be free to swing. That's where I'd go. The water was safe.

The dragonfly vanished into some reeds.

I chose to delay a while and let the kangaroo and dogs move on. My teeth chattered with cold from the inactivity but still I waited.

The Australian wild dog, the dingo, had been in this area for four thousand years. The dingo had in the last two hundred years mixed with other domestic dogs that'd been released or escaped into the bush. It was the high order predator in Australia.

Eventually I determined that enough time had elapsed and I shouldered my pack. Eyes alert, I hurried to clear the area.

The journey took me past Pockets Hut. It was a substantial building on the right. In the 1930s this now abandoned homestead was owned by a prosperous company that operated from the main regional town of Cooma. The homestead was notable in that even in the 1930s it had electricity and hot water that made it quite a bastion of civilisation.

The valley widened into a plain and I knew I was almost at the northern end of Tantangara Reservoir.

I came across a trail junction and a sign. The forty centimetre stake had a sky blue arrow with the words *Australian Alps Walking Track* pinned at its highest point. The Alpine Walking Track was a trail that extended from Canberra to Walhalla in Victoria, over some six hundred and fifty kilometres. It was a possible route through the mountains. Parts of it I'd follow in the coming days as I completed my trek.

Facing east with my back to the late afternoon sun, my destination was Oldfield's Hut. My legs powered onwards.

The historic hut was reached as the last rings of the sun disappeared behind Bimberi Peak that was now to the west and north of my location. I'd crossed over. I was on the other side of the range.

SHARING

THE SKY WAS SHADOWY as I opened the door of Oldfield's Hut. The interior of the building was even darker.

Stepping in, I was greeted by a flurry of noise underfoot and a hiss. In a reflex I jumped back, catching a foot and stumbling. Regaining balance, my gaze came upon a possum. He stood opposite the door watching me with big eyes. Drawn to full height he was postured for a confrontation. Possum's stance conveyed unhappiness at the unexpected late arrival to his home. He was letting me know it was his territory I'd just invaded.

'Shoo,' I shouted and waved my hands.

The possum replied with a hiss.

'Move on Ol' Possum,' I requested authoritatively with waving hands. I advanced a pace to demonstrate my commanding intent.

The possum advanced toward me hissing.

This caused me to retreat. I tripped over a broom and landed on the dirt floor.

Slowly I picked myself up. I was sheepish at this unexpected setback.

The potential of the broom was evident so I grasped it in both hands as I stood.

The next five minutes was a burst of activity. I ran around the hut yelling, broom waving in the air. The possum deftly avoided all of the advances and thrusts. He eluded the swishing broom and was unperturbed as he took up position as far from me as possible in the confined space. He was ready for my next attempt.

Panting at intervals of calm, I drew up mental plans on how to chase Ol' Possum out.

All of the tactics were fine though the execution was undone by the opponent. The composure of the possum throughout each round of our tussle was morale-sapping.

Tired and wheezing, I elected to reset the conflict. It occurred to me that it was his home after all. I was the trespasser.

'We can share, you know. If you hadn't been so combative when I walked in we might have come to this arrangement without such fuss. I'll just camp over here,' I announced, pointing to a place on the floor. 'And you can have the rest of the hut. That seems reasonable doesn't it?' I waved around the hut in a gesture that I hoped conveyed generous intention.

The possum stared at me unmoving.

They were big expressive eyes and I imagined they still contained annoyance at me. I guessed that in their depths there was a little pity for me. I imagined he was plotting vengeance at some point when I slept. It was a long night and the possum was nocturnal. I knew that once I went to bed that the odds were stacked in the possum's favour.

We stared at each other across the room.

'I'll go in the morning, I promise.'

Our standoff endured for a minute or more before the possum turned and climbed into the fire place. He vanished from view. The possum's tail was high in the air as he left. It was a sign that he wasn't defeated. He looked very dignified.

Hoping the disappearance was a kind of settlement and truce I unpacked.

First I put on the hot water for a tea and for use in rehydrating dinner. Then I stepped outside to try the mobile.

It was an exercise in hope. There wasn't a signal and I didn't expect one, given the location of the hut in a hollow in the mountains.

Returning inside, I was disappointed nevertheless. Still no contact with Arianne.

Oldfield's was a cattleman's hut. Inside it had a fireplace and no bunks. The walls had gaps between the timber slats. It was drafty. The flooring probably once all slats, now was partially dirt. I guessed that there'd be marsupials that scurried around at night and of course Ol' Possum. His dark sparkling eyes watched me from behind his pointy little nose that was partially obscured in the shadowy fireplace.

I measured some now boiling water into the dehydrated food pack and with the remainder I made a brew. I sensed I was in a routine though this was just the second time I'd completed this process.

Next I assembled the bed and then searched the ceiling with the torch. I found the hooks attached in strategic places for the food bag. Gratified by the discovery, I felt like an old hand.

Touching the hat, I adjusted it rearward so it perched lightly on my hair. Leaning backward I sat against the wall in the corner of the room. I sipped tea and ate food.

The shelter was built for Bill Oldfield in the 1920s. He had a sheep and cattle run in the area and had worked the local country until his lease wasn't renewed. Like all the huts I was going to visit from here onwards during the journey, it was maintained by the Kosciuszko Hut Association or KHA. Formed in the early 1970s, this association was set up by volunteers to assist with the conservation of huts and homesteads in the National Park. In the 1990s, the Kosciuszko Hut Association expanded into some of the huts and areas of the Namadgi National Park.

For many years the Kosciuszko Hut Association had attempted to preserve what the National Parks didn't necessarily value. At the time, the parks saw their role as returning the bush to its natural state. The huts were not part of nature. This philosophy evolved in time, and a cooperative partnership between the volunteers of the Kosciuszko Hut Association and the National Parks grew. They now jointly conserved the huts. Importantly for me as a historian, they did research and made it available for the use of others.

Fed and warm, I took the paper and pencil from the pack and climbed into bed.

It'd been a good day overall, I judged.

Nagging doubts about Ol' Possum's intentions tonight remained in the back of my mind.

I wrote the title *Home Invasion*.

Words came effortlessly and before too long my heavy and closing eyes were reading the last words.

> *Ol' Possum regally left the fray*
> *For now I'll retreat but you'll soon have to sleep*
> *Then havoc I'll reap*
> *Ol' Possum smiled at the hiker's coming dismay*

I fell asleep still worried about the possum.

Light coming through the cracks in the hut's walls was what woke me.

Immediately I registered my whereabouts. The next thought was that Ol' Possum had not disturbed me in the night. This was pleasing. I'd misjudged him. I decided that Ol' Possum was a fine fellow as I reached for the hat. Placing it on, I then lit the stove. I commenced the routine of getting packed and fed before the day's exertions.

It was just minutes before I was doing final checks for any equipment I'd missed. A quick sweep of the hut and then out the door of Oldfield's in grey light with the sun yet to rise. At this stage of the morning I couldn't tell whether the day was cloudy or it'd turn to blue when the sun rose.

My dreams had been of Arianne looking for me in the mountains. I was guilty. The note I left had explained plans though I hadn't expected to get this far into the journey without having made contact. It was apparent that I should've called earlier in my first day when my mobile was more likely in range of Canberra. I hadn't and I was kicking myself.

What was I thinking?

Why had I been so intent on making my getaway?

What was I avoiding?

Arianne?

This was not the case. I missed her and she'd been the one regret since leaving.

Could I be running from work?

Not really, I answered. It wasn't perfect, nevertheless I loved history and the museum and I enjoyed every day I spent there. Sometimes I sat at my desk, immersed in work, only stopping when my stomach rumbled with hunger. At that moment I'd look at the time and realise it was past three in the afternoon and I'd been at work since seven in the morning.

Society?

Maybe. I was an outsider. There was an ever-present sense that I didn't belong. The values I held were somehow different to everyone else's. I construed that most people I met guessed it. They all looked at me a little strangely and with good reason. Their suspicions were right, I didn't fit.

This last conjecture caused extra thought.

It didn't seem logical that I couldn't read what other people were thinking, yet somehow imagined that they could read my mind. Arianne would tell me to stop being paranoid if she was here.

At that moment I missed her so much that my chest tightened. Talking to her was special. Her insights and her company were priceless.

I determined that this morning I'd walk down Tantangara Reservoir on the eastern side. There was a road that was blocked off in winter that would be my route. This path would give me the best chance of picking up some mobile reception as it was nearer to the distant towns of Adaminaby and Cooma. Talking to Arianne today was the priority. She'd be at work and there was always the possibility that she would be in a meeting and unavailable. I was disappointed by this prospect. I'll get a connection I said to myself as if saying these words in my head would make it come true.

My toes were numb in the boots again. I walked as fast as I could. Unpleasant cold feet would be with me each morning on this journey.

The mood of the country was particularly apparent to me today.

At the start I'd walked up a hill into a dense fog. The moisture had been captured in the hills surrounding the valley. Grey gums closed in on all sides except for where the track made a narrow corridor. It was intimidating. Healthy trees towered over me and highlighted my comparative small stature. The restricted view into the grey of the fog filled me with foreboding.

Then I emerged from the forest and fog simultaneously. The open plains around Tantangara Reservoir were revealed. The sun was up. There was blue sky, contrasted with white frost and a dusting of snow crystals on the ground. The shards sparkled when light touched them. Above, across the blue, fluffy black clouds skated through the sky on unseen jet streams. From the position where I stood there wasn't a breath of wind.

I kept on down the chosen route and an hour later the blue sky disappeared. A squall of stinging icy rain buffeted me for ten minutes before it returned to bright sunshine.

Good progress was made as I enjoyed a few hours of fast walking on a flat wide dirt road. Sporadically I halted to check for phone reception. Efforts were rewarded about 10:00. A bar in the corner of the screen signified I was just in range of a tower. A mixture of relief and pleasure was the overwhelming feeling. Arianne would be at work for a few hours by now.

After dialling I pushed a button to put the phone on speaker. I heard briefly the tone that signalled connection.

At the other end the telephone was answered before one ringtone could complete.

'Hello ... hello Tim,' it was Arianne's voice.

'It's me Tim ... Did you get my message?'

'I can hardly hear you ... I received the message. I've got your note. It's OK. Are you OK?'

'We're OK. We're just walking ... thinking.'

'John called. He thinks the exhibition's the best yet. You didn't have to worry. People are streaming through.'

I paused and drew breath, 'How's John?'

'He's OK. I talked to him. He said he'll see you when you're done.'

'Are you OK?' I was conscious that I'd rudely not asked this of Arianne.

'I'm . . .' the response was never finished. The bar that indicated reception had disappeared from the screen.

I dialled again.

Nothing.

'I love you,' I mouthed to the phone.

For another half hour I hit redial and held the phone at different angles to get some reception. It was all to no avail.

I gave up. Time was disappearing and I needed to move ahead. There were many kilometres to travel if I was to get to my evening's destination.

The waters of Tantangara Reservoir were occasionally visible on the left as I trudged.

Despondency overcame me for a little.

Why had I left off the words *I love you* until the signal had cut out?

Why hadn't I spoken those words first?

I was melancholy and then the familiar rhythm of hiking enhanced my mood.

My fingers spontaneously stroked the brim of the hat. It was reassuring to the touch. My disposition improved.

I brightened further when the sun shone.

The gravel road I was walking down was easy to navigate as the big bends were shown on the map. My exact location was always apparent.

The road helped me make good time.

Lunch was eaten with a view of the Reservoir's waters while luxuriating in the quiet stillness.

I was acclimatising to the cold, I told myself.

This proved to be an illusion and I was soon shivering. Before long I walked on.

Shortly after lunch the road veered steeply downhill and I reached the dam wall.

Tantangara Dam captured the waters of the Murrumbidgee River.

The Murrumbidgee, the Murray and the Snowy Rivers were the three main waterways affected by the Snowy Mountains Hydroelectric scheme. Originally the proposal had been to divert the Snowy River from its eastern flow where the waters disgorged into the Pacific Ocean, to a western flow to provide more water for cattle and agriculture in the drier interior of Australia. The idea evolved to be a hydroelectric scheme as well and then a nation building exercise where workers were recruited from more than thirty mainly European countries. Begun post-World War Two, many of the workers came from countries that'd been at war with each other just a few years earlier. The new world offered a chance for these workers to begin life afresh. At the same time it changed the cultural face of Australia as well as the environment.

In the more than sixty years since the scheme had been planned, weather patterns had changed. The dry spells had become longer and evaporation had increased. In addition the Murray River and Murrumbidgee River were affected by the allocation to farmers of more water than what was currently flowing through the system in the drier years.

The outcome in 2015 was that the rivers were becoming more saline. They were rancid with blue-green algae blooms on drier years where the flow was less and the demand for water from farmers for their crops higher. The mighty Snowy River had turned to a trickle. The survival of native fish was threatened. Trees and vegetation along the banks of the river were dying.

Environmental flows were negotiated to return the Snowy back to health. Sometimes there wasn't enough water spare for them to be authorised to proceed. Political discussions talked about reducing water allotments and in some cases buying out farmers on the Murray and Murrumbidgee Rivers. Emotive and highly charged progress was made often only to be reversed at the change of government.

Analysis of the long-term trends by experts painted a bleak future for the iconic Snowy Scheme. The region was warmer and had less rainfall. The snow wasn't as deep. The seasonal flooding was altered by the dam system.

Man, ever adaptable, hatched a new plan.

Rain would be made by cloud seeding. Cloud seeding generators were installed on the western edge of the ranges with the idea of increasing snow fall. It was thought that silver iodide particles released from the generators would increase precipitation by more than ten percent. This would increase the water available for irrigation and electricity generation.

No studies were done into whether silver iodide would affect endangered native animals like the pygmy possum. No investigations were conducted into whether silver iodide would get into the food chain and have health implications. These risks were dismissed as negligible.

As I hiked, I marvelled at how deceiving the country was to an amateur like me. The Reservoir and creeks all looked so pristine to the eye. There wasn't any hint that underneath substantial problems threatened the delicate balance of nature.

Past the dam wall and towards the edge of the abandoned Kiandra goldfields I progressed.

In this area the plains had been denuded of trees in a few years of feverish activity from 1860. The rolling grasslands I was moving through were the result.

Thousands had descended in the hope of finding gold and making it rich. The land was still trenched and eroded by the mining that'd been undertaken one hundred and fifty years earlier. Patches of snow had gathered in dips emphasising the work of the miners even more.

The Eucumbene River curved through the landscape. It was beautiful when highlighted in the soft light of the winter sun moving to the end of its day in the west.

Taking off the boots I forded the thigh deep river. It made me gasp and grimace at the shock of the icy water on the lower body.

Stumbling onto the western river bank I searched for a place to sit and put on socks and boots. Part way through putting the socks back on the idea occurred to me that this would be a lovely place to pitch tent. There was no need to go to a hut.

I slipped my feet loosely into the boots to consider the idea. It seemed a reasonable decision. With nothing against it, I scoured my memory of the survival course for ideas on how to camp.

Choosing the right site was the most important task, I recalled. There was a need for a location higher than the river. It'd been explained to me that if I made camp too close to the river the rushing waters of the stream would generate cold air. This air being heavier than warm air would hang in the creek line area. As warm air rose, there was often a trap of air about two thirds of the way up the slope from the bottom. That was where I should camp. Too close to the top and the cold air would roll across the hill crest.

I searched for the spot that might meet these requirements. When I found it I walked across with the pack temporarily flung over one shoulder.

It was exciting to be pitching a tent. I was camping.

Just ten minutes later the tent was set, the sleeping gear rolled out and a pot was on the stove.

Pulling out the phone I checked for connectivity, saw there was none and put it away.

This was disappointing. It would've been comforting to talk to Arianne and share the events of the day with her. At the same time I wasn't frustrated as I'd spoken to Arianne this morning. I knew she was OK. She knew I was safe.

The pot boiled. The flame of the stove was extinguished. The tea was made. The remaining hot water was poured into the satchel of dehydrated food before resealing it. I waited. It was all automatic.

Adjusting the hat I leant backwards in a relaxed fashion. Fingers wrapped around the mug for warmth and I watched the still, quiet landscape with spots of snow seemingly glowing in the soft light.

Tranquillity engulfed me for the first time since I'd started this adventure. For the first time in a long time.

I sipped the black tea. The tea bag still dangled inside the water. The beverage would get more flavoursome as each mouthful was drunk.

The lavishness of the city life was far away and I had no choices over what to have for dinner or what to drink. It was a dehydrated meal and tea. There would be no searching the pantry or refrigerator to decide if anything took my fancy for dessert like I might do at home. The pantry was the pack and there were no confectionaries.

At first blush the austerity of this circumstance was restrictive. Counter-intuitively, I was finding the lack of choice to be freeing. Thoughts weren't being constantly consumed by the next decision. My brain was wandering like my feet had for a few days now.

I ran through the obstacles I'd overcome so far.

There was a satisfaction at what I'd achieved alone.

I'd negotiated deep rivers, long marches, steep trails, living in primitive accommodation and uncertain weather.

I had no companions to consult with or encourage me. It was just me.

Again I'd been given the gift of freedom by no choice. There was no taxi or car to flag down and take me home. There was just the option to keep going and I'd kept going. I'd been focussed on the goal. There was virtually no alternative except the destination.

My navigational skills had stood up. They'd been stretched, though not absolutely tested at this point.

Spontaneously I burst into song.

'I love to go a wandering along the mountain track, and as I go I love to sing with a knapsack on my back.'

I struggled through the first verse, sometimes stopping a line to recorrect a word, before continuing with the song. As I sang, an uneasy sense developed that I was being watched. I launched into the second verse even though the uncomfortable feeling persisted. This prickle of paranoia rose as the verse progressed and at the same time my voice faded. Confidence dissipated as the words trailed off into silence.

Spinning from left to right I searched the plains. It was as quiet and as empty as before. Artificially I segmented the view to my front into left, centre and right. Methodically I scanned each segment. Nothing.

Leaving the reclined position I stood and faced behind me. The process was replicated.

My eyes examined the distant tree line. It was grey and in shadow. Shapes were blurring in the fading light.

I found a human shape by a tree, standing and watching me. I stared back for an eternity. It didn't move. Not a twitch, not a muscle stirred. To get a better view I walked towards it. Still no discernible movement could be detected.

I was persuaded that my mind was playing tricks. I was as alone as I'd been since I left Canberra.

My observation was true except for the chance meetings with the bushman on the Murrumbidgee River and near Pryor's Hut. Then there was the ranger I'd met near the waterfalls.

Focusing, I tried to remember their faces and couldn't. The details were indistinct. It was so long ago. Then I mentally checked myself. *So long ago* was only the day before yesterday.

'Wow.' I exclaimed as an acknowledgement.

I sat back down.

The review of the journey restarted.

All of my spare time was spent maintaining personal health and in particular the feet. The right ankle was becoming sore. The uneven tufty grass and rutted track that constantly caused twisting was taking a toll.

I massaged the ankle to assist it in getting better but also to distract myself from the paranoid idea that I was still being watched. As the ankle had become sore on the right leg, I'd favoured my left. This extra strain meant the left leg was sore from cramping.

I committed myself to extra care from here. The plans I'd made in the garage needed to be adjusted to the reality of the circumstances on the ground. Preservation of physical condition was the priority. I had no ambulance to call and no doctor to visit. I needed my body to function and my mental powers to be at their peak. I wasn't yet half way. I needed to be measured and realistic.

Reaching for pencil and paper my mind turned to poetry. I'd come to think of the pages I'd been writing each night as a poetry book. A modern man's bush poetry. As the sun dipped below the horizon I began to write.

The simplicity of life here in the mountains was confronting. Without coming across other humans, I didn't have other ideas or opinions to reconcile against mine. I had the flora and the fauna and they offered no advice. I just had the thoughts in my own head.

I could see how stories of creation came about.

How gods were created.

The sun was a perfect example. It gave life. It was vital for me to achieve anything. When it disappeared, the cold of night drove me into the sleeping bag in search of warmth.

I continued writing, though every now and then the sensation of being watched returned to prickle me. I'd look up from the words but nothing moved.

I was confident I was alone and yet still I couldn't lose this feeling of being observed. I pulled the hat down a little further for warmth and wrote the words 'Sun god shine ...

THE WILD

SUDDENLY VIGILANT, I AWOKE with my senses engaged.

I lay in the sleeping bag with the hood wrapped tightly around my head and only my eyes and nose protruding. I didn't move. Racking the brain I sought the cause of my watchfulness. It didn't know. The alarm had started in the state of sleep and therefore it was the subconscious acting to defend, not the conscious.

Then I caught a sound. It was a stealthy footfall. It wasn't the heavy crunch of a man in boots. It was lighter and padded. Muffled. I heard another surreptitious step and then silence.

An instinct deep inside of me registered that I was being hunted. On the other side of the tent wall lurked something dangerous.

The rational side of the brain then countered by questioning the intuitive.

You've never been the prey of an animal before so how would you know?

The mind raced.

Was it imagination?

Was I just hearing things?

What could be stalking me in Australia? There were no big cats or bears.

More furtive sounds reached my ears and panting breath.

Dogs, wild dogs! Hastily I moved to unzip from the sleeping bag to defend myself. As I was going through this frenzied movement I heard the first threatening growls from outside.

'Ahhhhhh … Ahhh,' I growled back. 'Get out of here.'

There was sudden startled movement and I heard the dogs recoil. It sounded like five or six dogs had jumped backwards in fright and kept running.

A pack of animals meant that I was outnumbered. The hesitance of the dogs was a small advantage in my favour.

Now I was free of the sleeping bag and my hands were prodding at the floor of the tent to where I knew I'd left the torch. I was comforted for a moment by the light it emitted. Kneeling I combed the tent for implements to defend myself. There was very little and the torch light highlighted the precariousness of the situation. The tent was wafer thin nylon. There was no doubt that the paws and teeth of wild dogs would push straight through it if the pack attacked.

The pot was the heaviest item in sight, but a whack from it would hardly disturb the dingoes I'd seen yesterday. My gaze fell on a walking stick. I could swing and prod with this so I reached out and grabbed it. The light weight wasn't reassuring, but it was something. There were two walking sticks and I pondered fighting with both before rejecting the notion. I took the other walking stick and placed it between my knees so I could grab it swiftly if the first walking stick broke.

Spare clothes were wrapped hastily around my left arm. This arm then went through the back straps of the pack. The pack could be used as a shield, while the master arm would wield the stick.

The position wasn't good.

A tremor of fear went through my legs.

My heart was thumping but not from exertion.

I spied the hat from the corner of my eye. Reaching out I put it on.

I felt more secure.

My eyes darted around the tent in the hope of finding more tools for a defence. My gaze fell on the snowshoes.

How had I missed them?

They'd make a better shield with their sturdy frame and steel claws. The straps of the binding could connect the long shoe to the arm firmly. The steel claws in the centre could be used to push back towards a dog attack.

Dropping the pack, I reached out for the snowshoes.

One became the shield and the other was placed near the stick between my knees.

I saw the tent nylon pushed toward me. An animal had pressed against it lightly from the outside. I heard a whine from deep in a dog's throat. I imagined a dog nuzzling the tent as a test.

I adjusted position by pulling myself onto knees. I drew breath, focussed on calming the heart and prepared mentally for the nearing fight.

If the dogs broke through the tent I must stand. There would be more agility and mobility standing. The height might intimidate. There was no doubt that I'd be beaten on my knees. I judged that the assembled makeshift weaponry wouldn't be fatal against wild dogs. The image of the two large and rangy dogs chasing the kangaroo from yesterday was firmly in my head. I was in serious trouble if the situation deteriorated to a fight. The vulnerable parts of the dogs would be noses and eyes. Strikes must target the animals where they were most susceptible.

I could hear the sound of cautious steps outside. They now paced around the tent at what sounded like a few metres away.

'Get lost!' I yelled. I heard the dogs recoil.

Then the pacing resumed closer to the tent.

They were getting bolder.

Waiting on knees I was keyed to strike at any dog trying to breach the tent.

'Go away!' I screamed at the top of my lungs.

The dogs retreated and then returned to continue their growling and pacing.

Light. Maybe the animals wouldn't know what to make of light. I spun the torch beam in all directions. The hope was that it'd make an unfamiliar and threatening dance to the dogs outside the tent. Simultaneously I let out a piercing scream.

I heard the dogs take a short jump and stand still.

I was glad that Arianne was unaware of the situation I was in.

The shadow boxing of me yelling and the dogs circling their prey persisted for hours. Slowly the terror had to share space in my mind with my rising physical discomfort. The right ankle ached. The knees were sore from kneeling on them and eyelids drooped with tiredness. The discomfort was intense and I shifted my position frequently. Finally I settled on a sitting position. This wasn't as good for a quick defence. I just couldn't kneel any longer.

My head waggled in exhaustion.

Stay awake, I urged silently.

I blinked my eyes. I shook my head. I yelled to frighten the animals and to try to stay alert.

Eventually I succumbed to exhaustion and dozed off. The shield was still in one hand and the makeshift weapon in the other.

I napped fitfully.

A strange dream filled my head.

The lanky frame of the hatless stranger was outside the tent. His long oilskin coat that Australians referred to as a driz-a-bone reached to his knees. The coat twirled as he spun to chase away the wild dogs. He fought them, always standing between the tent and the dogs. It was the actions of a guardian.

The dogs cowered away and then suddenly turned on him while letting out frightful yelps. The stranger's driz-a-bone flapped furiously as his arms flailed at them. Dogs fell away from him, sometimes hitting the tent and causing more noise.

The sound of the terrible ruckus penetrated to my brain. This was real. The sounds were really happening.

I opened my eyes.

The nylon tent was bending and bucking.

'Ahhhhhh,' I yelled and raised the walking stick in a reflex action ready to strike.

There was no sound of a reaction from dogs. The tent flapped and was buffeted.

It was a few moments before it dawned on me that the tent wasn't about to be breached. It was extremely strong gusts of wind causing the tent to shake.

Relieved but worried, I assessed the situation for some time.

It was minutes before I lowered the stick.

The dogs had disappeared. At least I couldn't hear them.

The weather had changed and the coming storm was clearly now the threat. The nylon might be torn if it wasn't lashed down with extra rope.

I sat procrastinating, afraid of the dogs and afraid of what the wind might do to the tent.

The tent flapped urgently and still I dithered.

A gust of wind howled and the tent bent till the tip of the nylon brushed the hat that I still wore. The touch energised me.

Stretching out I unzipped the tent entrance with the left hand. The right hand held the walking pole high. It was ready to strike.

I crawled and stepped outside.

There were no dogs to be seen. In fact, except darkness and driving flecks of sleet that were being hurled in my face, I could see nothing. The wind was so strong that the sleets trajectory was almost horizontal to the ground. It stung exposed skin with cold and force as it hit.

Turning, I faced the tent. Bending into its entrance I fumbled to find the torch. Next I found the sack that contained some extra-long tent stakes and ropes. Once I'd placed these in the jacket pocket I whipped around the tent's exterior and commenced the process of tying it down more securely.

Thrusting stakes into the ground, I then tied the tent to these additional anchor points. When this was complete I moved in a clockwise direction standing on each stake to ensure they were all secure. I stumbled off balance on a few occasions as my sore ankle hindered me and I attempted to compensate. It was a while before the ropes were stretched satisfactorily tight.

The tent was steady when subjected to a gust of wind. Pleased I was confident enough to re-enter the relative warmth of the tent's interior.

Once on the inside I attempted to speed the process of returning feeling to the hands by rubbing and beating them together. I did this underneath the covers of the sleeping bag that I'd dived into. It was a while before they were warm again.

I'm safe and the dogs are gone, I thought with relief. My thinking then turned to the predicament I was in. I should have kept going to a hut. I'd be safer from the dogs. I'd be not as cramped. Try as I might I couldn't push this negativity aside. I drifted to sleep still admonishing myself.

Dawn's light filtered through the yellow synthetic dome of the tent, waking me. The interior was cosy and warm, much warmer than a hut. The small confines of the tent were trapping some of the expelled air and therefore some heat.

I listened.

The wind was still blowing hard. It caused a whooshing sound.

No dog sounds were evident.

The tent resisted each blast of air.

The gale still raged.

Rolling out of the sleeping bag I unzipped the entrance of the tent to satisfy a curiosity about the outside.

I poked my head out of the flap into a white world. Bleached sky. Bleached snow. Patches of yellow on the tent where snow hadn't yet fallen were the only visible objects of colour.

During sleep it appeared as if the world had been cleaned and painted.

Snow covered the ground and was already half a metre in depth. The amount of snow that'd fallen and was still falling was a surprise.

The sky was silvery-white.

Snow whipped around me.

I swayed as I searched for focus on a reference point. I found none. Visibility was down; my depth perception and spatial awareness had become impaired just sitting still. It would diminish further when moving.

Packing up the tent and walking into the storm was an option that held little appeal. The open and exposed ground offered no cover. The wind would penetrate clothing causing dangerous loss of heat. It was foolhardy.

I determined that I should stay put.

Assessment now turned to the tent and surrounds to see how I was placed to wait the storm out.

There was some risk that the tent would become buried in snow, I guessed. This was undesirable as I needed to be able to break camp and continue the journey when the storm subsided.

I took the plastic shovel and stepped outside. I dug snow away from the tent. Still fresh and soft, the shovel penetrated the surface easily. When it was swung away it was a pitifully small amount. Shovelling snow was a task I'd never done before and I was surprised to find that after fifteen or so minutes my heart was thumping from the exertions. I wasn't warm, I was hot and I'd made relatively little progress.

Returning to the interior of the tent I ate some food for energy, recovered composure and reflected. The activity in the last hour had made me conscious of how stiff the right ankle had become. Massaging it, I attempted to get the blood flowing to assist in the recovery. As I rubbed, I decided on ten minutes of snow shovelling each hour for the remainder of the day. The chime on the watch was set so it'd beep as a reminder. In the intervening period I'd think. It was a luxury that I rarely had time for in the city. Someone was at me or I was diverted by the many entertainment events or possessions. Thoughts about the distractions and how I might regulate them better raced around my head. Perhaps I could quarantine some thinking time, just for me, each day. Doing this I realised didn't necessarily mean that I'd take better control of my life, though it was a start.

The watch chimed. Out into the wind I went, shovel in hand.

Ten minutes later, my heart racing, I crawled back inside the tent and sat.

My mind turned to Arianne. I recalled her soft beautiful hair. Her deep eyes that looked back steady and true. She was so sure of herself. But how did someone as certain as her end up with someone as tentative as me?

Could it work? I was flighty and she was assured.

We were opposites in so many ways. Was it a case of opposites attracting each other but in the long term it held no future? I hadn't met her family. That was by design on her part because the opportunity had come up. What did that mean?

She'd never declared her position by saying, 'I love you.'

I dismissed the notion. I'd never conveyed to her that she made me a better person, that she was the most important person in the world to me, and I loved her. It was unfair to expect the same thing from her when the best I'd done was sending a text saying 'Luv u,' not 'I love you.' The text was feeble and I was frustrated with myself again.

Arianne always supported me. She always anticipated my thinking. We shared common values. She wasn't the kind of person to stick around if she didn't think that we had something!

But why had I left her for this?

Massaging the ankle was the next task. I was tired. It wasn't just from the restless sleep between periods of exertion through the night. It was from the cumulative effects of the effort over the past few days. This trip was hard work and I had a long way to go if I was to achieve journey's end.

The wind dropped and the tent stopped bucking around.

The watch chimed the next hour. Taking a moment to compose myself, I was primed for the draining challenge of ten minutes of shovelling snow.

Unzipping the tent, I crawled out into a world of lightly falling snow flakes. They floated ever so gently. Watching them, spellbound, I remembered that they could fall at a rate as low as six or seven kilometres per hour. Sometimes a flake could take an hour to fall to earth.

Bending at the waist, I shovelled. The snow on the ground was now almost a metre deep. Around the tent was a pronounced hollow. Evidently my effort was achieving some results.

Burning from the exertions I re-entered the tent when the allotted time had expired.

I snuggled into the sleeping bag even though I was warm. If I'd known how hard this trip was going to be perhaps I'd never have started. In this regard I guessed I was like many pioneers who went into the wilderness with limited knowledge and skills. They too might have had the very same thoughts in the Australian bush. A miner on these very goldfields in moments of despair could well have empathised with this thinking. It was sobering to realise that once here the miner was possibly out of money and isolated. He probably didn't have a choice and had to continue, just like me. Like the miner I couldn't call for help. There was no mobile reception. I had to accept the challenges head-on, whatever they might be. Test myself. At times push to the absolute limits of endurance and physical abilities. Take fate into my own hands and grow.

The watch chimed the next hour. Sighing, I reached for the shovel again.

The day wore on in this routine. The light faded and the dark returned and still the snow fell. My schedule that I had left for Arianne was now well out and there was no knowing when I could continue my progress south. There was no way of telling Arianne.

The watch was oblivious to the darkness. It emitted a beep and out the tent I'd dutifully emerge to begin exertions again. Then back inside to rub the ankle.

This pattern repeated until past midnight.

On the next chime I climbed outside into a world of starry skies and white glowing snow. It glistened under the twinkling light from above.

I'd never seen the stars so near. A dome. My arms extended in an impulse to touch them.

Searching, I found the constellation of the Southern Cross. Exhaling, I relaxed at the familiar spectacle. The recognisable pattern was reassuring.

The closeness of the stars was palpable.

The storm had blown the dust from the continent of Australia out to sea. The southerly winds had ushered in pristine air from Antarctica that now surrounded me. Both of these combined with the thinner atmosphere at altitude to allow undistorted views to the heavens. The stars' vibrancy surprised and held my attention. The Milky Way was luminescent and the reasoning behind its name was apparent. It was obvious to me here. This had never been so evident in the city.

Tracing the shape of the Milky Way, I used my limited knowledge to imagine it in the same way as Aboriginals. The sky and earth were interconnected. Many creation figures were in the sky above. It wasn't just the stars I should see but the subtle shades of black. Darker areas in patches between the stars. Without reference to time, distance or quantity the changes in the night sky guided understanding of seasons and hunting and gathering. The Milky Way was shaped like an emu to many of the first Australian nations. I could see this outline clearly. To the Ngunawal people it had been a reminder of why the emu could not fly. The Great Spirit when creating birds had run out of long feathers. This meant that the emu could not leave the ground for the heavens which was the Great Spirit's intention. The Spirit left a reminder of the incomplete plan in the sky and then gave long legs and strong feet to the emu as a compensator. The emu could still be safe by outrunning predators.

I wondered how many Australians tonight could see the Milky Way.

How many Australians could see the Emu?

My eyes remained fixed skywards in awe.

Wouldn't it have been incredible if all Australians could see both the Milky Way and the Emu? The blaze of stars burned into my consciousness the vastness of the visible universe. It challenged me to answer how significant I was to the whole of all this.

The answer was obvious.

I wasn't.

This led me to think about ego. Had I been taking myself too seriously? Had I been drawn into some kind of competition with those around me, either wittingly or unwittingly, to get recognition for myself? A means of boosting my self-worth?

Here in the bush, rivalry didn't exist. It was just me in all of my smallness in the enormity of the world. In this moment I was an organism that was entwined in the landscape. I wasn't a tourist looking at nature.

After a little period I realised I'd been holding my breath in wonder. I concentrated on breathing again.

I knew from research that at night in these mountains the heavens were one of the darkest skies in Australia. In the modern world the lights from the built environment affected the night sky, obscuring the beauty of the stars. Hiding the universe. Research had made me aware that there was a group of people that regarded this light from cities as pollution. A Dark Sky movement existed and it lobbied to have light pollution reduced from cities. Here in the Alps I understood why. I could almost touch what they fought to preserve. A view of the stars that had existed for millions of years was my heritage. It was a birthright that had unwittingly been taken away.

I'd survived the wild dogs and a storm. Now I was seeing the stars like I'd never seen them before.

I thought of my hidden DNA.

What did a *Bemeringal* know about this country? What lesson would the first Australians have imparted to me if they had accompanied me on this journey? Letting the question linger I didn't pursue an answer.

I looked down at the high-tech polyester tent. Its unnatural man-made yellow colour was discernible under the light of the Milky Way. The illusion of being *Bemeringal* fell away.

THE LOST VILLAGE

IN THE MORNING I EMERGED from the haven of the tent into a changed scene. Sapphire skies stretched unbroken from horizon to horizon. Reflecting the hue above, a blue gleam shone out of the brilliant white of the snow that enveloped the rolling undulations of Wild Horse Plain. All the blemishes and scars left in the landscape by mining had been covered.

The sore ankle was temporarily forgotten.

The storm had caused me to add a day to the schedule I'd left for Arianne. My calculations needed to account for this and I hoped that Arianne would as well. The seven day timetable had turned to eight days. I was ninety eight percent sure that Arianne would be watching the weather and would guess that I couldn't move in the big storm. I couldn't be certain. Without having a way to check I had to assume that there was a small possibility that she may not know. I would have to try to call her.

I had a moment's pause to ponder why time was still important to me out here. It was quite clear that it wasn't as important as it was in Canberra. I knew when thinking of Arianne and the schedule that time was different for me. A realisation had occurred that I was so attuned to deadlines and KPIs that when a hierarchy at work wasn't setting them, I set them for myself.

In reality, out in the bush, it mattered when the sun came up and when the sun went down, when a storm started and a storm ended.

Still I chose not to explore this idea too much. The truth was that it was important to me because right now it was important to Arianne.

More significant was the fact that I was now short of a day's food and perhaps fuel for the stove. I needed to be more careful with both even though I had not been reckless with either to this point.

I cast my eye around the countryside. The biggest lesson from the last few days was that the weather can change rapidly. It was important to make the most of the good weather when it was available. Unlike the city where bad weather was an inconvenience, out here it was deadly.

My concentration shifted to packing up the tent. Though relatively clear of snow due to the regular digging, this was harder than I'd anticipated. An audit of the tent showed a layer of ice near the top of its dome. This I guessed was the warm moisture in my breath rising and freezing on the fabric. The tent itself was relatively clear of snow, though I needed to dig down to expose each of the guy-ropes and pegs.

Packing up commenced in high spirits.

Time disappeared.

But progress was slow and enthusiasm dissipated.

Once digging was completed I fumbled with the knots on the ropes. It was easy to deduce that with gloves still on I wasn't dextrous enough to achieve my goal.

I took off a glove to make the task easier.

The fingers were soon stinging. The knot remained intact. I cursed the fumbling fingers. I hastily replaced the glove and blew into the cupped hand to return some warmth. I rubbed my hands together and the friction created blood movement again. The stinging persisted.

I eyed the pegs and ropes. They were my nemesis and needed to be overcome or worked around.

They could remain attached to each other, I determined. Leaving gloves on and pulling with all of my strength on the ropes, the pegs were worked free.

I started folding the tent. It was covered in crystals and droplets of moisture. I swept the fabric with the gloved hand in an attempt to brush most of it away. The snow stuck to the fabric. Worse still, the gloves were now damp and losing their warmth-giving properties. If I kept going the gloves would progress from damp to soaking and that was going to be uncomfortable and perhaps dangerous.

The remains of the moisture could stay on the tent.

I folded the nylon fabric into the carry bag with difficulty, stuffing the pegs and ropes in on top. Shoving hard, I squeezed the tent into the base of the pack. The poor folding and ice meant it'd grown in size. This would've been a problem a few days earlier. I wouldn't have had space. Now having eaten down some of the food it could be squeezed inside the pack. It was a certainty that as the temperatures rose during the day that any frozen water would melt, making the gear damp and uncomfortable.

'Yuk!' popped out of mouth.

I restrained from checking the time to mentally record this job stretching out further than I'd expected. It'd take what it takes to pack up, I declared.

The packing concluded. I pushed the load with one gloved hand while tightening straps with the other. It was a more awkward process than on the previous mornings. All that was now left on the snow was the bulging pack, snowshoes and walking poles.

I stepped into and adjusted the snowshoes. I swung the pack onto my shoulders and drove the walking poles into the ice. I stood still and assessed the abandoned campsite on the expanse of the plain. It stretched to forever and left me desolate. A panic rose as the situation I was in came to focus. I was tired and cold, my ankle was sore, my gear was likely going to get damp, the storm had put me behind schedule and still I had no contact with the world. No options for rescue and no way to let Arianne know of my circumstances. I raised the hat, rubbed my hands slowly back through my hair, replaced it and made first stride towards Kiandra. I must not dwell on the negatives. I focussed on what I was doing.

These first footfalls were without rhythm. The tempo of the day had to be created and that took time. Yesterday the beat had been established quickly. Today the cadence was not found. It was like the brain was a monitor of each part of the body. It was required to do full assessments about how the day's hiking would go. In snowshoes there was extra information to factor into the calculations.

The heavy appendages stuck on each foot and the stiff right ankle needed to be included in today's computations.

The shoulders, legs, back and arms were showing no signs of unusual aches. The ankle was a little inflexible though less swollen after the rest and massaging. The snow surface was even and the twisting on grasses and rocks wouldn't occur. The ankle would hold up for the remainder of the day, was the preliminary assessment.

Just as I was getting comfortable in the lilt of hiking, the sensation of eyes watching me returned.

I halted.

All noise died away. I was alone on a large open plain.

In the silence I scanned in each direction for dogs. A prickle of fear roused the hair on my head. The idea of being caught in the open by the pack that'd been outside the tent was disconcerting. I was exposed, I wasn't very mobile in the soft snow and my weaponry was flimsy.

The thud of a snowball landing on the ground drew me to alert. The rustle of leaves as a branch sling shotted back to its natural position followed. The weight had been removed. More snow fell off some distant branches of gum that'd been weighted down by the fall, causing them to rebound and make more noise.

In response I swung towards the new reverberation.

Was there movement? Was it dogs or was there a man standing behind that line of trees?

It was most likely just gravity. I couldn't make out the shapes of either a dog, man or any other living creature.

There were just trees.

I returned to the beat of tramping.

Thinking was turned from the threat of dogs to the abandoned town of Kiandra that I was now heading directly toward.

The name Kiandra was a derivation of the Wolgal peoples' word that was used for the locality. *Giandarra* was the original term that described the area. It signified to the inhabitants that the stone in the region could be used for making tools. This description was an insight into the value the region held to the Wolgal. For the Europeans who settled in the vicinity, the name Kiandra was synonymous with gold. Kiandra and surrounds were the sites of a short-lived gold rush in 1860. For a brief period the population reached seven thousand. A frontier mining town attracted adventurers and seekers of wealth from countries all over the globe. There was unruliness, alcohol abuse and of course hard work.

As I approached the town a few stone chimneys rose out of the snow as a reminder of the constructions that were once here. Two complete huts stood next to each other, nestled into a gully on the south side of the Alpine Highway that ran through the middle of town. These huts were near the point where the Alpine Walking Track headed in the direction of the Jagungal Wilderness. This was the trail I'd follow.

I paused to observe the track.

I pulled out the map and checked the curves of the hills to satisfy myself that the ground matched the contours. The track was partly obscured by snow, though by reference between the map and the landscape I could trace its faint path.

Taking off the pack, I detoured east and downhill a few hundred yards to where the crosses and fences of the town cemetery jabbed above the surface of the snow. A cluster of graves clung together. It was as if this lonely windswept frozen hill had driven them into a huddle.

Through the cemetery I wandered. Stopping at each grave I read the headstones. I stood motionless at the grave of Catherine Wortz and beside it a post that marked the burial place of Tom Ah Yan.

The Chinese miners had numbered about seven hundred at Kiandra's peak. Tom Ah Yan's grave was one of the few evidences of this important community. The Chinese had customarily returned their remains home. It was an indicator perhaps of their feelings towards the foreign landscape and their place in the community.

In Kiandra the Chinese miners had lived in a separate camp on the outskirts of the town. This segregation wasn't unusual for an Australian goldfield where Europeans outnumbered other races. This allowed the Europeans to assert themselves as having more right to the wealth. The marginalised Chinese miners were often left to rework areas already abandoned by the European diggers. Through being meticulous they often achieved success by using this method. This fuelled envy and further disharmony.

In the Kiandra goldfields the winters of 1860 and 1861 were particularly cold. Deep snow meant loads of supplies needed to be carried in by porter. The Chinamen were the people who completed this arduous job. Their achievements in the conditions still didn't bring acceptance.

Tom Ah Yan arrived about this time. He broke through the barrier of racism and after a long life he died a prominent citizen of Kiandra in 1925. He lived around eighty years. He progressed from gold prospector to owner of a store. A lone miner, he became the husband of Catherine Wortz and the father of a large family. This family had contributed greatly to the life of the district and here in this spot Tom and Catherine were beside each other for eternity.

Tom Ah Yan had prevailed against what modern people described as discrimination. In the 1860s the idea of racial tolerance hadn't yet had its time. Still I mused that perhaps stronger leadership and governance might have helped build a more integrated community.

The appointment to Kiandra of a Gold Commissioner, Frederick Cooper, who was in his mid-twenties, was never going to be the leader this isolated township needed. From a wealthy family in Sydney, Cooper was reputed to be the first undergraduate to be expelled from Sydney University. It was suggested his presence in the goldfield was to save his family any further embarrassment. Cooper's colourful life was unaffected by his move to Kiandra. Allegations of harsh justice, mob rule through intimidation and assault were a feature of his leadership. In 1861 he was reported to have visited the goldfields at Crackenback, shouted the miners' grog that he later refused to pay for and addressed a crowd while drunk and nude.

I touched the brim of the hat. It was a small sign of respect for Catherine and Tom. Somehow they'd found a way to live and love during and after the gold rush in this toughest of places. It was a triumph in the circumstances.

Leaving their graves, I slowly retraced my steps to the Alpine Walking Track, retrieving the pack as I went. I was deep in contemplation. Catherine and Tom were different, yet they'd succeeded.

What did that mean for me and Arianne?

I stopped briefly to draw strength before stepping up a steep ascent. This was the first tough pinch of the day. Gaining altitude, I stared at the gully and imagined it full of skiers. Kiandrans had referred to skiers as *snowshoers*.

Norwegian miners introduced skiing. Carnivals had been held, with the first recorded in the winter of 1861. In fact, the Kiandra Snowshoe Club was recognised as holding the first organised ski races and claimed to be the oldest in the world. This distinction was jointly shared with a Norwegian Ski Club at Holmenkollen near Oslo. The Kiandra club attracted much prestige and it would have had a number of luminaries on the board over the years including Banjo Patterson. Patterson wasn't the only poet drawn to the novelty. Barcroft Boake penned a work named *The Demon Show-shoers* in the late 1800s.

In the first carnivals, entrants came from around New South Wales. Later in 1908 the club sponsored an international and intercontinental downhill skiing carnival with America winning, Australia second and England third.

Perhaps this very gully I was walking through had hosted the daughters of Tom Ah Yan and Catherine Wortz when training for the ski competition. Barbara, Margaret and Mary Yan were the winners of the women's races for many years. The Yan sisters dominated the racing and possibly could claim themselves Australia's first female ski champions.

I kept hiking south, still climbing. Vigorously I drove the walking poles into the snow. The legs were burning and the soreness in the ankle was evident as the steep pinch tested the movement at the joint. I had twenty kilometres of hiking to do before I reached my next destination, Happy's Hut.

I imagined the thousands of people who'd once been on this ground that I now traversed utterly alone. The miners had used the land for their purpose and when it was exhausted they moved on. They moved to another place to use up. The search for a new patch of land to live in and to exploit was endless. All in all there was little evidence of their passing.

Like the miners I was transitory. The evidence of last night's tent site would melt into the snow and the tracks behind me would disappear. I was gone and the signs of passing were going with me. Besides the pack and its contents all I carried was hope and confidence that I'd deal with the challenges of tomorrow when they came.

I was reassured by my navigation. It was meeting the test of trails obliterated by snow. Referring to the map I traced a path towards

Tabletop Mountain. I just needed to find this feature in the landscape. It wasn't visible immediately.

I moved ahead, searching the area where I expected the mountain to appear.

On achieving a crest, I spied a flat, level mountain. Covered in snow, it reminded me of what we Australians called a vanilla slice or the French called Mille-feuille. Morale soared at the discovery. Still I pulled out the compass and cross checked just in case there was another feature that I could've confused it with. The visual compass bearing when applied to the map matched my initial assessment. I determined that this was the mountain. As I interrogated the map I noted that a mountain on the right of Tabletop was called Round Mountain. I peered in that direction and saw a feature that looked like a muffin with icing. The only thing missing was a cherry on top. The pioneers had named it suitably.

Confident of my location, I rested and examined the surroundings. The drab olive colour of the gums distinctively contrasted with the snow. The drooping branches of the trees left an attractive filtered light underneath. The waxy leaves of this species were always turned away from the sun to limit loss of moisture. It was an uplifting mottled light that shifted subtly as I moved beneath it when the shadows of the tree crossed the path.

The mono colour of the gums could seem uninspiring next to the shades of greens and sometimes red of European trees that'd been planted in Canberra. In the Australian bush, autumn didn't mean a change of colour as the nation had just a few stands of native deciduous trees. Still I liked the gum tree. The monotonous droopy leaves induced a reflective melancholy. They were a mood changing tree. Spirits changed, dependent on whether I focussed on the leaves or the light beneath.

A squawk from above caused me to stop the meditation on trees. I stared skyward. A black cockatoo flew overhead. Contrasted against the sky's colour, the enormous outline of its wingspan was on full display.

In silhouette against the sky the creature looked more like a flying dinosaur than a bird.

Illogically, I was fearful. It was as if I was to be the bird's next meal. My smallness in this moment was palpable. I was isolated and vulnerable in this white world that dauntingly stretched forever. I was the sole visible living creature except for the massive bird looking down on me.

The composure drained from me.

The hat was jammed further on my forehead by an instinctive hand movement. I put my head down and started moving. I hiked with purposeful strides.

The black cockatoo squawked again as if demanding my attention. I refused to give it to the bird.

I adjusted the brim of the hat to give more protection.

DEEP INTO THE SNOW

IN THE EARLY MORNING I TREKKED on crisp snow. At each step the snowshoes were held on the surface for a moment before breaking through a crust. The flat ground and the hardened snow were allowing me to make good time.

Happy's Hut, where I'd spent the night, was an hour behind me. Power lines of the hydro scheme that cut the valley in two were also left in my wake. Happy Jack's Plain was spread before me.

The area drew its name from an ebullient miner who'd found gold in the region.

Yesterday it'd become evident as the day wore on, as the temperature climbed, that the snow had become softer. It was wetter and more difficult to walk across in the afternoon. This observation, I guessed, was caused by a combination of the altitude, the latitude, the continent and its weather patterns.

Embracing this information, I adapted. I'd get up as early as possible and walk in the half-light of the pre-dawn to ensure I maximised the usage of the conditions when the snow was hard. Make good time when the chance presents itself, I'd resolved the night before. I couldn't control the snow getting soft in the relative heat of the day and becoming more demanding to walk upon. The time I left the huts was in my remit.

The area I was currently passing through had been at different times home to pastoralists, miners and botanists. The botanists had been researching the species of trees that might be introduced into the region. No trees had been planted. Tough gum trees remained as ever the dominant vegetation between wide expanses of snow. Grass poked through the surface to indicate I was moving through summer grasslands. This plain area was a frost hollow and it was evident that most vegetation would find it difficult to flourish.

The end of the plain area was marked by a knee-deep stream that was forded. The trail climbed towards Mackey's Hut and very soon I was hemmed in by gum trees again. The Mackeys' had run a lease in this area using the hut as a base. With as many as fifteen hundred sheep and some cattle they were successful from World War two to the late 1950s when the lease expired. Now the hut and some fence lines were all that remained of their enterprise.

My gaze was drawn to the left where Mount Jagungal was located. As I closed in on this orphan mountain it filled my vision. Jagungal was far north of the other main range features that were of comparable size. At a height of two thousand and sixty one metres I'd spied it when looking south from Mount Gingera on the first morning of this trip. Now three days walking and four days later I was on the approach.

Today I planned to skirt its base on this track in the valley floor. Next I intended to cut up onto the plateau south of Jagungal. From this position I'd have an easier hike to get access to the final high ground before Mount Kosciuszko.

This area had been the pathway for at least the Ngarigo and Wolgal peoples in the summer months. Europeans who first came to the area recorded the local name for the mountain differently. Some variations in early records were spelt *Targil*, *Jar-gan-gil*, and *Coruncal*. It was reputed to mean 'Mother of the Waters.' The map shows rivers heading from the mountain on all sides. The Aboriginals were right.

Jagungal was a destination for the Bogong moths and therefore Aboriginals for the purposes of feasting and ceremony. At some time round the 1870s no further record of this annual pilgrimage exists. People searching the sky for the guide of crows flying in large numbers, the indication that they too should return to the mountains for Bogongs, ended. The moth feasting and accompanying rituals ceased.

Disease introduced by the settlers to the Aboriginal inhabitants devastated the population. Isolated for millennia, there was no resistance to the ravages of influenza, measles, tuberculosis, small pox and syphilis. The Ngarigo people, hindered by the changes to their health and hampered by settlers in getting access to land, gave up their traditional lifestyle. The Ngarigo began living in proximity to the Europeans around Cooma and, like the Chinese at Kiandra, found themselves on the fringes of town.

The Bogongs migrate down the north-south Great Dividing Range to the Snowy Mountains of New South Wales and Victoria. Journeying thousands of kilometres the moths avoid summer in the northern breeding areas of Queensland's Darling Downs. With a wing span of around four centimetres, the migration is a tremendous feat.

During winter in Queensland the moths build fat reserves giving the tiny creature energy for the migration and to survive through the summer in their new home in the Southern Alps. Resting in rock crevices they do the opposite of hibernate. They aestivate through the summer.

The fat reserves on the moth and their abundance is the reason this annual event became so important to the Aboriginal inhabitants of the High Country areas. From the mountains near Canberra to the mountains north of Melbourne, the Bogong moth played an important role for food and ceremony to the groups who lived in the region.

Each year as winter approaches the moths return north to Queensland to feed and breed.

I hiked searching for clues of the Grey Mare Fire Trail. A routine developed where I looked to the distance to detect the slight shadow caused by the furrows of the trail underneath the snow. Then I traced a path backward to where I stood before stepping off on another bite. This process was repeated over and over. Every thirty minutes I'd stop, pull out the map, and memorise the next kilometre or so.

The trail always had another set of tracks on it besides mine and sometimes many. Rabbits, possums and wallabies all aided me a little by leaving prints. Their winter migration patterns, by some sixth sense, followed the summer migration patterns of four-wheel-drive vehicles. This the animals managed even though the ruts of the trail were a metre beneath snow.

There was an abundance of rabbits in this stretch of the walk. At one point I was following a lone rabbit's imprints on the track when it abruptly came to an end as a splotch of bright blood. No other footprints of a predator were evident. I searched for what had happened. No more clues could be discerned so I assumed that a bird of prey must have swooped down. Perhaps an eagle. The blood was so bright that I knew the attack must have happened recently. The sight of blood and its association with death was sobering.

This was tough country for all that passed through it.

I stepped away from the blood. Perhaps because of revulsion, possibly out of respect. I pulled out the map and memorised the next stretch.

Slightly downhill for four hundred metres to a creek crossing. The trail then veered right, climbing steeply for two hundred metres. At that point the track turned a quarter left with a gradual climb for another six hundred metres before levelling out.

The site marked on the map as Farm Ridge came and went. No farm had been in this location for sixty or more years.

Next, O'Keefe's Hut appeared on the left. I halted momentarily to enter my name and time of passing in the hut log.

On I strode, always in my well-developed routine. Check map.

Memorise route. Find the trail in the distance. Trace it back to where I stood and start walking.

Five hundred metres uphill was the first bite. Then the trail twisted right. Three hundred metres of gentle downhill would then follow, before a steeper four hundred metre climb to the top of the next crest.

Direction was always south and with the sun in the northern sky my shadow was a constant companion. It was prominent from the other shadows because of the outline of my head and hat. The silhouette on the snow seemed to be leading me to my destination.

At a point where the Grey Mare Fire Trail was well beyond Mount Jagungal, I took a sharp turn east to begin a steep climb. I chose a prominent ridgeline and slogged ever higher. This slope of about one and a half kilometres in length was the chosen route to higher ground.

Fatigue was building in the muscles. I did a mental check of the reasons for the lethargy. Dehydration was discounted. I'd been drinking well and wasn't thirsty. Energy was also discarded. I'd been snacking on food bars at regular intervals in an attempt to keep the sugar fuelling my muscles. The fatigue was partly the result of a long day's hiking already behind me and the cumulative fatigue of the previous day's exertions. The tiredness was contributed to by the steep slope and altitude where the thinning air was causing me to puff hard. Halting, I allowed my heart rate to steady before stepping again. I took the climb slowly.

As I stopped for another break I tangled the extremities of the snowshoes against each other. This caused me to stumble to the left. The snowshoes and centre of gravity moved a fraction off the ridge.

I arrested the fall by jamming the poles into the snow and standing upright. I was pleased with my quick reactions for a second. Then, noticeably I felt myself sinking gradually into the snow.

The ground beneath me shifted and refused to hold my weight. I'd stepped into a drift.

Moving the walking poles to what looked like a firmer position,

I dug them in again. I supported my body weight through arms and shoulders onto them.

This made no difference.

I kept sinking steadily and the process appeared to be speeding up as I was now at least knee deep into the drift of snow.

Frantically I shifted the poles again.

The downward movement didn't slow for a moment.

An attempt to move sidewards towards the ridge was thwarted by the cumbersome snowshoes.

Stumbling, I was now past waist depth in fine powdery snow and sinking ever faster.

I was powerless to stop the pull of gravity. Helpless, I stood still, not wishing to make matters worse by thrashing around.

Next the shoulders were below the surface of the snow and still I sank. Eventually the descent into the snow came to an end. Beneath my feet was crushed and condensed snow. Above the hat's brim the blue sky was visible through a hole in the surface of the snow. It was more than a foot above my head.

I shifted my legs in a climbing movement. The snow gave way under my weight and I remained frustratingly where I'd begun.

Panic set in as every movement upward was countered by gravity and I was left in the same position.

'What the hell are you doing here? You're an idiot,' I exclaimed out loud in anger.

I needed assistance. Someone help, screamed inside of my head. It was an instinctive response and a useless response. I was alone.

The mind raced so I forced it to slow.

Keep going, I urged. There's no one to give sympathy or to blame. No one is here to help—I must help myself, I instructed inside my head. Composure returned.

I closed my eyes. I expelled air in numerous sighs.

I opened my eyes.

Clearly the load in the pack combined with my weight was too much pressure for this drift of powdery crisp snow.

Removing the pack, I placed it by my feet.

I reasoned that without the encumbrance of this item I might be able to compact the snow by compressing it with the shoes. I'd then create firm enough steps to climb out.

Once I'd determined on this course, the execution was surprisingly simple. A few minutes later my head was poking through the surface. Then my shoulders and then the waist emerged back into the light. At this point I lay onto the snow to maximise the surface area and spread my weight distribution. Carefully I inched back towards the ridge.

It was with relief that I was able to stand again.

Powdery snow that was covering me from head to foot was brushed off. The last of it fell away with a shake.

I surprised myself by laughing out loud. It was relief at finding a solution to the unforeseen event.

Lying back on my stomach, I reached down into the hole to where the pack could be seen below. It was out of reach. Worse still, I sensed the snow shifting beneath me and I envisioned falling into the hole headfirst.

I edged back to the ridge.

The next strategy was to gingerly edge ahead, compacting the drifts of powder by patting it with the snowshoes as I went. Inch by inch the surface snow lost height. It became compressed and firmer. When I judged that the snow was sufficiently trampled I lay back down. Again I reached into the hole. This time I managed to hook the strap of the pack in my hand.

Carefully I raised it towards me. Underneath me the snow shifted. It gave way a fraction. I held my breath.

It held.

A minute later I was relieved to be lying on the ridge with the pack beside me.

It took a little while to compose myself, stand on shaky legs, lift the pack onto my shoulders and feel ready to climb again.

To resume the ascent was the spontaneous reaction. To continue on my path was automatic. I'd been raised to be stubborn and to persist. In my workplace these characteristics were admired. Out here they could be fatal.

Should I climb?

How dangerous was this if it happened again?

Would I have been able to get out if I'd sunk in deeper?

In another section I might continue to fall off balance and injure myself. Should I retrace my steps to the bottom and search for another route?

The initial reaction was to turn to someone, preferably an experienced bushman, for help with these questions. There was no one. I was the expert. My judgement was all that I had.

Taking off the hat, I rubbed my temples.

I conducted a review.

Only so much snow had fallen in the storm so it stood to reason that there was a finite depth to a drift.

Drifts formed on the downwind side of a ridge. The wind in the storm had come from the south so the northern side of the ridge was where the drifts should be. The drift I'd just fallen into conformed to this reasoning. If I carefully stayed on the ridge I should be OK.

The snow had held my weight when I was flat on my stomach with no pack on. I surmised it'd hold me in other sections if I did similar.

I placed the hat back on my head. I'd continue warily.

This time I advanced with caution. My feet were testing if the snow would support my weight at every quarter step.

Safety was the main aim.

I eyed the ridge suspiciously. It now held fears for me that'd been unimagined just a few minutes before. Prodding the snow with the walking sticks, I stepped and put body weight on the next section.

Short step by short step, I edged upwards.

Occasionally, I found soft sections where the snow crumbled away before the probing sticks. At these, I took off the pack and tied it by a short cord to the lower leg. I'd then lie flat to spread body weight and crawl across the unstable area. Inch by inch, I progressed this way until I hit stable ground again. Then I'd retrieve the pack by pulling on the cord, shoulder it and continue uphill again.

I climbed over a lip of snow that'd been blocking the view and I found before me a plain.

I slumped to take a rest. My heart was thumping from the exertions and adrenaline.

I was desperate for a hot chocolate. I could almost taste its sweet revitalising warmth.

I savoured it for an instant.

In the next moment I realised that it was a function of fatigue and adrenaline that was causing this association with sugar and warmth to be made. It was also clear that nothing was to be done about it. I hadn't brought any hot chocolate with me; a café to solve my dilemma didn't exist. The craving for gratification couldn't be met and the desires would have to be postponed. I'd add it to the list of things I wanted, that I might get, when I returned to the abundance of town.

I looked back at the broken snow that marked the trail I'd blazed upwards. No neat snowshoe tracks here. It was satisfying to see the areas where I'd sunk in, where I'd crawled and where I'd prodded forward. It was the record of a man's solitary progress in the bush. Perhaps it was witness to the route of the first man. The path in the snow was a trace of achievement that only I knew about. It'd disappear in the next storm or in snow melt.

It had been hard work. I'd doubted myself. In the end, problem solving was the way out of the mess. Falling into the snow was an unpleasant surprise and a test. I permitted the conceit of a pass mark.

For a moment I considered walking up Jagungal as a reward. I might climb it and look back to Mount Gingera. Back in the direction I'd come and savour the progress on this trip so far. The peak of Jagungal was just off on the left and north. I eyed it and noticed wisps of clouds resting against its summit.

It was likely that detouring up there wouldn't deliver a view. I still had a way to go today if I was to make this evening's hut.

Redirecting attention, I focussed on the destination. To the front was gently sloping virgin snow inviting me into its endlessness. An easy route as payment for the challenge just now overcome. This was the path south to Kosciuszko. There would be no drifts in this flat country, nowhere for the powder to accumulate as it was whipped along in the storm. This would be easier going.

Far to the left, on the edge of the plateau, gentle curving creeks coiling and twisting to three rocky mountains were in view. I consulted the map. I assumed that these mountains were the Bulls Peaks. These mountains were mainly protrusions of granite.

At my front were two other mountains. I decided one mountain looked like an upended cup and the mountain next to it was flat like a saucer. These were marked on the map as Cup and Saucer Hill.

Beyond these features already visible were the Kerries. Behind them and out of sight was the Main Range.

As I studied the landscape, the First Nation's creation-narrative of the Copper Head Serpent was captured in the folds and curves of the ground.

In the Dreamtime, the earth and heavens slept. Nothing moved or grew. Then the Serpent awoke from her slumber. She travelled far and wide awaking the world. The Serpent left the marks of her tracks and these became rivers, while other areas were pushed before her massive body forming hills.

Life came to earth and the Serpent provided laws to care for Country.

Those that were true to these laws became humans and those that were not were turned to stone and formed mountains.

Looking at this scene, the account of the Serpent had an undeniable authenticity.

I faced south. This was the shorter route towards the main range, providing navigation was good.

Lost

THE SNOW WAS FIRM AND HARD and the slope marginally downhill.

More features were revealed as I progressed. On the right I spotted a rounded, triangular-shaped flat-topped hill. I assumed this was the aptly named Strawberry Hill I'd noted on the map. On the left I identified a spire of rocks that stood out from every direction. This must be what appeared on the map as the Post Box. In the middle between these two features was the Cup and Saucer Hill. Steering this central path I closely observed the changes in view as I advanced.

Overhead, a jet stream of a high-flying passenger aircraft left a long chalky white dash in the sky. Another white line slightly behind and parallel showed the path of the rival airline.

I guessed that the origin of the aeroplanes was Sydney and the destination Melbourne. Since the first passenger flight between the two cities in 1920, and the first regular airmail service in 1925, this air route had become one of the busiest in the world. Almost two hundred passenger flights occurred each day between these two major Australian cities. Annually up to seven million passengers flew from one city to another above these mountains. City to city. Touching the bush wasn't necessary anymore. Country was flown over by many Australians. In the modern urbanised world, it was in cities that human activity and entertainment was concentrated.

I'd been on these flights. Each time I hoped for a window seat. I'd peer below and pick out rivers and mountains. The excitement that a glimpse of snow gave me was always an extra reward for these efforts. Dependent on the sun's position, the snow reflected back at me. So rare in this hot, dry continent, it was like looking down on a diamond. I'd twist and turn my neck in the cramped space of the plane to get the best view from the porthole. Sometimes the passenger next to me would display annoyance at the jiggling. My exasperation was with the manufacturers of the aircraft. The windows were never placed in the right spot of the fuselage for easy viewing.

On the flights I'd travelled, few were enthralled with what was below. To me, the valleys, the forests, the peaks, all seemed to have possibilities because of their emptiness.

How many of the three hundred or so people directly above me now were looking down?

At the altitude of the aircraft I wouldn't have been a speck. No one above would ever guess that in the endless valleys and mountains a lone person hiked.

I guessed the passengers of the plane assumed that they were having no impact upon the wilderness twenty thousand feet below. They were hopping over the bush not leaving any roads or tracks. They possibly had little idea that the warming planet was causing the snow cover in the Australian Alps to decrease. The emissions from the plane they were in contributed to that warming.

The rarity of snow in Australia was becoming scarcer as the winter season shortened and the depth of the snow decreased.

Was cloud seeding the answer?

I marched on. One foot forward. Then the other. One foot forward, step another.

Now I was climbing a slight rise and the leg muscles strained. The ankle ached. This ascent shouldn't have been causing me such effort. The obvious conclusion was that the muscles were tiring.

Halting, I did an assessment of Cup and Saucer Hill in comparison to the map. Adjusting direction, I headed towards the western end of the feature. Slightly right of the Cup was the aiming point as I looked at it. I expected if I reached the Cup and Saucer at this point I'd have a view steeply down to the Valentine's River and then onto Mawson's Hut.

Mawson's Hut was nestled in a well-protected valley with the mountains known as the Kerries on the south and west. The range would be behind the hut from the direction I was approaching. I'd stay west of the hut, crest the Kerries and then follow a ridge down to Valentine's Hut. There was still ten kilometres to go.

Confident in where I currently was, I enjoyed the crisp snow of the high plain beneath my feet. The snowshoes glided across the surface on this leg of the trip. The sun bore down on me from behind. The glare off the snow caused me to squint despite sunglasses. My shadow was in front of me and as the day wore on, it progressively shifted to the left. The sun was moving to the west over the right shoulder as it passed into the afternoon. Finally it'd fall below the horizon, and to sleep for the night. I had hours of effort in front of me. This crude method of tracking my shadow became the stimulus to put urgency into each stride.

My desire was to spend the night in Valentine's Hut. No tent tonight, I promised, as I revisited the uncomfortable time spent packing up the tent on the plains before Kiandra. There would still be patches of damp in the tent and this intensified the need to reach the shelter before nightfall.

A line of east-west fence posts crossed the path at right angles. The remains of an abandoned summer pasture. The long shadows from the dilapidated posts reaching out across the snow were disappearing and haunting evidence of the cattlemen. These leases I knew had been uninhabited on the opening of the hydro scheme fifty years before.

The snow moved beneath my shoes. The shadow with the hat continued to move towards the left.

It was another hour before I stood beside the rocky hill that made up the Cup and looked down a steep hillslope towards the Valentine River.

Satisfied that the view was as I expected, I sat on a rock without taking off the pack and checked the map. A crossing point for the river was marked. Raising my eyes from the paper, I scrutinised the valley below. Right where it should have been was a pole that I guessed marked that spot. Consulting the map again I guessed that Mawson's Hut should be visible. I looked up and found a square shape nearly obscured by a copse of trees. I was pleased.

I now had a choice. Should I follow the river towards Valentine's Hut or cut over the Kerrie Range? I wrestled with the decision. The river bank looked flat and negotiable. I guessed it might have swampy sections hidden underneath the snow, where flowing water seeped from the river into the flat ground. From a distance, this looked like the easiest place to walk.

The Kerries on the other hand were a sharp climb and this didn't look inviting. Tired legs and my sore ankle were to be considered if this was the chosen route. In the Kerries' favour was the fact that they'd hide no surprise and from the high ground I expected a bird's eye view. This would make navigation easier.

I chose the high ground.

Somewhere deep in my psyche was the lesson of Blaxland, Wentworth and Lawson. Go the higher ground. Avoid the valleys and ravines. Water flow always was on the steepest terrain. It was simply gravity.

With this decision made, I stood. The sun was in the western sky and low. Time was running out. I steered a path well to the right of Mawson's Hut. With the advantage of height I spied a snow bridge in the snaking path of the Valentine's River. A stretch of snow had formed across one of the river's bends in such a way as to suggest a route across without becoming wet. Heading straight towards it, I hoped it'd be strong enough to hold my weight.

The sheer downward walk to the river was enjoyable. Snow, disturbed by the shoes, fell in front of me and rolled past in little balls. I took the time to look to the left and spy the roof of Mawson's Hut. Someone had long ago made the effort to paint a large M on the galvanised iron roof.

A mountain myth had it that the famous Australian Antarctic explorer, geologist and academic, Sir Douglas Mawson, had used this hut to train for his expeditions. I knew this wasn't true. In fact, the hut was built by Herb Mawson of Bobundra Station with some friends in 1930. Sir Douglas Mawson had completed his earlier expeditions to the Antarctic in this year and was actually on his last trip to the frozen continent.

Reaching the site of the snow bridge across the Valentine's River, I scrutinised the crossing. It looked OK. Surveying to left and right I ensured that no other point offered better access to the far bank. This rudimentary assessment showed it as the best option.

Next I analysed the path of the river. Though largely obscured by snow, the point where it disappeared under the bridge to the front would be the weakest point.

Prodding with the walking poles, I gauged the stability of the bridge.

Satisfied, I took one small step, then one more, and then another.

Cautiously, I padded onward.

All was going to plan until the right snowshoe unexpectedly broke through the surface of the bridge. My body weight crashed down to the right. There was a splash as my leg dipped into the frozen waters of the river up to the knee, then caught. One leg was on the bridge and one in the water.

I winced at the cold.

Adjusting the awkward position, I was able to raise the right leg from the water and back onto the snow bridge.

I crawled onto the bank cursing under my breath.

Wet and cold, I determined to keep moving. I needed to warm up and get to the hut.

I made a path to climb the Kerries. I ignored the throbbing ankle.

Leaning heavily on the walking poles, I sucked in air while looking back in the direction I'd travelled. As my chest heaved, I admired the snowshoe tracks. The trail disappeared down the valley to the Valentine's River and up the other side to the Cup. In the distance, now far behind, was Jagungal. It was a satisfying view. I'd gone somewhere. I wasn't standing still. Facing west, I was mindful that the sun was now at a height just above eye level. Gold coloured, it was running out of punch for the day. Me too, I thought. My legs ached with cumulative exhaustion and lactic acid.

Each weary stride was motivated by the knowledge that the comforts of a hut awaited.

There were twisted snowgums in the area. Each tree had different contortions and colours. They had endured. Storms, snow, and the heat of summer - all had impacted upon the tree in its habitat. The snowgums were here to stay and their seeming permanence was reassuring. The twisted trunks sent a message that life can flourish even when all conditions were hostile.

There was longevity about the landscape that was altogether different to Canberra. In the city, new buildings and roads were built. Others were altered. Growth, growth, was the mantra as the economic system was reliant on the idea. The museum put on different exhibitions to attract visitors. It must keep the patrons coming. The media had a cycle of news that was ever changing. They must, to titillate the consumer and sell and grow.

The bush was dissimilar to the unsettling changes of urban life.

The bush's reassuring permanence built confidence.

I was starting to know it. Survive, survive.

Reaching the high point of the Kerries I stopped to take in the view and to stare in the direction of Valentine's Hut.

The structure wasn't visible. I was deflated. The map had a note informing me that it was painted bright red. It therefore should contrast sharply with the never-ending white of the snow. I guessed it was hidden in a fold in the ground, and so predicting its position, I pressed on.

The steep westward descent off the Kerries was conducted carefully. Picking my way ever downward I maintained direction to where I envisaged the hut to be. At this height, the sun was directly aligned with my line of sight. Fading, its gold had turned to orange and was now almost touching the tips of the distant Grey Mare Range. No more than half an hour of light before it disappeared, I estimated.

I examined the map.

To the right and the north was a view of a bend in the meandering Valentine River. Still there was no vision of the hut. I was certain that it should be evident when I looked at the relative height of the hut to where I stood. Its absence from the landscape was disconcerting.

I trudged on.

Peering first to the left and then to the right, I still couldn't see it. I remained confident I was heading in the right direction. The navigation had been good today, I reassured myself. It didn't seem possible that wrong decisions had been made in this last section. I'd navigated perfectly across country to reach Mawson's and then skirt around it.

You're on track, I reassured myself again.

I travelled forward to the spot where I expected the hut to be. All the time I lost altitude. Big steps were taken. Progress was a half falling motion on the steep descent.

Down, down, down. Snow whooshed behind me as I let gravity pull me to the bottom. Still the hut was undetectable. Anxiety rose inside of me. It must be there.

I walked into a minor re-entrant.

Then I trudged up a slope to where I assessed the fire trail should be. This was where the normal route to the hut was shown on the map.

'Of course it'll be obscured in the snow,' I remarked. I still expected to see two long parallel indents where the snow had settled into the wheel ruts. These clues had been the pattern of the journey to date.

On the ridge-rise I conducted a review. No wheel ruts. The tell-tale symmetrical evidence of human alterations to the landscape couldn't be seen.

I peered to the right. Towards the Valentine River and where I anticipated finding the bright red hut.

Zilch. No hut and no trail.

Twisting at the waist I oriented to the left.

Nil. No trail.

Though logic dictated the hut wouldn't be in that direction, I'd started to convince myself that this afternoon's navigation was marginally off and it'd be there. It wasn't.

I moved a hundred paces to the right to change perspective.

Back several hundred yards to the left.

Zero.

Wistfully, I thought of the broken GPS at the bottom of my pack.

Anxiety and doubt welled inside of me.

Maybe I'd screwed this up and was out by a whole bend in the river. I pulled out the map and referred to it in the fast fading light.

I can't be out, I affirmed desperately.

Calm down and gather the facts. Make a decision. Don't beat up on yourself if it chooses to be the wrong one, the inner voice urged.

The inner voice had no positive effect.

All of my calculations indicated that I was standing on the location of the hut. My eyes informed me that there was nothing here except snow and some gums. I should have been able to see some evidence of a track. There wasn't any.

I swore under my breath.

The navigation was out by a whole bend in the river, I convinced myself, though even as I thought this, it just didn't make sense.

I swore louder this time. This did not have the calming effect I desired.

My hands came to my head and I screamed, 'Ahhhhhh!'

I looked at the sun. It was now three quarters obscured by the mountains of the Grey Mare Range that it was behind. There were minutes before the sun was gone, its last light fading to shadows.

I swore again, this time loudly.

I made up my mind. I was out by a bend in the river.

Head down to concentrate on the footing, I raced down a snowy slope, through a creek and up the next rise. My breath was anxiously short. I drove on frenziedly.

At the top of the hill, I looked over the curves of the Valentine's River and row upon row of mountains heading to the horizon.

A little grey in the sky was all the light I had left.

The view was breathtakingly beautiful. The vastness of the ridges and snow that stretched uninhabited for tier after tier of ridge was incredible. In the circumstances it terrified me.

I dared not take a second to admire it.

The mountains had swallowed me.

The navigation was out. I had to accept this even if I didn't know how I'd become lost. Could it have been out all day? Distrust of my map reading skills started to rise. Doubts crowded in. Was I miles from where I should've been?

Taking off the hat, I wiped my brow. It was part resignation and part exasperation. The familiar abrasive touch of the rough old felt in my hand was the only comfort.

Groaning, I bowed my head.

I was tired and not thinking straight. This needed to be acknowledged.

Navigation had been spot on all day. Somehow, something had gone wrong on this last leg and I didn't know what. I knew I wouldn't be able to work it out logically when I was as fretful as I was in this current moment.

I needed to resign myself to the fact that I was camping in the tent again for the night. In the morning I'd be retracing my steps to Mawson's Hut, the last known point, and renavigating from there.

'Where would you camp around here?' quizzed a familiar voice.

My head came up. I spun searching for the source.

'What would you look for in a campsite?' the voice probed. 'Where would you make camp?'

A tree not too far away was thicker than it should be. Perhaps someone was leaning against it.

My mind deliberated on the questions.

Tired, I wiped my brow and placed on the hat. With my fingers on the brim, I leant it back to think. I was taking my time. I had an urge to fill the awkward silence but I overrode this as I wanted to sound half sensible when I spoke.

'I'd make a campsite like the mountain men have done for each hut I've seen in the last few days. The site would be protected from the southerly and westerly winds by a fold in the ground. Frost and cold settle so it wouldn't be at the bottom of a hill. It'd be about two-thirds of the way up a rise. It would face east and north to catch the morning and daytime sun. It'd be near permanent water.'

All of this sounded sensible and was consistent with observations of the mountain men's huts.

'I'd camp there.' I pointed. Then I noticed what was at the very tip of my finger. Obscured by a cluster of gum trees and a drift of snow was the faintest regular form. Straight lines.

I looked away and then back at the spot again to ensure that my eyes were not deceiving me in the gloom of imminent nightfall.

The symmetrical shape remained.

In relief my legs involuntarily broke into a run. Down the hill, back across the small creek and then up to a location where I'd been only minutes before.

Valentine's Hut. Buried in snow. I raced towards the door.

I'd been at the hut site. I'd probably been standing on the hut's roof looking over it.

I used all of my strength to yank the door open against the weight of snow. I made an inch of progress and had to drop to my knees to dig with my hands. Into the sharp cold snow they clawed to make a hollow for the door to swing into. Eventually I was able to open it enough to squeeze inside.

In the doorway, I took the time to search over my shoulder into the dark for the man behind the voice.

He wasn't in view.

He'll come in later, I convinced myself, and went inside, shutting the door behind me.

The hut was cosy with three small rooms and a potbelly stove. A wood pile was stacked by the stove.

Built in the 1950s for a surveying team, reputedly it was originally painted in red with hearts. This gave it the name Valentine's, but the hearts had long since disappeared from its paintwork.

Unlike Oldfield's there were no holes ventilating the side of the hut, so I guessed unlike some of the other huts it'd hold its warmth.

My eyes revisited the kindling. The invitation for me to light it and release its energy was irresistible and for the first time on this journey I was tempted to light a fire. The stove would generate heat, the hut would hold a little and there was plenty of wood. More than that, it'd help me with preserving some of the fuel I'd brought with me that I suspected was running low. This sealed the decision and so I busied myself.

'I'll put on a brew for two,' I muttered.

To the Man From Snowy River Country

I FELT AS IF I WAS GLOWING when I left Valentine's in the morning. The potbelly stove had created good warmth in the confines of what I'd discovered was a well-insulated hut. The snow encasing the roof and external walls helped, I guessed.

The boots this morning were completely dry after sitting near the stove. The ritual of defrosting the leather and laces to pull them on wasn't needed. The socks inside the boots were also dry. They'd been hung above the stove and every hint of dampness had evaporated. The tent had been taken from the pack and aired overnight. All moisture from it was gone when I packed it away.

A quick evaluation of circumstances was overwhelmingly positive.

The sky was blue, the wind still. My body was warm and it'd take an hour or two before the damp of the snow pushed its way through the leather of the boots, the wool of the socks and onto the skin. Excepting the first day's walking, and the fact that the ankle was still sore, I was starting a day in the best conditions possible.

Today I'd climb endlessly. Only the slope of where I walked would vary. Mostly it was steady uphill, though there were a few steeper pinches.

The sky looked clear and the wind was still. I guessed that unless the weather changed I'd be warm for the day.

I ascended with deliberate steps to stretch my muscles out.

Internally I revelled in a freedom that was so pure. I had a vision for the day's activities and route that was mine. It didn't have to be explained to anyone. I had no compromises to make with others. The experiences I'd gathered on the trek in these last days provided me with absolute clarity about what was achievable. Everything I needed was on my back.

I was independent.

Navigation was easy as I kept the Valentine's Creek on the west. Last night's map reading trials and frantic searching for the hut were forgotten as I enjoyed the crisp air and the cold crusty snow underfoot. Each step of the snowshoes left a satisfying audible crunch as my weight was transferred onto it. I had time to enjoy the valley as I turned my mind to Schlink's Pass and the Main Range beyond.

Ambling along the Valentine's Creek ever upward was meditative. I was now well past sixteen hundred metres in altitude.

At the end of the Valentine's River I found myself on a highpoint.

I consulted the map. The trail progressed downhill from this point. Eventually after losing much altitude it turned sharply to the left, the direction of east, and regained all of the altitude I'd taken so long to climb this morning. Alternately cutting east now, following the contours to the road, would save what looked like wasted effort descending.

From the map, the path I outlined in my head was sensible. The direction I was supposed to follow looked like it needlessly added distance to the journey. Still I hesitated. There must be a purpose behind the track being placed in such a way, I reasoned.

The memory of being unsure of my whereabouts the previous evening flooded back. Take a shortcut or follow the route? Minutes ticked by as I battled indecisively over the course to take. I followed my instincts, or was it conditioning from classroom lessons? I'd stay high, rather than lose altitude, the shortcut.

Progress on this chosen route was excellent for ten minutes. Very soon after this I was in a boulder field surrounding two converging creek lines. Thick scrub added to the obstacles. Hopping from rock to rock, I balanced on snowshoes and steadied teetering with the aluminium poles.

It was quite dangerous. If I injured myself when off the trail it would be hard for searchers to find me. The decision to leave the path was poor. I was getting over-confident, I decided. There was a need to exercise more caution. I needed to slow the pace and regain the safety of the track.

Picking each stride carefully, it took me more than an hour before I safely stepped back onto the trail. It was wide and good. A skidoo had been through, flattening the snow and making it easier for me to walk.

After a rest I resumed the climb. Using the groomed skidoo tracks, my movement became speedier. I was in a narrow valley climbing upward to Schlink's Pass. Mountain peaks towered on each side of me. Power lines on massive pylons crossed the trail first on one side of me and then the next.

The Pass when I reached it was a narrow gap joining two ranges across a valley. In the middle, where the power lines and trail converged, a sign announced the altitude at seventeen hundred and eleven metres. This Pass was named after Herbert Schlink. An avid skier in the first decade of the twentieth century, he was a foundation member of the Kosciuszko Alpine Club. Sir Herbert, known as Bertie, enjoyed fine food, wine, cigars and good company. The Pass had been used in a winter crossing from Kiandra to Kosciuszko in 1927.

Schlink and his adventurous companions Hughes, Fisher, Laidley and Gordon, were the first party to be recorded as achieving this feat. While initial impressions were of a man of privilege, I'd discovered that befitting a man of the mountains he did overcome and persevere through adversity. During the Great War, he'd served his nation as an Australian Army Medical Corps captain. His German parentage was obvious from his name and this was to cause him grief. His allegiance to Australia was impugned and he was unceremoniously removed from duty despite Schlink's declarations of loyalty. Schlink was undeterred by this setback.

He was a man who wasn't to be discouraged easily. He went on to make many contributions as a pioneer in cancer treatments. He wrote extensively on diseases affecting women and was a founder of the Australasian College of Surgeons. To cap it all, he became advisor to Australian Prime Ministers on medical matters and was recognised for his commitment by being knighted Sir Herbert.

I climbed the steep slopes at the south of the pass and made my way onto a ridge that faced east. A thin edge of snow snaked up to the heavens. First, the pristine crest deviated to the left and then to the right, before straightening and disappearing into the distance. The path was illuminated in gold by the sun behind me to the west. A long slow climb to the summit drew me into the gentle ridge.

The snow, exposed to full sun, was deep and soft. I slogged on, realising that I'd be lucky to get to the Guthega Valley this evening as I'd planned.

I resolved to camp on the high ground as the weather was fine and there was not even the slightest of breezes.

I'd find a sheltered spot on the ridge near Consett Stephen Pass. It'd make a fine place to watch the sun go down and rise in the morning. The headwaters of the Snowy River would be visible.

The sunrise would be the last of the trip. Tomorrow I'd reach Kosciuszko, Thredbo Village and the journey's end.

Storm and Mortality

SLEEPING FITFULLY, I WAS SENSITIVE to the merest changes of colour in the darkness. I zipped the tent flaps open at the suggestion of dawn. I beheld the darkness as the black of night turned to navy blue on the eastern horizon.

In the cold, I fumbled to light the stove. The sound of gas rushing to the flame wasn't as urgent as it'd been at the start of the trip. The flame appeared anorexic and had flecks of orange where once it had all been blue.

Huddling back into the sleeping bag, I watched the stove and the eastern sky.

The stars faded and died, though I had no time to mourn their passing. On the horizon the gold glint of pre-dawn replaced them with promise. At the coldest moment, the first sun rays poked upward over the mountains. As time elapsed, a tip of the gold orb of the sun appeared. Another day was born.

The water in the pot still showed no signs of boiling.

The gas flame had reduced in size further and the rushing sound of gas had decreased to a seeping sound.

Then, without warning, the flame died.

Sitting up, I poured lukewarm water into a mug with a satchel of sugar, skim-milk powder and instant coffee.

It was sweet to the taste but grainy from where the sugar and coffee had only partially dissolved. It provided energy and moisture to a dry mouth, though it didn't satisfy in the same way as when the water was piping hot. As always, I pressed my hands against the mug, trying to suck warmth through its sides and into my body. This morning this habit had little effect.

If there was an emergency, I'd have no fuel left to warm water. This was definitely a worry. I consoled myself with the knowledge that I wouldn't need fuel in Thredbo tonight. I congratulated myself on the decision to light a fire in Valentine's. If I hadn't done that I'd have run out of fuel last night.

The pleasure was diminished because I was on the edge. Everything I'd done on this trip was extending food, fuel, and physical abilities to the absolute limits. It was sobering. I reaffirmed my commitment to be cautious. I'd put no slack into the planning at the beginning of this journey. Now that I'd exhausted my supplies I had even less leeway. The mitigation to the diminishing resources was a lighter pack, newly gathered experience and a pledge to an even more careful approach.

On the horizon, the sun exposed itself a portion at a time until it was almost a complete ball. A sunray reached out across the top of the ridge on the far side of the valley. It extended across the gap before touching my face with its warmth.

Below me, the Snowy River wound through the shadowed valley. This mighty river had been impeded by the Snowy Scheme and a dam was visible beneath. The pondage of water held by the walls was black. The sun's rays hadn't penetrated to the floor of the valley.

Work for the dam and accompanying power station began in 1951 and was completed in 1955. This power station was built by a Norwegian consortium. At the time, the largest number of Norwegians living outside their country of birth was at Guthega. Locally it was known as *Little Norway*.

The Snowy River was at very least known to all Australians because of the famous Banjo Patterson poem, *The Man from Snowy River*.

Patterson never identified the Man from Snowy River. This fuelled speculation. Many attempted to attribute the identity of the character to a real person of the region. Some believe that the poem was based on a story Jack Riley had conveyed to Patterson when they'd camped together. As a boy of fifteen years, Riley found his way from Ireland to the Kiandra goldfields before leaving and picking up work in the adjacent Monaro district as a stockman. He then managed a station at Tom Groggin, an upper Murray pastoral run to the south of Mount Kosciuszko.

It was during this period that Jack Riley was said to have guided Patterson through the country and shared with him tales of his adventures. It wasn't long after this that the poem by Patterson was first published in 1890.

Another version of the origin of *The Man from Snowy River* was that the story Patterson conveyed was of a ride undertaken by the son of Jack Riley. Born to Jack and his Aboriginal wife, Alec the stripling was an Aboriginal stockman and by all accounts very skilful.

There had been other claims that the story Patterson captures is of a ride undertaken by Charles McKeahnie, an Adaminaby resident. The young stockman conducted a solo chase near the Eucumbene River area between Kiandra and Adaminaby. This location was near where I'd camped surrounded by dogs. Proponents of this renowned rider note that in the late 1800s the Eucumbene River was referred to by many as the Snowy River.

All of this conjecture led me to believe that the Man was a composite character. He was a means for Patterson to capture the essence of the High Country stockmen.

Staring into the valley at the Snowy River, I imagined it in days past. Patterson had described the terrain in his poem: 'Where the hills are twice as steep and twice as rough,' he'd written.

Beholding these steep slopes, I formulated my plan.

I'd stay high on this north-south ridge. The summits of many of the mountains were visible in a line. This was where I intended to hike. I'd hop across each peak, ever upward until Kosciuszko.

I'd walk many of Australia's two thousand metre mountains as I headed for Kosciuszko. I rattled the names off in my head. Mounts Tate, Anton, Twynam, Caruthers, Townsend, and then lastly Mount Kosciuszko. After the last and highest summit, I'd turn for Thredbo Village and the journey's end.

I grinned as I considered the barely known Mount Townsend. It was in fact this more visually imposing peak that the Polish explorer Paul Strzelecki had named Kosciuszko and declared as the highest mountain. He'd erred. Measurements later confirmed that this peak was marginally lower than the peak next door so the names were swapped to maintain Kosciuszko as the highest peak on the continent. For adventurers who knew this story, a custom existed of taking a rock from the bottom of Mount Townsend and placing it on the summit. The idea behind the tradition was to make this summit, once again, the taller of the two mountains.

Any Australian knew instinctively that Kosciuszko was Australia's highest mountain, though in fact Mount McClintock in Australia's Antarctic Territory held that honour at almost three and a half thousand metres. Then on the far distant Australian Territory of Heard Island, Mount Mawson at over two thousand seven hundred metres was also substantially higher.

Yet Kosciuszko was the highest peak on the continent of Australia. I knew from previous visits it would appear more as a round bald hill after millennia of weathering and erosion. It was named in 1840, after the explorer Strzelecki saw a resemblance to the General Tadeusz Kosciuszko burial mound in Krakow.

The General was a hero of the American war of independence and a national hero of Poland. After the war, and on return to Poland, he fought several unsuccessful wars against Russia. One of these is remembered as the Kosciuszko Uprising. Kosciuszko died in Switzerland in 1817 and was buried in Krakow. The General's admirable and adventurous life had nothing to do with Australia except the link a Polish explorer made in his mind.

The Ngarigo people's name for the tallest mountain area is said to be *Targangal* or a similar sounding name meaning 'Table Top Mountain'. Another explorer recorded *Muniong* as meaning 'Big White Mountain', though this was disputed and it might have meant a place for corroborees.

I searched the sky. A few isolated and menacing clouds scudded across it. They were moving at pace well above me from a high altitude wind. At the elevation of the camp, the breeze stroked my cheeks. It was chilling. I had no weather reports, though it was reasonable that following the stable weather I'd enjoyed since leaving Kiandra that a change was on the way.

I assessed this information against the plan. On the ridge I'd be exposed to deadly winds. Still I'd conquered so much to be here and if I moved fast I'd beat the weather and achieve the safety of Thredbo village.

The long thermal underpants I'd slept in could stay on. They'd keep me warm on this exposed slope. There was no need to change. They might chafe, but raw skin wasn't going to be a handicap tomorrow. I would've reached the end.

Hastily I bundled my equipment away. No neat folding of the tent or sleeping gear. I shoved them urgently into the pack. Wasting time removing moisture when I didn't need the tent tomorrow wasn't sensible.

I shouldered the pack for the last day's adventure. First the waist belt was tightened around my hips. There was more strap dangling from the buckle than before. I'd lost weight, I guessed. Bouncing a little in an up and down motion from the knees, I caused the load to shift. The shoulder straps were adjusted. Like me, the pack was lighter than it had been. The food was now almost all eaten and the fuel gone.

I left the Consett Stephen Pass area and walked on at a good pace to Mount Anton and then Mount Twynam. Soon these two summits were well behind me. All the while I looked down on the Snowy River. Over on the east across a valley and over a hill was Charlotte Pass. This ski resort was accessible in winter only by snowmobile. It was the coldest locality on mainland Australia, with a recording of minus twenty three degrees. Temperatures regularly fell below minus ten degrees Celsius. The Pass was named after Charlotte Adams, who in 1881 became the first European woman to climb Mount Kosciuszko when she accompanied her father on a surveying expedition. Who was the first Aboriginal woman? How long ago was that?

After a while I spotted an icy body of water. It was nearly all white except for a small patch of black where the water had not frozen. According to the map, this was Blue Lake. Clearly it'd been named by a summer visitor. It was a remnant feature from the last ice age. Glaciers flowing from Mount Twynam had carved out a basin in the granite rock forming the lake.

I pushed on through the snow. The day was predominantly a steady uphill walk. The snow was soft. Quadriceps and hips worked under the constant strain of lifting up the snowshoes and driving myself and the pack upwards.

The sun was high in the sky now and more clouds scooted in from the south and west. On a clear day from this ridge I'd have seen Mount Bogong, the highest mountain in Victoria. Not today. The Victorian Alps had been enveloped by a wall of cloud. Not black but white. A coming front.

A pang of fear went through me. This approaching white wall was bad. My association of bad with black was visually challenged. The approaching white was menacing.

I moved with ever more urgency.

My eyes kept being drawn to the clouds.

They were closer.

Ever closer they appeared.

The cool breeze that had been present at the beginning of the day was now wind.

I passed twisted and gnarled snowgums. Their appearance was sobering. There was no tall proud majesty in any trees up this high in the Alps. The conditions would smash pride and make a mockery of any misplaced vanity. Better here to bend and twist and live.

The wind now varied in strength. Gusts cut through the outer layer of clothing and to the thermal layer on my skin.

The first scuds of icy snow were driven into my face.

There was a dull stinging feeling from this. My face was painfully screwed up and I squinted from behind the sunglasses that I still wore to protect them from glare. The cold was numbing.

Leaning into the wind, I walked forward.

The falling snow was icy, like beads of glass. It hit the ground and was whipped along in swirls. At pace they raced towards me and then passed me. I didn't turn to see where they'd gone. More swirls of ice were skimming the ground towards me and holding my attention.

I'd seen sand on a beach behave the same way on windy days. It was beautiful at the seaside but terrifying in the wind chill at this altitude.

I came to a standstill. Taking off the pack, I pulled out a windproof shell and poncho. The wind made slipping my arms into the garment clumsy. Then the zip stuck. I was tugging and wrenching at it as my waning strength was used to control the flapping. Eventually it was closed.

Removing the hat, I secured it by squeezing it between my knees.

I pulled on a balaclava. Then I placed the hat on over this before squashing it into place and pulling the hood of the poncho across it. The hat was secure.

I was safer.

The hat was stopping some of the snow and moisture from hitting the sunglasses. The poncho covered nearly my whole body as it fell to the knees. Underneath I had a layer of a windproof shell, a shirt and a skivvy.

I should've been toasty warm. I wasn't. As always I was reliant upon the warmth generated by movement to keep my body away from the dangers of hypothermia.

I struggled on into the wind towards the summit. Strength started to wane and the snow became heavier. Stopping frequently, I checked the path. Another bite of ten or so paces was taken. A short period later I took another halt to regain breath.

Ten more paces.

I was gasping for air and squinting at a distant form. At first I mistook it for a snowgum and then I heard a familiar voice.

'You're almost there.'

'I know,' I yelled. The noise was whipped away by the wind as soon as it left my mouth.

'Another thirty minutes and you'll have achieved the summit of Kosciuszko, or you'll be dead.'

'What?' I screamed above the noise of the wind.

'The mountain will still be here tomorrow. You may not be.' He lingered for effect, letting the words sink in like the cold. 'You know what to do.'

'What?' I screamed it as if it was the only word I knew.

'Respect the elements.'

A burst of snow came down and I lost all sight. The whole world went white.

'Use everything you have to survive now. Everything.'

I twisted awkwardly in the cumbersome snowshoes and unsettling wind to face east. This was the direction of the sheltered Thredbo Village.

The wind was now at my back. It wasn't in my face. Immediately I was degrees warmer. I wasn't squinting into the wind.

Visibility improved a fraction.

I considered the last advice for a moment.

Use Everything.

I dismissed it. I took half a pace before checking it. In my mind I revisited the counsel. I was using everything. Everything I possessed that was warm I had on.

I took another step and halted.

I reconsidered the recommendation.

I ran through every item in my pack.

There were spare socks. I could use those as an underlay to the gloves.

I dropped the pack to the ground and began a search inside of it for the socks.

I pushed items aside. At last I found the socks sitting underneath my first aid kit.

I was in the act of shoving it aside when I stopped.

Was I going mad? The space blanket and the hand warmers were out of sight but inside of it.

First the space blanket was ripped out of its package. I shoved it up under my jackets and shirt against the skin. It'd trap warm air against the foil barrier and radiate it back. The foil would also block completely any cold wind that penetrated to it.

I took off my gloves and placed a sock on each hand as an inner layer. Then a chemical hand-warmer was placed in each hand before the gloves were pulled across the top.

Grabbing the pack from my feet I put it back on, adjusting the load.

The world had turned white. My head spun. I searched for any reference point. There was none. The ground was white and the sky was white. The boundary between them was white. The border had disappeared. A rise of panic churned my gut.

Fighting for self-control, I suppressed this emotion. It wasn't going to be of any use.

How could I find direction?

I was stumped.

What should I do?

Bewildered for a moment, I gradually grasped the realisation that I had turned to face Thredbo Village. The wind was over the right shoulder and back. If I kept the wind hitting me at this angle I'd be walking relatively straight.

I drew a deep breath. That was a plan.

My mind turned back to the stranger. 'Who are you?' I screamed desperately. The wind was snapping at my ears, hood and collar, causing a frightful noise.

With all the background clatter I heard no reply, though I listened intently.

Long moments passed and then I thought I heard, 'Just a man who had a roving fancy take me.'

This didn't make sense. I wasn't even certain I'd heard those words.

I yelled, 'Follow me.' Then stepping blindly but cautiously, I moved towards Thredbo.

SAFETY AND CIVILISATION

MY PACES WERE GUARDED. Keeping my steps and arm movements short, the idea was that if I fell, I'd roll into a ball and hopefully limit any damage. The pack on my back blocked the wind and the hat's brim kept the snow directly out of my face. Despite this I had limited visibility. The ground a metre or less in front was discernible, though not much else. Occasionally I saw the shape of a large boulder or cluster of rocks.

My memory of the map was that it had shown flat terrain to the chairlift at the top of Crackenback Ridge. This chairlift would take me steeply downwards to Thredbo Village. More importantly, near the lift was a Café that'd give me warmth.

Moving the walking poles forward, I placed them firmly shoulder-width apart. I speedily assessed if they were level, and when satisfied I was on flat ground, advanced the feet until my whole body was safely between them again.

I persevered with this method.

First I conducted this process cautiously, then more swiftly as my proficiency increased.

Step by step.

Time slowed. I was uncomfortably cold except for inside the gloves. The little balls of warmth from the chemical reaction worked magically.

Having the pack on my back between me and the wind was perhaps the most effective protection from heat loss. But I was still at risk of hypothermia if I stayed out too long.

It felt like hours of walking had passed, though I suspected this was an illusion. I couldn't check the watch on my wrist as it was buried in layers of clothes. The same sequence of motion repeated over and over made time indeterminable. The disorienting conditions were playing tricks on my mind. The wind whipped at me in gusts, sometimes creating a frightful noise around the ears. The snow swirled in the limited window of vision.

An enormous dark shape appeared in the murk directly in front.

My heart skipped in excitement. This had to be the chairlift building, I convinced myself desperately.

The system of movement I'd devised was forgotten. I leant forward at the waist in anticipation. Automatically my legs tried to catch up.

I was in a half run before I knew it.

Stumbling, almost losing balance, I was saved from a fall by the strength in the arms as an extension of the walking poles.

I'd become one with the few tools I'd carried into the bush.

I steadied and stared. The café was an enormous pile of rocks.

I'd fooled myself. Calm down, I urged. Back to the method, I admonished. This isn't the time to lose concentration.

I moved the walking poles forward of the body placing them firmly shoulder width apart. I was back in the beat. Stay steady, I urged, and took another cautious step.

Time disappeared.

The process took over. Vision intermittently swam. When this occurred I'd pause, balance and begin again.

Abruptly, by some unknown force, I found myself at a door.

I blinked.

The door was still there.

I fluttered eyelids and the door was still in my field of vision.

'Are you going in?' a voice questioned over my shoulder.

Pushing into the building, a blast of warmth hit me. An unfamiliar gust of human sound tore through the air and burst into my ears.

I was jostled by people struggling in and out of layers of clothing and tromping in ungainly boots.

The smell of abundant fried food and beer filled my nostrils.

This was the Eagles Nest Café and Restaurant. I'd made it.

I took off the snowshoes.

A skier with a group of friends provided comment in passing.

'You know how to make life hard for yourself don't you mate? You should get yourself a set of skis.'

I smiled self-consciously. I was shy about my unkempt appearance. I was on the back foot instantly. I hadn't felt like this since stepping into the bush.

My overwhelming sense wasn't of elation at having reached safety. It was embarrassment at not fitting in. I reached up and tipped the brim of the hat downwards as a defensive gesture. The hat was a shield against the bustling sights and sounds that were overwhelming me.

I was more assured.

This protective measure encouraged the skier. 'No really, skiing is a lot of fun, you should try it.'

I tipped the hat backward. As I did this a surge of confidence coursed through me. The bigger the angle, the bigger the attitude, popped into my head from left field. A quote from Frank Sinatra, I remembered, before dismissing it.

Though I was willing my legs to move me on, surprisingly I heard my voice responding.

'I don't think that I would've made it from Canberra on skis. The snowshoes have been very reliable, thanks.'

The skier and his group stared at me and then walked off.

'Wow, walking from Canberra,' I heard one of them say.

'I reckon he's taking the piss.'

'Walk from Canberra? As if,' exclaimed another.

'Did you check out the hat? A cowboy's hat on a day like this!'

I reached up and touched the brim of the trusted hat. Suddenly I was self-conscious about it. Taking off the hat, I looked at it.

I was tempted to put it away.

It was a unique piece of apparel in this café. All around me were beanies and head coverings in a range of trendy and gaudy colours. This season's colours. The faded fawn-coloured hat with sweat stains, holes and tattered brim was definitely out of place.

Then I realised that trying to blend in by taking the hat off wasn't going to work. I was still out of place in the bedraggled hiking equipment.

As I considered the hat, I noticed the hole on the crown had become bigger since I'd left Canberra. I'd caused this wearing. Some of the sweat stains were new and there was fresh white salt in little waves near the old perspiration marks. My sweat. I put the hat back. It was very comfy. If anything, its ease of fit was even better than when I'd first put it on a week or so ago. It was evident that the hat had moulded to me when I wore it. Then I reversed the observation. Alternately it might have been me that'd grown into the hat during the trials of the last week. Did the hat fit me or did I fit the hat?

In a flash I was certain that I wasn't going to blend in and this wasn't an offence.

I tromped into the café and ordered a hot chocolate. The craving I'd developed near Mount Jagungal was at last to be satisfied.

The drink was served with a smile from a cashier and I returned it. He looked happy and this reflected the mood of the building. The taste was sweet and warm and worth the long wait.

I found a chair in a corner. Overlooking the protected valley that contained the village of Thredbo, I watched the still-falling snow, feeling satisfied.

I needed to defrost and this was the perfect place.

I reached into the pack and found the mobile. Calling Arianne was a priority.

The greeting was a mechanical voice. 'The number you have dialled is switched off or out of range.' I hung up and tried again. Maybe my cold fingers had pushed a wrong button. The same voice message was conveyed to my ears. I hung up disappointed.

A sleek black square pinned to the ceiling flashed images of news. A television. It was supposed to steal attention.

It showed a bomb blast, followed by pictures of confusion and terrified faces.

Next, pictures of a flood were shown, shot from a helicopter. Then the editor cut to disoriented and crying families.

Tragedy.

Footage of a dog pulled from a drain swollen with water.

Happiness.

Film of an interview with a belligerent politician then flashed onto the screen. Then another politician popped onto the television, this time from the other side.

Conflict.

A celebrity with a cap hiding his face ran into a car. The caption screamed 'scandal'.

I forced my eyes away from the TV. It was scripted. Transient emotions packaged so that the audience were up and then down. The whole bundle was designed to prime the viewer for another dose tomorrow.

I was detached. The isolation in the bush had disconnected me from the news cycle. Most of it had nothing to do with me; it was a kind of voyeurism.

I forced myself to stare out the window at the valley. Trees and a river were far below. A large outcrop of boulders was in sight on the left. Solid rock. It represented the permanence of the landscape that had become reassuring to me.

Skiers swayed and zigzagged down the mountain. The smoothness of their run was a small insight into the beginners versus experts. It was a beautiful view.

I was pleased at achieving the journey to this point even if I hadn't summited Kosciuszko. I'd failed in that milestone, though on the way I'd found other versions of success.

It was a while before I was warm. Hands, fingers, nose, and the blood that flowed through my body all had to have thawed before I was ready to leave.

Eventually after another hot chocolate it was time to go. I pulled away from the view that'd entranced me for an hour or more and headed for the ski lift.

I waited for a chair to rumble slowly behind me. Then with the pack on my chest, I adjusted onto the seat. My feet found the stirrups below and I pulled the safety bar across. The lift was full on the way up the hill but I was the only passenger taking it down.

I watched below as the slope and skiers passed. Further and further downward I was propelled effortlessly by the machine. Into the ski village I descended. I was returning to modern Australia as if somehow I'd been in a time machine visiting the past for a week.

I was stiff as I stepped off the chairlift. Efforts to get out of the way of the ever moving contraption were lurching and slow. The chair pursued me for a few moments of alarm.

My walking was barely a hobble and I did a quick mental check. No muscles appeared to have been pulled. It was probable that I'd stiffened after the trip on the lift or maybe the body was relaxing after the long days in the mountain and it knew instinctively rest was near.

A wave of tiredness hit me and I wiped my face with a gloved hand. The touch brought blood to the cheeks. After losing a thousand metres of altitude, the sheltered village was warm. I took the gloves off and rubbed my eyes with the palm of my hand. Taking the time to wipe my eyes made me more alert.

I hobbled past skiers dressed in fashionable clothes.

Some of the holiday makers half turned to look at my dishevelled appearance. My face was unshaven and the hair poking out from underneath the distinctive beaten bush hat was matted.

I was a spectacle no doubt. I couldn't do anything about that but I didn't care.

I shambled on my way. Now that I was safe, the body had run out of energy. As step followed step the stride length shortened. Each was harder than the one before.

Across a bridge to the main village I shuffled.

All of humanity going onto and off the mountains passed on this narrow footpath. I was hemmed in on all sides and carried along by the crowd. I was forced to stand in the steps of the person in front with others occupying the place my feet had just vacated behind me. Walking was now the complete opposite of blazing a path across the snow.

On the far side of the bridge I extricated myself from the stream and found a bench to sit quietly.

What next? Should I look for a bus back to Canberra? Should I get accommodation for the night? It'd be dark in an hour and I needed to make some swift decisions.

The most important thing to do was to call Arianne. Letting her know I was safe was the most urgent task.

Digging into my pocket, I found the mobile phone.

Fumbling fingers turned it on. It took considerable concentration for my fingers to cooperate with my brain.

I waited impatiently for a network signal.

This was eventually received with a beep of recognition being emitted. I pushed the buttons to commence dialling home. Not more than three or four numbers were entered when I was interrupted by another electronic tone. A little envelope appeared signifying that messages were waiting.

I stopped dialling. I navigated to the icon that'd provide me with the message service.

'You have five new messages.'

'Hi, it's Arianne thinking of you.'

'Hi, me again, stay safe in the storm, it's hit Canberra hard as well.'

'Hey, hope you're well.'

'Me again, call me when you can.'

'Hi, keep well. Thinking of you. You must almost be at Thredbo.'

I hung up. It was lovely to hear her voice, to know she'd attempted to contact me each day. It was good to be in her thoughts.

Then doubts resurfaced. She'd said so little. This thought came into my head and killed the positive thoughts from seconds earlier.

Stop being a paranoid idiot, I admonished. Message banks were a very crude way of leaving information. For a start, the answering service provided for a simple ten second message.

I dialled Arianne's number again.

The telephone was answered immediately.

'Hey, where are you?' Arianne's pickup greeting was almost shouted.

'I'm safe. I've just made it into Thredbo.'

'Where?'

'Thredbo. I'm just by the bridge near the chairlift. I'm deciding what to do next.'

There was a long pause. I filled the silence.

'I was thinking about seeing if there was a bus tonight back to Canberra,' I offered to the telephone.

Again I was met with silence.

'Tim!'

My head swivelled towards the sound of Arianne's voice in a reflex reaction. It hadn't come from the phone. The noise came from behind my left shoulder.

I contorted a creaking body to see better and caught movement from behind some people. The next moment, Arianne was running towards me.

She threw herself into my arms and I hugged her tight.

Her soft lips met mine.

She pulled her head back.

'Did you mean that text?' Her eyes explored mine intensely.

I understood what she was asking of me. I considered saying 'yes', though under her scrutiny I knew that wasn't the right answer.

I drew breath.

'I Lo ... ' was all I managed. Her finger came to my lips. 'I know what you're going to say. Let's say it together so both of us can say it first,'

'I love you,' we whispered in unison.

We both laughed.

We kissed for long moments.

'I'm glad you came through safe.'

I nodded. 'I told you we'd be OK.'

Arianne appeared puzzled. 'You said the same thing to me on the phone.' The crease on her forehead deepened. 'We're OK. We're just walking ... thinking. Who's we?'

I pondered what to tell Arianne about the man in the mountain. Everything. I should have no secrets.

'Me, myself and ... ' I trailed off. I'd tell her a little later, I assured myself.

'And I?' Arianne finished.

I dropped my gaze under her examination. I'll tell her later, I promised silently. Squeezing her hands in delight, I felt pressure as she squeezed mine right back.

LOVE

ARIANNE WAS WELL ORGANISED. She'd booked a room in a chalet high on Crackenback Ridge.

When she led me through the door, a burst of warm air greeted me. She had placed clean clothes on the bed. Shaving gear and toiletries were next to them.

'You've planned everything,' I acknowledged gratefully.

'Now have a shower and shave. I love you. I'll love you more when you aren't so stinky.'

I hobbled to the shower, undressed and climbed under the spray of hot water. Standing perfectly still, I let the water drip down my face into an open mouth and then over my body. I'd never luxuriated in a shower like I did in this moment.

The invention of the shower was amazing.

The common every day event of washing had extra meaning today. The heat and pressure were adjustable. The water first sprayed me tickling the nerves before I turned the stream into a deluge, lightly pummelling aching muscles. The shower, that I'd taken for granted all my life, was unexpectedly novel to me after this trip. The luxury of plumbing was worthy of celebration.

I thought of the hotel room with the warmth and softness of carpet underfoot, an extravagance. Beds and mattresses, chairs, heating, and insulation it was now apparent to me were treats.

I had new appreciation for these inventions and innovations after having experienced life without them. I was privileged to be living in the modern world. Developments like water on tap, sewerage and electricity were not just modern. They were part of the contemporary urban landscape. Town life had wonderful advantages.

Later, I lay in bed stroking Arianne's long soft hair. In the shadows of the room her glinting eyes watched me back.

'I want to show you something,' Arianne whispered, before jumping out of bed with an explosion of energy that contrasted with her gentle voice. Bent with her back to me she opened her suitcase. I admired her hair and the beautiful curves of her body as she did this. Finally she straightened, holding in her hand a tablet device.

Returning to bed, Arianne plonked down beside me and pulled up the covers. She held out the tablet so that we could both see. She tapped with her fingers and there on the screen was a picture of a queue. I recognised it as being out the front of the museum. The crowd of families snaked across the length of the photo and clearly stretched beyond the range of the camera lens.

'I took these for you.'

Her index finger stroked the screen and the picture changed.

This time the picture was of the front desk at the museum with still more files of people purchasing tickets.

My hand reached out and I held the tablet on the left while Arianne steadied it on the right.

Arianne flicked at the screen again and there was a photograph of a family in front of an exhibit on brumbies. A little boy was pointing at the horse and his mother was leaning down whispering in his ear.

'Not bad, eh?' Arianne enquired.

'Great photos,' I complimented.

Arianne beamed and then her face turned to a serious expression. 'I'm not talking about the photos. I'm talking about the crowds.'

I smiled. 'Yes, it's fantastic. Thank you for going down to the exhibition.'

'It was a way of connecting with you when you were gone. It's a really good exhibition.'

'No bias in that assessment.'

Arianne's finger pushed a button and took the device to the home screen. She then pressed a link to the newspaper *Canberra Times*.

A page came up and I saw a headline, *The Mountains that Changed Us*.

My finger pointed in a reflex.

She nodded. 'John said that you would like the title of the article. He spent hours with the journalist repeating those words in the hope they'd be picked up.'

'Wow,' was all I managed.

'John's pretty proud of himself, don't you worry,' remarked Arianne. 'Read on,' she urged.

> The Snowys exhibition at the National Museum is a beautifully presented and curated show that has opened this week to much critical acclaim.
>
> The retrospective on the Snowys has captured the imagination of the public, said the Museum Director.
>
> The response has been overwhelming. The first three days has seen more people through the door of the National Museum than in any other seventy two hour period. Momentum is still building as word of mouth spreads the news about the excellence of this exhibit.
>
> The museum has engaged more staff and requested volunteers to help with the crowds. The Museum Director has announced extended hours for the exhibition from next week. From Monday, visitors can enter from 8am -8pm. A ticketing system has been adopted to ensure the crowds are spread across these new hours. Please check the museum website for details.

Arianne reached across and kissed me on the cheek. 'Congratulations.'

I touched her hand and pressed it lightly as a gesture of thanks. I had a sudden urge to kiss it and brought it to my lips.

I reread the article. I caught Arianne smiling at me out of the corner of my eye.

'There are more articles and the museum website has additional news. I saved them in Favourites for you.'

The afternoon disappeared rapidly. Arianne made coffee for both of us before returning beside me.

'Are you happy?'

I considered the answer. I sipped coffee and Arianne watched me.

'Yes of course,' I eventually responded. 'I'm just trying to work out whether enjoying external validation is the same as needing it. I don't want to need it anymore. I want to be more self-contained like I had to be in the mountains.'

Arianne's hand touched mine.

'I think you are. How else could you have walked from Canberra to Thredbo? I also think you're introspective and you need to cut yourself a break.'

I frowned. 'I'm working on that.' The light was fading through the curtains and Arianne switched on a bedside light before urging me to dinner.

I dressed into tailored chinos and a blue striped long sleeved shirt that Arianne had selected from my wardrobe before coming to Thredbo. I revelled in their comfort after days in the one set of dirty gardening attire. The cotton was finer and the cut was fitted, hugging and comfortable.

Arianne's clothing matched mine. Her fuchsia jewellery was simple and highlighted the deep blue of the dress perfectly.

'You look stunning.'

She smiled a thank you. 'You're looking pretty good yourself, considering the mess I picked up this afternoon.'

I held out an arm, Arianne took it and we walked out the door. The outside cold hit me and wrapped around the forehead. I was exposed. Unprotected.

I'd left the hat in the room.

'Just a moment,' I requested of Arianne before ducking back inside. Retrieving the hat I put it on my head. My nakedness was fixed with this simple act. I caught a glimpse of myself in the mirror. I stopped and took the time to appraise what I saw. I was thinner around the face. My skin was darker in shade than I had ever seen it. It was beyond a tan. I was black from long exposure to the elements. I looked like the quintessential Australian bushman. I took off the hat. I still looked like a bushman. I put the hat back on.

'Really?' Arianne remarked in surprise when I re-emerged.

'It keeps my head warm,' I offered as explanation.

After a brisk stroll, we found ourselves in a nice restaurant in the village. Only two tables were free. We chose the corner for privacy, and taking our seats, I propped the hat on the table.

With my back against the wall, I watched the doors and windows. With so many people around it was difficult not to feel some anxiety. I was on alert but why?

The cacophony of sounds assaulted the ears. Snatches of conversations were absorbed.

'I've never gone so fast.'

'Did you see that poor fellow fall?'

The flashing of lights and movement of people assailed the eyes. The invigorating smell of garlic came from the kitchen. My mind tried to process all of this unfamiliarity. The brain pulsed 'overload' at me.

I was on the verge of headache.

It was way past bush-bedtime, I realised. Possibly I was just out of sorts as by now I'd have been fast asleep.

A menu on the street near the door attracted couples and families to peruse before they made a decision to enter. The menu offered many choices. A stark contrast from the restricted eating I'd become used to in the last week. Lamb, beef, seafood, chicken, duck, pasta, vegan, gluten free and vegetarian were options. There was an extensive drinks menu to compliment the food. This choice wasn't satisfying to all groups. Many continued down the street to another restaurant to begin the process again.

The décor of this restaurant was subdued, unlike others we'd walked past. I guessed the owners were trying to achieve a romantic ambience for the customers'. In contrast, the mood of many customers was exuberant and so the intimate atmosphere wasn't achieved. The incongruity was unsettling. I was disoriented by the noise from conversations buzzing that became ever louder.

How could I hear myself in the noise of the town after all those empty days and nights in the bush?

The meal distracted me. Oysters textured and creamy were a wonderful change to diet. Chicken with chili olives provided heat and spice that sent tingles through my mouth. The smell of the steam with the rich mashed potatoes caused me to hold my breath and close my eyes for a moment of pleasure. It was a wonderful change from the dehydrated meals.

Eventually my spoon played with the Crème Brulee I was eating for dessert.

Arianne watched me. I still hadn't disclosed the story of the man in the mountains and now doubted I would. She'd think I was mad, just when everything between us was so perfect.

'I'm sorry you didn't make it,' Arianne's voice was full of empathy.

'Thank you. I'm not.' I stopped to think. 'I learnt more by turning around and admitting that this wasn't the time to complete the goal. The mountain is still there. It will be there tomorrow and the next, to forever. I can still do it another time.'

'You'll try again,' Arianne stated without judgement in her voice.

I used the spoon to poke more holes in the dessert.

'Possibly. I don't know.' It was at this moment that the jumble of what I was thinking made sense. I verbalised it. 'I'm thinking about walking back.'

Arianne stiffened. Her lips imperceptibly creased into a straight line.

She fixed me in her eyes. They bored into mine and I was uncomfortable. I held her gaze with effort.

Arianne's head shook before she quickly controlled it. Finally, when I was paying complete attention, when the full import of what she was about to say was apparent to me, she spoke.

'It's dangerous. You're a city person with limited experience, even though you've done so well to get here safely. I'm very proud of you. You trying to walk back to Canberra would be tempting fate. Surely you're tired after this arduous trip. You looked done-in when I first saw you today. Maybe you should recuperate.'

Arianne was laying out facts honestly and was accurate in every statement. She didn't speak out of selfishness rather out of concern for me. I loved her more.

I considered my response for a long time. I touched the hat. The answer wasn't necessarily pleasing. It was the truth though and Arianne deserved that.

'I was so alive, Arianne. In a way that's hard to describe.' I dwelt on the next words. 'I don't want to sound dramatic or worry you, but there were circumstances in the last week where if I'd made a poor decision or made a mistake I could've lost my life. To be able to see what you've to lose, life, and to live because of the decisions you make, is invigorating.'

Arianne sat very still.

I went on. 'More than anything, out there,' My head nodded to the window, 'I have a sense that I might find a piece of the puzzle about who I am. Something that can't be achieved by a family tree or DNA test.'

There was an urgent need to fill the silence between us. 'You told me John was fine with my absence. The exhibition is not over for another week. I've some unfinished business in the mountains. I know it's a lot to ask. I need your support. If you say no, I won't do it.'

'You want to climb Kosciuszko after all,' Arianne's shaky voice suggested she was trying to control her confusion.

I shook my head.

'I haven't completed all that I set to achieve on this trip. I've learnt to become comfortable with that. Sometimes beautiful things elude and that's what adds to the mystery. So I won't climb Kosciuszko.'

Arianne bowed her head. She waited.

'This afternoon you asked me who was *we*. There was a bushman out there.' I turned to face the window. Snow floated down gently and romantically. The ski slope beyond was bathed in soft light and it all looked so benign. The mountain beyond the slopes was steep, but the chairlifts made the grade look exciting, not exhausting. It was a world away from the storm I'd battled today. How could I explain? I drew breath.

'This bushman watched over me. Every time I was in trouble he would come out of the wilderness and calm me. He offered me wisdom. At other times he questioned me. The right questions at that moment. It was lifesaving. During the storm today I was on the edge of making poor decisions. I was going to persevere when I shouldn't have. His clear thinking was the difference between me being here with you tonight and me still being on the mountain. I need to find him. I need to thank him. He is the *we* you asked me about.' This time I'd divulged everything and I didn't have the uncomfortable urge to drop my eyes.

Arianne stroked my hand. 'Could anyone survive out there in the snow tonight? Surely he is in danger. Should we tell someone there's a man on the mountain?' she queried with concern.

'He's a real bushman. He sent me to cover this afternoon and I know he would've done the same. Right after he looked after me.'

'Who is he?'

I shrugged. 'I don't know,' I confessed. 'I think he told me his name. The noise of the wind took it away.'

I detected doubt in Arianne's expression so I added, 'It was horrendous, the wind and the noise.'

'How will you find him?'

In my heart I knew the answer and that was he would be there when I was in trouble. I wrestled with this for a moment and then answered.

'I won't find him. He'll find me. I know it.'

Our hands touched. Her fingers softly played with mine for a little period. Then she nodded her agreement.

Back to the Bush

After two nights in Thredbo, I was the first passenger on the chairlift at seven in the morning.

The pack beside me was bulging from food and fuel that had been purchased on a trip to the regional town of Jindabyne the day before. I was sure I had too much food. Certainly a lot more than when I'd left Canberra. Arianne was insistent as we walked the aisles of the supermarket. I wasn't in any position to object. I was grateful for her support and thankful of spending a special day with her. After buying food we wandered the stores. Cafés provided breaks to talk and the shores of Lake Jindabyne were an opportunity for quiet time where we could walk arm in arm. Over dinner she'd presented me with a new GPS that she must have purchased unseen on one of our many stops. 'For the top of your pack please.'

I twisted backward on the chairlift to catch the last glimpse of Arianne as she waved goodbye. The warmth of her last kiss still sparkled on lips. The lingering glow from her gentle stroke of my cheeks reassured me. Her eyes screamed *take care* even from this distance.

Then she disappeared from view. I turned to face the front. The steep mountain loomed over me and in the instant I was daunted. This time it was not by the unknown but the known challenges. I knew snowshoeing was arduous and I would sometimes need to walk until exhaustion to achieve the safety of a shelter. The dangers of snowdrifts, whiteouts and storms could only be managed not controlled completely. The chairlift cables reaching for the summit, revolving around a wheel, and returning from the summit offered an entry and an exit. I dismissed the temptation.

After alighting from the lift back at the café, I stepped a few paces onto the snow, adjusted the snowshoes and without a backward glance, trekked northward.

A weather check before I'd left had declared the temperature as minus ten in the village. It would be even colder where I was higher on the mountain. The freshness in the air stung my nose, yet the feet inside the socks, inside the boots, were agreeably warm. My core was comfortable, and the turned up balaclava under the hat was keeping my head cosy. From toes to top, I was in good shape.

Tromping a few hundred metres north, I admired the view.

It was dawn as I looked from the top of Crackenback ridge. I was alone again. Me, a pack, some snowshoes and a hat.

I could feel the strength Arianne had transferred to me through her last hug. It willed me to come home safe. All of me. Body and mind. I knew this without it being spoken.

After the noisy village, the silence in the bush was audible. It shouted: this is what the world has sounded like since forever.

The hush of dawn was familiar and calming.

The still-shadowed mountains, immovable and majestic, stood in all directions as far as the eye could see. Thredbo Village was below in a valley. I was looking down on it and so were the peaks.

I'd discovered spaces like this on the outward journey. Alone in the moment, I was entranced. It was a beguiling feeling that'd enticed me to recapture it. I'd enjoyed the instants in the bush when I wasn't fearful. I wanted to progress this developing relationship further. Taking my glove off I knelt and put my hand above the surface of the snow. Its cold radiated. I reverently stroked it. I was grounded.

Leaving Thredbo Village for the bush was a tug-of-war.

I'd lain awake in the early morning, tossing and turning next to Arianne, still debating the merits of embarking on a journey just as I had the night before leaving Canberra. I was more conflicted about walking back to Canberra than the conversation with Arianne over dinner had suggested and it still continued now.

Tug towards the city. I wanted to stay with Arianne and enjoy her company every minute. We'd finally said I love you. Now I longed to show my love to her, the way she showed hers to me.

Tug towards the bush. It wasn't as momentous a decision to head for the Alps when I'd been there and seen its moods. I now had knowledge from the journey to this point. Experiences had been accumulated and the bush didn't hold as many fears. I'd become more comfortable with nature.

Tug towards the urban life. I acknowledged that unfamiliarity with the bush had caused me anxiety on the expedition to Thredbo. This could not entirely disappear. Storms could catch me out despite my plan to find cover and wait until they abated. Navigation had been good enough to get me to Thredbo, though I still harboured reservations about my abilities.

Tug to the bush. I had a stranger to meet. In my keeping was a hat that had some special hold over me that I didn't understand yet. The hat was going somewhere and taking me with it. I still needed to know where the journey would end.

The tug-of-war stopped. I stared instead at the birth of dawn. The sun was popping over the eastern ridges in a reddish pink ball. The black silhouettes of trees on that ridge contrasted in such a way as to be reminiscent of the survivors of a bushfire. As I scanned from the vantage point in the west, the colours of the morning display softened to pinks across snow. Layers of mountain ridges then extended into the distance moving from shades of mauve to purple and then blue.

I recalled the sunset over the Brindabellas that I'd witnessed from the office just over a week before, the event that had ushered in this journey. I'd been privileged to see the gold-pink sunset then. An ending. And I was honoured to be seeing this dawn.

I stepped off downhill and north towards Charlotte's Pass. The shoes shwooshed a song on the hard, early morning snow. The squeaks from each step told me the snow was at least as cold as minus ten degrees Celsius. Higher than this temperature, the pressure caused by the step partially melted the snow causing a flow. That step would be silent. Colder than minus ten the ice crystals were crushed by each step causing the creaking noise.

A plastic wrapper from a chocolate bar lay on the snow. Time was on my side. I stopped to pick it up. I put it in my pocket.

I was by myself.

I thought of Arianne's love. John supported me. I was very fortunate, I acknowledged. I wasn't really alone.

The ankle had no soreness. It held my attention for a little but I could tell it was strong.

I could simply have turned westward and included *Targangal* in today's hike. Climbing the mainland's highest mountain didn't seem important anymore. My goals and values had been transformed in the experiences on the walk from Canberra. I noticed that my brain had started using the name for the mountain that had been used since the Dreaming. It seemed natural. I looked across the Alps. It was like I was at home in a way that hadn't been possible a week ago.

This morning, the frantic pace that'd driven me south into the mountains as I left Canberra wasn't needed. Now I was rambling north. Back to the city on this clear, wind free day. I had confidence in where I was and what I was walking towards. Arianne's GPS accessible and safely stowed near the top of my pack as instructed was backup.

The last week had taught me so much about the wilderness. I'd become more comfortable there as I'd grown in familiarity yet I'd learnt it was harsh, really relentless, and it could kill a city person and unprepared traveller. I'd been unprepared, naïve and silly to take on this task. I'd made it through with assistance at key moments. I doubted that I'd have made it through without the advisor. I needed to find the stranger and guide.

The snowshoes skimmed over the surface. Down I progressed towards my first milestone.

Understanding of the National Park had developed by being in it. It was not attainable from the office and looking at the mountains.

Before this trip I knew how this park had come into existence with the declaration of the National Chase Snowy Mountains on the fifth of December 1906. When Australia was fighting in World War Two it was still important in April 1944, for the passage of the *Kosciusko State Park Act* to occur. It provided a new protected area for all Australians. At this time, the summer cattle grazing were sustained throughout the area of the State Park, though a battle to stop this had begun. Erosion in the high altitudes of the park made catchment management a threat to the proposed hydroelectric scheme. The cattlemen were depicted by the media as self-interested and standing in the way of a national project. In the main, the snow lease holders believed the campaign to oust them was run by city dwellers who threatened their livelihood for the odd occasion that they might travel to ski or visit nature. The city-country divide was the fault line this battle was waged on for another quarter of a century until grazing was concluded in 1969. The State Park transitioned to the Kosciusko National Park in 1967. It was changed to what was considered a more correct spelling Kosciuszko in 1997.

The philosophy of the people who managed the Park had changed since 1967. The initial idea had been to concentrate on the natural landscapes. Preserving nature and returning it to a pre-settlement state had been the original goal. This viewpoint meant that evidence of European occupation was to be removed.

In time this perspective shifted, though not before much of the evidence of the settlers history had disappeared. The huts, some forlorn fence lines and some rusting parts of steam engines used as part of mining equipment were all that remained.

On the outward journey my belief that a National Park would keep the country safe in perpetuity had changed. Rubbish, introduced animals, weeds, development of ski areas were all impacting upon the environment. The impact of humans was still occurring.

The ski fields and many species of animals were at risk by warming temperatures. Broad-toothed rats and pigmy possums were in dangerous population decline. Scientists had recently accidently introduced a waterborne fungus while doing research. It had caused the extinction of four Australian frog species. It was speculated that it'd further endanger the southern population of Corroboree Frog that was already in a precarious position.

Establishing a National Park was just the beginning. The campaign to allocate an area for conservation for the benefit of future generations wasn't the only battle. In the long-term, future generations needed to keep valuing and protecting the Park. I'd not understood this completely when curating the exhibition. An opportunity had been missed. I made a note to improve future exhibitions I curated by visiting the landscape and immersing myself in it more.

The walk progressed downhill and north. It was a different route to the one taken on the journey to Thredbo. This time I headed directly towards Charlotte's Pass, ten or more kilometres downhill. Morning tea would be eaten in the comfort of the resort and then I'd cut onto Mount Twynam. Finally I'd wander along the ridge to Consett Stephen Pass before snaking downhill to a hut at White's River.

The sky was clear from horizon to horizon. The morning was now advanced enough to describe the sky as blue. I watched a plane make its mark across the sky as it sped by at altitude. As usual, another plane parallel to the first and behind it was making a similar smudge. The lines stretched like a finger of fate, the smudge of man.

The steep downhill through patches of snowgum to Charlotte's Pass was negotiated effortlessly.

Entering the ski resort at Charlotte's Pass, I found a Café.

A hot chocolate and raisin toast were pleasurably consumed.

It was still before nine when I shouldered the pack again and headed towards Mount Twynam. The first skiers of the day were already gracefully skimming down the slopes.

It was a steep pinch to the ridge. This caused me to puff hard and to stop at intervals. Eventually I was once again on the crags appreciating views of the Snowy River and Guthega.

As I sauntered, I realised that lunch time could be had at the old campsite on Consett Stephen Pass from the night before I'd reached Thredbo.

The camp couldn't be found.

The indentations left by the tent, the place where I'd dug the snow down to make a stable footing for the stove, my footsteps, had all been obliterated in the storm. It was like I'd never been there, though I had. On the pure snow it was like man had never been there, though they had.

I brushed a rock free of snow, sat on it and enjoyed lunch regardless. A fresh ham and cheese roll made by Arianne.

Just past Consett Stephen Pass I found some cross country ski tracks heading towards Schlinks. I followed these and started the long steady descent west towards the Pass and the White's River Hut where I'd stay the evening. The walking was pleasant and uneventful. I made certain to stay in the middle of the ridge so as not to sink into any drifts.

The skiers' tracks curved whimsically on stretches, though mine stayed on the shortest path between point A and B.

At some point I had to leave the ridge to get to the hut in the valley below. This decision held my attention. I would need to negotiate drifts and steep terrain. I scrutinized the map frequently to ensure I selected the right location. My goal was to find the place where the contour lines on the map were the furthest apart indicating a shallower decline.

I chose a location to walk into the valley and so left the high ground. Within a short distance I was staring over a cliff. I assessed the terrain and could see no safe route. I turned one hundred and eighty degrees away from the precipice and retraced my steps back up to the central point.

Once on the ridge I reconnected with the skiers' tracks. This time I saw them with new eyes. I kicked myself. Surely they were going to the same valley as me.

After a short walk, this deduction proved to be true and so I didn't have to make a decision. The skiers' tracks dived off the ridge towards what I determined to be the hut.

It was a measured drop they'd chosen and I guessed that the unknown skiers had been on this route before. I picked my way down the precarious slope. Snow displaced by shoes raced downwards, pulled by gravity. In the sheerest sections I found that if I turned and faced into the hill, it was safer to step backwards and down. This gave me better balance and grip.

It was an hour before I found myself staring at the back of a hut from across a stream. A skier kneeled at the creek scrutinising me. He was immobile, frozen in the motion of filling a water bottle.

I greeted him cheerily. 'G'day.'

The salutation was returned with a grin and some guidance on the best route across the fast flowing stream.

'No, don't put your foot there, or the snow bridge will give way. Go to your left to that rock and jump across this way. That's it.'

Once on firm ground, I shook hands with the tall stranger. My head was level with his shoulders. Brian introduced himself as my hand was pumped in his large paw. He pointed me to the hut.

'Lachie and Harry are inside lighting a fire. I'll join you when I've filled the other water bottles. Do you want some bottles filled?'

'Most of mine are empty. I'll do it.'

'Don't be silly, go inside and warm up.'

I left my water bottles with Brian and followed his directions.

Inside the hut I was greeted by a much younger Lachie and Harry, who were attempting valiantly to light a fire from damp wood. They were teenagers. With enthusiasm and persistence they succeeded. A waft of pungent smoke was the initial outcome, though in minutes it had turned to flame.

Brian returned and produced a battered and blackened billy-can full of water.

Brian was a seasoned camper. He was bringing his grandchild and friend on an introduction to snow camping trip. He was full of stories from previous trips and the teenagers full of excitement about the experience.

Before long, laughter filled the hut as Lachie and Harry recounted the day's events. Brian had chosen a snow bridge to cross a creek on the way into the hut. He'd shepherded Lachie and Harry safely across, only to step on it and have it give way under the weight of his much heavier frame. Fully immersed, Brian had yelped from the shock of the cold water and the teenagers had yelped with delight. They were all still chuckling about it.

The hours drifted by at the fire. Laughter was never far away.

The merit of a piece of camping equipment I'd brought with me, against a piece of equipment they'd brought, was worked through in minute detail. The benefits of the tinned food Brian ate over my rehydrated meals took a good period to discuss. Taste versus weight required a complex evaluation system that led to no resolution.

As we ate, I complained about the lack of spicy heat in the rehydrated chilli con carne.

Brian looked at Lachie. 'You know how to fix that. Do you remember what I showed you this afternoon?'

Lachie nodded and then, torch in hand, disappeared out the door into the dark.

Five minutes later, Lachie reappeared with a handful of long leaves that he'd clearly taken off a local bush. 'Mountain Pepper,' he announced, as he tore a leaf up and put it into my food satchel.

All watched as I dipped my spoon in for the next mouthful.

Tears flowed down my cheeks as a hot pepper sensation filled my mouth.

More laughter as I wiped my eyes.

After dinner, Brian offered a whisky from a well-used flask.

I nodded.

Brian tore up another leaf of Mountain Pepper into my cup. He poured the whisky on top. 'We'll call this a Tim-Toddy,' he announced with a grin. 'A little extra heat to warm your inside.'

We took out our maps to use as a reference as we discussed the routes each of us intended to take the next day. The *How It Was* map was pushed to the side. Brian offered bits of advice from his years of walking in the country.

Brian turned his attention to my unfinished *How It Was* map. I explained the idea behind it. He nodded.

'I schooled in these parts, but the knowledge I have about this country is not from school. It's from my father and experience, and it's all up here.' His hand tapped his temple. 'If I don't pass it onto Lachie and Harry how will it get to them? Your *How It Was* map makes sense even if it's impossible to complete. It's important so don't give up.'

Shortly afterwards I yawned and apologised that I needed to go to bed. I retreated and settled into the sleeping bag on its thin piece of foam. It was adequate, though nowhere near as comfortable as last night's accommodation.

I missed Arianne. Alone with my thoughts I imagined being with Arianne. Her soft hair, her fragrant smell, her sweet taste.

Distracted I reached for the pencil and paper. I'd not needed to write in Thredbo. Here though, it was once again the right thing to do.

After the nights of aloneness in the mountains, tonight's company had been a pleasant and happy surprise. I considered the evening and how joyful the comradeship had been. Brian was from an older generation, the teenagers from a younger generation, nevertheless conversation had flowed in the confines of the cosy hut.

Words came in a torrent.

> Cheers for that coffee,
> No worries, she'll keep out the cold,
> Mate I'd kill for a tea,
> Hey listen to Lachie, since when's he been so bold
> Give me a break I'm cooking the feed
> Is that what you call opening that tin
> Shush ... the poetry to you I'll read
> Good luck! It'll never be heard over this din

The sun's light was poking through holes in the wall when my head emerged from the hood of the sleeping bag. The hut was empty. I looked around but there was no sign of anyone except for myself. My heart skipped a beat.

Had I imagined last night?

I sniffed the residue of smoke clinging to the air. There had been a fire, I hadn't imagined that.

I kicked urgently with my feet and wriggled to free myself. I strode to the hut door. Opening it, I looked out into a landscape of snow.

Across it were footprints other than mine. My heart rate slowed.

Returning inside, I found a note on a bench.

Safe Travels—all the best, Brian, Lachie and Harry.

Searching for Clancy

WALKING HOME WAS EASIER than into the unknown wilderness. It almost felt the same as hiking downhill even when the trail was on an uphill grade. In a physical way it was a descent. *Targangal*, being the highest point of the mainland and Canberra at an altitude two thousand metres below, added to the strong sense that I was always on a downward slope. Of course this observation in a two hundred kilometre journey wasn't true. There were some steep climbs.

Occasionally I found parallel lines in the snow from skiers who were crossing the ranges. Some ski tracks intersected my path and others were heading in the same direction as me for a section. It was simpler to follow in tracks of others when I could and so I took advantage. Blazing your own trail, with all the accompanying doubts about your current location and destination I had learnt was much harder.

On the journey south I'd faced the prevailing cold sou-westerly wind. The advantage though, was that the sun being in the northern sky was behind me, illuminating the path. Now I was walking north. The wind was at my back. This was warmer, as the cool breeze wasn't on my face and chest. On exposed ridges of the range, the push of the persistent airstream behind sped me towards the start point. Now though, the sun was in my eyes, causing me to squint even through the filter of the sunglasses.

The circumstances of all the variables of terrain and weather were rarely entirely in my favour. If there was a lucky coincidence where all of these factors came together, I'd learnt to enjoy the moment. Perfect conditions in the bush were infrequent and short-lived. When the situation I was in wasn't in favour, I was learning to find the positives and accentuate them. Focusing on the negatives ate at my will.

I had space to consider the journey south. I'd cleared out of the city searching for my own air. Air that wasn't shared second hand or stale. Over the expedition, finding room to breathe had become a quest. I'd set and achieved my own goals. Something that was exclusive to me. To be an adult was to set my own objectives from life, not merely to follow the direction of superiors or society's pattern for me.

Progressing north, my shadow was now to my rear. It was a shady double that followed just a few steps behind me looking over my shoulder. Checking I was OK. Sometimes when I rested I'd turn and look at the terrain I'd passed over. Then with eyes drawn to the shadow I'd raise the hat. It had become a habit to confirm that it was really just me. It worked, but it left me with the feeling that I was doffing the hat out of respect for a fellow traveller and they'd returned the compliment.

I'd begin each day by speculating if this was the day I'd see the bushman. I'd pause in the hut door, admire the ever widening holes in the crown of the hat, put it on and begin the day's effort.

After a long time I'd come to acknowledge that the bushman I was seeking needed a name. The name for me was Clancy. I hadn't searched for that name, it just felt right.

Where are you Clancy? Are you going to show today?

I wasn't looking for trouble, though I knew that Clancy always showed when I was in distress.

New challenges were never far away.

Ice gave way underneath me when crossing the semi-frozen Eucumbene River. I staggered, my knees buckled, the walking poles slipped off some rocks and I plunged head first into the water. Panic overtook me and arms flailed to find the bottom and push myself upright. I surfaced gasping for air. I regained firm footing, stood, realised the water was just over knee deep and then made for the bank. I trembled on the river's gravelly shore.

It was then that I realised that the hat had slipped from my head. Frantically I faced the river catching a glimpse of it being swept downstream around a bend. Desperately I ran and then dived after it. The hat eluded my grasping fingers.

Picking myself off the rocks I chased the hat again.

The speed of the flow took the hat further away from my pursuit. The distance gradually widened. Puffing hard I slowed and nearly stopped in surrender when an eddy captured the hat. My heart quickened in excitement and with a final effort I was able to retrieve it.

I tromped out of the water.

I redressed, my hands fumbling with the boot laces. Water dripped down my face from the wet hat I'd returned to my head.

Move like a startled brumby until all the cold has left your limbs. Go.

Coping with this challenge built confidence. This trip had been a hunt, and still was, to find who I was as an individual and an Australian. This search couldn't be undertaken by driving through or flying over. I had to experience the temperature. Fording rivers, cowering from wild animals, falling, stumbling and persevering over ups and downs were part of discovery.

I was required not just to know history, but to live it and begin to understand the unique way the distinctive landscapes shape the character of a people. The way Country had made an authentic Aboriginal narrative as well as a distinct settler discourse. Finding out where I was going was easier when I knew where I'd come from. Perhaps I would stop working on the *How It Was* map and start making a *How It Could Be* map.

As I progressed closer to home I sometimes heard kookaburras laughing. I had a strong sense they were laughing with me. I recalled the first day's climb up from Corin Dam to Pryor's Hut when I was certain they were laughing *at* me.

I had begun to notice new objects. Even the smallest orange fungus on bone dry fallen timber popped out at me. I hadn't even noticed the fungus on the tramp south.

In the early morning, rather than cursing the cold, I'd come to accept it. I'd included in the morning pack up ritual a birdbath. I'd go outside to the creek that was inevitably by the hut. I'd kneel by it and splash my face with water. The tingle at the shock of the icy touch invariably caused a shudder down the length of my body. Next the hat came off and I'd dip forward dousing my hair. Hands then were run through the hair in a quick comb. Drips inevitably found their way down my neck under the collar and along my spine. A shiver would rack me before I took off my shirt, dab at my armpits in a quick attempt at a clean, put the shirt on and return inside to the hut. Only then would I shoulder the pack and get on my way.

North of the Eucumbene River the snowshoes became unnecessary. I tied them to the pack and continued toward Canberra. They were not needed again.

In the fog one morning a rainbow appeared. It was a complete white-silver luminescent arch across the trail. The yellow, reds, blues and greens were barely discernible. I could see each end of the rainbow. There was no pot of gold that one part of me searched for. I sped up as I tried to walk beneath the arch. The rainbow retreated in front of me. I forgot about the famed treasure as now the semicircle reminded me of the creation serpent.

As the morning progressed I admired the winter light in the forests of eucalyptus. There was texture to shadows. I found substance to the shades and depth to the gloom. I searched for Clancy.

In one section of the track a family of Brumbies stood and watched me from a safe distance. I kept on the path heading in my direction and then they trotted slowly off in another.

I retraced steps back hoping that Clancy would be on the same route that he'd been on during the outward journey. Each day I was disappointed.

I noticed that some changes had taken place about how I calculated progress in the day's walking. I rarely checked the watch. The Key Performance Indicators that I'd imposed upon myself on the way south were largely absent. The checks in my head such as comparison between kilometres and time had fallen away.

I now recognised the self-imposed goals as distractions. They were detracting from the pleasure of enjoying the here and now. Key Performance Indicators were for work and I didn't need to take them into every aspect of life. These artificial goals did not add to the experience. They diminished appreciation of the sweet air, the vastness and the beauty.

The goldfields of Kiandra were at my back and still there'd been no sign of Clancy. I hazarded a guess that he may have gone elsewhere. Conceivably, he was more to the lowlands avoiding the danger that storms posed on the exposed higher ground.

I revisited the map and chose a different path to Canberra. I'd head east and then north. I'd skirt to the right of Bimberi Peak as I looked at it, cut through the Yaouk Valley and join the old Boboyan Road. This would take me on an altered route through Namadgi National Park. This path, from the number of known archaeological sites, had been a track for the Ngunawal and Ngarigo nations and later a road for the Europeans.

Once on this new course I made good time.

The views were expansive in grassy valleys and the water in the numerous streams was clean. The destination for the evening was Westerman's Homestead where I expected a comfortable evening's sleep.

The Westerman's had taken up land in the area in 1882. Two cottages had been erected before the bigger homestead was built in 1916.

As I left New South Wales and entered the southern part of Namadgi, the forests of gums looked taller and healthier. I spied a wattle tree about to burst into flower. The return to the Australian Capital Territory invigorated me. A return to Arianne.

A pair of juvenile crimson rosellas winged through the forest tweeting as they went. Moments later more rosellas flew past behind and in the same direction. Green with flecks of blue and red, they were a portent of spring. This seemed a silly observation for a moment as spring was a month away. Then I remembered the Ngunawal six seasoned calendar. This time was the cross over from late winter to early spring. The time when wattle bloomed. Cool and getting warmer, for twenty thousand years.

I stopped and stared at the endless gums.

Silently I said my respects to the traditional custodians of the land, the Ngunawal people. I was about to re-enter their Country and so I asked for safe passage.

I was nearing home and Arianne was on my mind. Time with her had grown in importance since we'd been apart. I would think of particularly beautiful parts of the journey and promise myself that I would return to share the location with Arianne. These places would be better with her, everything was better with her.

The repetition of stride became a meditation of the trail. A unity with the mountains and the sky above was real. Scribbly gums were everywhere and I had time to admire the trunks.

The indent, a scribble, was caused by the larva of a moth wriggling beneath the bark. Then, when the larva was half grown, it reversed direction and made a new mark back and parallel to the first. It was not known why the moth behaved this way. Research was still to be completed on this matter. It all enhanced the allure of the countryside. The mystery of the still unknown. I looked around appreciatively. I walked to a gum and touched the bark. The squiggle could be felt. It was brail. There was a message.

There were lyrics in the sweet cold air. The whispered ebbs and flows of breeze. Messages were in the bark of the trees.

BEMERINGAL

PAINTED BODIES DANCED. It was a special occasion, though it was certain it was not meant for me, just for me to know about. To be curious and respectful. The joyful sounds of the gathering filled the forest. Sticks clattered and the song's rumbles came and went.

My brain latched onto the sounds. Awareness dawned that they were real. I forced myself awake, at the same time as I comprehended I was on the floor of Westerman's Hut. A day was beginning and thunder was filling the valley. Sticks of gum were blown against the hut.

I climbed out of the warmth of the sleeping bag. A quick peek out the door showed dark clouds, a strong wind and no rain. I went back to light the stove and begin the morning's routine.

Leaving Westerman's Homestead, it was a short stroll over the hill to Brayshaw's Hut. The wind had dropped and some threatening clouds hung in the sky, but I sensed that I was not to be rained upon.

My fear of this country had dissipated.

A healthy respect for the dangers that existed because of the country's isolation still was present inside of me. This was of course the case when I reflected upon the lonely death of David Brayshaw, resident of the hut. He died from injuries and exposure after a fall from his horse in 1931.

The still cool of morning energized me.

A settlers trail for tourists had been built from here to Waterholes Hut, some four kilometres distant. The trail featured benches to sit and gaze at Grassy Creek. I'd been here before on strolls and picnics with Arianne. On this morning, the second last before returning to Canberra, I stopped at each bench for a few minutes. I reviewed the journey and what the future held. I considered the part Arianne had played in my life and how I wanted her to play a larger role.

Patches of snow, swirling mist on the surface of the water of the creek and grey gumtrees made for an enchanting view.

On the water's edge, healthy Cumbungi grass drew my attention. The distinctive long, brown, spear-like seed heads meant that I could recognise it. The plant had been known to the Ngunawal. It was used for weaving, string and tobacco substitute. The white rhizomes at the base of the plant were baked or chewed as food.

Drawn to the grass I knelt, pushed away the grass to expose the rhizomes and picked a few stems. I continued on my way while contemplatively chewing and savouring the slightly sweet earthy taste.

Waterholes Hut was shabby. Never meant to be permanently occupied, it was a hut for working stockmen. The floor was covered in a layer of water, so its name appeared appropriate.

I wasn't here to see the hut. Just a few hundred metres from the rear of the building was an old stockyard, one of the last left from the era of the cattlemen. It was at the stockyard, rather than the hut, that I halted for a quick snack and to admire the roughly hewn timbers that in some parts had tumbled down. It was an enclosure roughly a hundred metres across, surrounded by what was termed a drop-log fence.

Stockmen had gathered and been mates. Horse breaking might have happened here with a few jackaroos doing the dangerous work while others watched and called advice. Some of the stockmen had been European and others Aboriginal.

It was a tough life for graziers on the edge of the Alps. The size of land holdings revealed the story. Farms on the grasslands of Canberra were a thousand acres or less. Properties in this area were likely to be four thousand acres or more. Stock would've been run around the grassy valley floor and also into the scrub of the lower slopes to ensure enough feed.

How long before even this reminder of the cattlemen was gone? One bushfire and it'd be erased.

The miners were gone.

What would go next, the ski fields and the Hydro?

I left Waterholes Hut, thinking deeply.

I'd come to the bush steeped in simple arguments.

Cattle grazing in the High Country versus no cattle grazing.

Brumbies belonging in the Snowy versus eradication.

Conservative Bushmen and progressive urban dwellers.

The decline of the Dreamings versus the rise of European narrative.

Arguments were formulated in mind as opposites, as if that was the natural state for discussion. Contrariness was the narrative of Australian politics, media and popular film and story. It was instinctive for me to formulate discussion in this way. I knew that what I was doing amplified the dramatic qualities, and wasn't necessarily maximising the potential for an informed discussion.

Why did it have to be *either, or*?

Why couldn't it be *and*?

Surely what this trip had taught me was that it wasn't one or the other. That it wasn't the idealised pure bush and the soul destroying urban environment. Australians could belong to both. One didn't have to be better than the other and Australians could learn something from both lifestyles. We could straddle the divide created by Patterson and Lawson. We could see it for what it was; a dramatic device.

What would happen to these musings when I took them back into the urban home? Were the ideas overextended and unsuitable to stand the test of the city? Or were they going to shed new light on how to live? Was the poetry I'd come into the habit of writing each night in the bush just going to stop when I returned home?

I hiked on through the early hours of the morning.

The sky changed to blue and clear. Wispy cirrus clouds were a portent of future fine weather. The sun and the exercise of walking warmed me pleasantly.

A short climb up a hill took me out of the little valley of the huts and onto Old Boboyan Road. I was heading due north.

First the path of the road took me uphill and then downhill. The dryness of this country was evident. In a rain shadow on the eastern side of the range, even now in winter the country looked stressed from lack of water. The previous ten years of drought had clearly taken a toll.

Would the drought ever break?

It was certain farmers were pondering this. For me the question was academic. My livelihood didn't depend upon rain.

I spotted some wallabies and in their pouches were the tiny heads of newborn joeys. The young wallabies needed the warmth and tender care of their mothers to survive. Science had taught me that a characteristic of the marsupial group was that they gave birth to less developed babies that lived in a pouch sucking on a tit.

Evolution science and the Aboriginal narrative of how the wallaby came to have a pouch ran around my head.

In the Aboriginal story of *Bynamee*, a wallaby mother with her two babies came across an old wombat that was unable to move, was hurt and needed water. The wallaby was happy to help. She went to the possum and asked her to watch over her two joeys while she went for water. The possum permitted the joeys and her children to play together.

The wallaby used a bark container to take water to the old wombat, but the wombat was so old he couldn't sit up and drink.

The wallaby went back to the possum. They both decided to help, so they then left both groups of children in the care of the saw-tooth rat. The wallaby and possum were now free to go and help the old wombat.

The wombat was helped up to drink. Suddenly he kept rising and transformed himself into *Bynamee*.

Bynamee thanked them for being so kind. He inquired after the children. The wallaby and possum explained the arrangement they'd made with the rat.

Bynamee told the wallaby, the possum and the rat that he could understand the problems they'd encountered when helping him. Particularly the difficulty they had with child care. *Bynamee* then gifted these creatures a pouch so that they could mind their children. This meant that their hands were now free to do other things.

The science was linear and my education had informed me of its method. It was logical.

The Aboriginal narrative contained logic from observations. The addition of the account of charity and reward spoke to me.

I kept walking and thinking about the stories these mountains contained. Could the Dreaming and post-colonial history ever come together?

After a few hours, the trickle of the Gudgenby River could be seen. No more than ankle deep, its pebbly bottom was speedily negotiated. Across it and on the far side were open grasslands full of families of Eastern Grey Kangaroos. Some were lounging in the rays of the sun, others stood and scratched themselves. I noticed that two of the kangaroos were scratching with their left paws. In my presence they froze mid-scratch. Most humans were right-handed and most kangaroos left-handed, whizzed through my head.

I rated a tilt of the head from the kangaroos. Not for these kangaroos to hop away as I approached. I was within fifteen paces or so before they stood and lazily moved a little distance. The Gudgenby River valley was a popular day walking venue for Canberrans and the kangaroos were used to the passage of many humans.

Xanthorrhoea bushes grew on the valley slopes. The grass tree. The stubby trunk with a head of bushy grass and a long flowery stem was distinctive. Some believed this tree was a reminder of a great ancestor warrior who'd been recognisable for his head of flowing hair. A maker of the best spear shafts, he produced many for the people. Even as he died he wished to continue making the best shafts to help the families. *Bynamee* granted him his wish by turning him into a grass tree. The long flowery stems still made the best shafts for fishing spears.

I chose the track to the west. The Yankee Hat Mountain on my left was the dominating feature in view. It was well named, as viewed at different angles it had the shape of a tri-corn hat, reminiscent of headwear used around the time of the war for American Independence.

A plastic water bottle lay abandoned. I crushed it with a boot, picked it up and put it in a bag of other rubbish I'd collected. It was bulging.

At the base of the mountain, I followed a track to the site of rock art. The paintings were hidden between huge boulders that'd formed in such a way as to leave a walking path under an overhang. The sheer stone wall was adorned with bright ochre and chalk-white clay depictions. The reddish ochre clay was highly valued and known as *gubur*. The white clay was *gubbity* in the Ngunawal language. The illustrations showed life as it had meaning to the people of this valley. Up to four hundred years old, the pigments depicted an emu, lizards, people, kangaroos, and in a later painting, what may have been a horse. I stared at the beauty and marvelled at the age. Some of these paintings were at least twice as old as the time since European arrival into the area.

Both the exhibition at the museum and my journey were full of remarks about the settlers in the past two hundred years. Much less information was available about the thousand or more generations of Aboriginals who'd lived in this region. There was such disproportion in the information available. I'd struggled with this inequity when curating the exhibition and I was no closer to reconciling the disparity now.

My direction of travel was west as I walked deeper into a grassy valley towards Rendezvous Creek. The going was initially easy, though on crossing the creek the trail disappeared and I was left to bush-bash upwards. It was slow frustrating work on the steep mountain sides.

The process was to catch breath, steady my heaving chest, balance, decide a route, pull and scramble upwards for six or eight paces, pause and begin again.

My path was to stay on the ridge until I reached the crest. Then I intended to move along it until I came across the markers of an ancient ceremonial place. I'd chosen to spend the last night of the journey nearby.

The ceremonial site wasn't well understood.

This may have been where tribal rights were administered. Possibly the ritual in this location made the moth gathering expeditions so special. There were many plausible explanations for the stone arrangements.

For me, this location would be an end and a beginning. I'd leave Country by paying respects to the traditional custodians of the land. It was the end of my personal journey through the mountains and the past. It was the beginning of a return to the contemporary and the future.

After a few hours of slow struggle upwards, I was at sixteen hundred metres with the shrub giving way to grass and boulders. I negotiated the crest. I made a path over one knoll and then down a saddle and onto the next. On a big slab of granite-like rock I found a seat on a boulder. I'd found the place I was seeking.

I could see rows of rocks that had been moved in parallel lines.

I could feel beauty and power.

After a while I moved a distance from the site and pitched the tent at what I believed was a respectful distance. Once the camp was established I returned the ten minute walk to the site. I sat to observe the stone arrangements as the sun was going down. I checked the time 5:15. The sunset had a faint orange glow that bathed the black-grey of the rocks in an eerie light. I sat in awe, not because it was the most spectacular sunset, nor the most panoramic view. It was just beautiful in its simplicity. Not showy, yet unique. This evening, this place, had power. Time stood still as the sun disappeared in increments. In the end only the rim of the sun was visible and it hung for eternity.

The hush of the mountains was a presence that surrounded me. Not a bird cheeped, nor an animal stirred. No wind moved. The air was thick with meaning, I knew this though I had no way of translating.

'I'm leaving now,' I stated. It travelled from me in stereo in all directions. Strong and confident like I'd never heard my voice.

A gentle breeze blew from the west tickling my skin.

Words carried to my ears. 'Country has touched you and I have seen you gently touch Country. You know something of the *Bemeringal*. Their story is hidden not lost. It can still be found if you keep searching. Save their story for everyone. Use your skills as a historian but mostly keep touching Country.'

Staring, I saw a man in ranger uniform. I raised my hand in a reflex greeting. 'James it's me ... Tim.'

A hand raised in response, or farewell. We seemed to stare at each other for eternity and then he turned his back and broke the spell. He disappeared into the scrub. I made to call out but restrained myself.

I stood still as the light disappeared. I checked the time 5:19. Four minutes had gone by, how could so much happen in so little time?

I picked my way carefully back to the campsite.

I enjoyed a cup of tea as I lay on the grass. The ground was cold, but I was used to the chill now and it didn't worry me.

It was a clear night and it'd be icy at this altitude on this exposed mountain. Eventually I crawled into the tent and zipped into my sleeping bag. Tonight I elected to leave the flap open and watch the stars. The Emu in the sky and the Southern Cross were in view.

Wriggling a little to get comfortable, sleep overtook me.

Hours later, I came awake with a start. I didn't know what caused this, although the brain was registering movement. Straight away I fought to push back the hold of sleep. I was on alert.

My eyes opened wide.

There were shadows shifting. Listening intently I could detect no sounds of movement.

Unzipping the bag gradually and smoothly, I was careful to be silent.

I reached for the hiking poles as a form of defence and headed for the entrance. As I crawled into the night I looked up for possible danger and froze.

The sky was full of pink sheets dancing in the sky. They subtly shimmered like the movement of a curtain.

It was an Aurora.

Minutes went by and the show continued. Sometimes there were shards of white. In the main it was pink. To the far south I spied some movement in green. After a while I realised that I'd been holding my breath. I made a note to breathe.

It was as I took this first breath that I saw a figure sitting on a rock not thirty paces away. He was a dark silhouette, though I knew who he was.

'Long time no see,' I called. 'Where've you been?'

'Oh ... around. I was keeping an eye over things though not needed,' was the deadpan response.

'But I did need you. I lost footing in a stream. I fell and all of my clothing and equipment were drenched.'

'You've been through worse. What did you do when you fell?'

'I picked myself up and moved like a startled brumby.'

I thought I saw the silhouette nod his agreement.

'So why are you here now?' I asked.

'I might ask you the same question.'

I deliberated for a long time, eventually answering. 'First, because I was beckoned into the bush, and now because I've come to love Country.' I paused and then repeated myself. 'So why are you here now?'

'Just to share this night. It's a treasure.'

'It is,' I agreed. 'The wondrous glory of the everlasting stars.' I quoted whimsically the words of Banjo Patterson from *Clancy of the Overflow*.

'A star spangled dome,' remarked Clancy in reply. 'Over there is Mount Tennant. Some people still go there in search of the loot of the bushranger. The real treasure is this sky. The greatest of all is being able to rove amongst this country, just like you've done.' He tailed off. Then more quietly, as if I wasn't there and he was remembering words from long ago, I heard, 'A roving fancy took me, which has never since forsook me.'

Silence fell for a long period and then he broke it. 'I gave up droving once. I hung up my hat so to speak. After watching you, I'm feeling like I might get back on the tracks. Get back to the days when I needed a good hat.'

A swirl of light whirled across the sky, demanding attention. It went white, and then pink, before the dark of night returned with the only light from stars. Long seconds passed before pink streaks reappeared. Next white lights became visible shimmering and merging with the pink before coming apart. The whole sky was filled. Slowly sheets of white developed with a pink swirl providing enchanting contrast. I knew what I needed to ask even though my attention was being held by the show, 'Who are you?'

'Your obedient servant,' I half heard. The dancing lights were having a hypnotic effect and I could feel my eyelids droop though I willed them open.

I couldn't look away from the spectacle. 'The Aurora Australis it happens this far north occasionally, maybe once every ten years or so. You have to be here, in a dark place, to have any chance of seeing it. How lucky are we?'

Hearing no reply, I turned to see if he'd heard. He was gone. 'What the ...', the drowsiness fell away. I jumped to my feet. The sky was forgotten and it was the dark of the bush that drew my attention. Shadows moved but each time I concentrated on that place it was just an illusion caused by the light in the sky above. 'Hello,' I yelled.

Silence.

'Hello.'

No response came. I was completely and utterly alone.

The lights shone faintly for a little while and then they faded away.

Almost at the same moment a cold southerly wind blew up and my cheeks and nose were freezing. I raced back into the shelter of the tent.

I zipped up the tent flap and then the sleeping bag against the cold. The wind whipped at the tent, causing a creaking sound as the nylon was pulled against the guy ropes and the poles flexed.

I dozed. Vaguely I registered the sounds and then I slept.

The next morning I awoke freezing.

It took effort to leave the sleeping bag. This is the last morning, I confirmed as motivation. You can be with Arianne this afternoon, was an extra happy encouragement.

The wind from the night before had dropped when I exited the tent and crawled into the grey light. I was grateful for this small mercy. I turned my mind to thoughts of falling into Arianne's arms. Holding her, kissing her being embraced by her warmth.

I shoved the frosty tent unceremoniously into the pack ignoring my stinging fingers.

I'd be home tonight, nothing else really mattered.

Frequently I rubbed my hands together and blew warm air onto them.

I was ready for the trail in extra quick time.

Shouldering the pack, I picked up the walking poles. These were checked to ensure they were sized right. It was a familiar start routine.

Something was not right. I felt out of sorts.

The hat.

It was nowhere to be seen. I realised that I hadn't put it on first thing as I left the sleeping bag as was my habit. I was so caught up in thoughts of Arianne and packing. I couldn't recall seeing the hat this morning.

I twisted my head left and then right. Down on the ground by my feet and to the middle distance I explored.

I hadn't noticed it during the pack up. Could I have left the hat outside last night? Could I have been that distracted? Perhaps the wind had taken it away, I speculated.

Wider afield I looked between rocks and shrubs.

I felt sick in the stomach and my vision blurred. I started to panic, my breath coming in short gasps.

I tried to compose myself. Vision slowly returned to normal, though the acid in my stomach remained. I kept searching.

The hat had taken me somewhere unexpected. I'd travelled from the city, through the bush and now back to the very edge of the city. It'd taken me from the present to the past and shown me a way to the future. I didn't want to lose it now. Not after all that we'd been through.

My eyes darted near and far.

It was with relief that I saw a faint round object. The crown of the hat catching the light. My fingers tingled with anticipation of the touch.

I strode towards the hat, restraining myself from breaking into a run.

My hopes fell as I neared. It was dew glistening on a rock. I stopped. There was a sense of loss that was palpable. I resumed the hunt.

My eyes roamed. It was nowhere to be seen.

AFTERWORD

NOTES FROM THE AUTHOR ABOUT *Clancy's Hat.*

Clancy's Reply is an Australian poem written in 1897 by Thomas Gerald Clancy. It's a response to the famous *Clancy of the Overflow* by Banjo Patterson. To my knowledge, no original copy of *Clancy's Reply* exists at the Australia Museum or anywhere else. I think I'm safe in saying that Thomas Gerald Clancy had a hat to keep the sun off his head. The fictional idea of Clancy sending that hat to Banjo Patterson with his poem was created by me.

The tip of Bimberi Peak cannot be seen from the Australia Museum where the fictional Tim works. Bimberi Peak is visible from other parts of Canberra, however the most obvious snow-covered mountain that can be seen from Canberra in winter is Mount Gingera.

Tim's walk on the first day when he leaves the southern suburbs of Canberra and makes it to Pryor's Hut is a superhuman effort. Some of the other legs of the walk described are equally superhuman.

Poor telephone coverage in the Australian Alps makes Tim more isolated in this book. He has difficulty getting a message to Arianne on a mobile telephone when in the bush from Canberra south to Mount Kosciuszko. Mobile telephone service coverage is better in the Australian

Alps than this story suggests. But it should be noted that there are many areas where no coverage exists.

I do walk alone in the Australian Alps. Unlike the novice Tim in this book, I've been walking in the Australian bush for more than thirty years. I take a satellite telephone and an emergency beacon with me. The fictional Tim could have made life safer for himself and made it easier to contact Arianne if he'd taken a satellite telephone.

Many of the trials Tim confronts in this book are challenges I've faced in the National Parks in years of snow expeditions. I've walked from Canberra to Kosciuszko in winter. It takes planning and six or more months of hard physical conditioning. I always have a road crew to provide support. I navigate with a map and compass. A Geographic Positioning System provides back-up if skills come up short. They still do from time to time.

The rural/urban divide remains important to Australian culture.

I've tried to make the history presented in this book accurate and apologise if any is wrong.

The fusing of Aboriginal and Settler stories into one Australian narrative is still a dream.

www.ingramcontent.com/pod-product-compliance
Lightning Source LLC
Chambersburg PA
CBHW050126030726
47505CB00007B/2060